PRAISE FOR

The Bone Houses

An IndieBound Bestseller

An Indie Next Pick

"dark, mesmerizing fairy tale reminiscent of the
imm Brothers, the Brontës, and Neil Gaiman in
The Bone Houses is a haunting and hypnotic novel
I drank deeply and savored. Emily Lloyd-Jones
an author who should be on everyone's radar."

—Mackenzi Lee, *New York Times* bestselling author of *The Gentleman's Guide to Vice and Virtue*

ed around a truly epic journey, with a satisfying
d slow-burn love story complicated by the walking
Bone Houses is a horror-drenched fairy tale. Emily
nes spins wit, longing, and loss into something
agical as the creatures that haunt the night in
llis's world, and the result is a careful, beautiful
examination on the impression love leaves behind."

—Sarah Henning, author of *Sea Witch* and *Sea Witch Rising*

"*The Bone Houses* is a dark and beautiful book, full of magic as quiet as death and as powerful as love. Lloyd-Jones gives us a beautiful setting full of vibrant characters that's resonant with gorgeously eerie mythology, plus my absolute favorite literary goat. I loved this book." **—Kat Howard, Alex Award–winning author of *An Unkindness of Magicians***

"A deliciously monstrous novel, full of the magic of ancient Wales. Reminiscent of Juliet Marillier and Marion Zimmer Bradley. Expect the unexpected in this funny, scary, mysterious, and ultimately unputdownable story!" **—Dawn Kurtagich, author of *Teeth in the Mist***

★ "Ghostly prose. . . . Filled with breathless moments and occasional humor. . . . This melancholic horror novel digs its way into the heart." **—*Booklist*, starred review**

★ "Both exciting and imaginative. Inspired by Welsh mythology, this stand-alone novel is both a classic quest saga and a page-turning horror story. . . . A required purchase for collections serving young adults, this fine novel will especially appeal to those who enjoy fantasy with more than a touch of terror." **—*VOYA*, starred review**

"A new and magical journey, filled with the best parts of a fairy tale. Monsters, curses, love—both slow-burn and familial—beautiful descriptions of an eerie mythical Welsh setting, and a streak of humor make this stand-alone novel a must-read." **—*SLJ***

"[Emily] Lloyd-Jones creates an evocative world of magic... and plays with the conventions of fairy tales and horror.... The story serves as a meditation on the complicated relationship between the living and the dead, combining fear, humor and enchantment in equal measure." —*Publishers Weekly*

"Emily Lloyd-Jones has crafted a world of myth and magic, legend and lore, fantasy and fairy tale that has a quality of timelessness about it.... Readers who enjoy fantasy, adventure, horror, and/or folklore will certainly enjoy this novel with its engaging characters and unusual premise." —*School Library Connection*

"Readers... who prefer their fairy tales touched with darkness, will find satisfaction here." —*The Bulletin*

"This Welsh-inspired story is haunting and compelling.... A stand-alone dark fantasy that readers will want to sink their teeth into." —*Kirkus Reviews*

"[A] gorgeously eerie, lushly written fairy tale." —**Book Riot**

THE BONE HOUSES

THE BONE HOUSES

EMILY LLOYD-JONES

LITTLE, BROWN AND COMPANY
New York Boston

Little, Brown and Company
Hachette Book Group
1290 Avenue of the Americas, New York, NY 10104
Visit us at LBYR.com

Originally published in hardcover and ebook by Little, Brown and Company in September 2019
First Trade Paperback Edition: September 2020

Little, Brown and Company is a division of Hachette Book Group, Inc. The Little, Brown name and logo are trademarks of Hachette Book Group, Inc.

The publisher is not responsible for websites (or their content) that are not owned by the publisher.

The Library of Congress has cataloged the hardcover edition as follows:
Names: Lloyd-Jones, Emily, author.
Title: The bone houses / Emily Lloyd-Jones.
Description: First edition. | New York; Boston: Little, Brown and Company, 2019. | Summary: "When risen corpses called 'bone houses' threaten Ryn's village because of a decades-old curse, she teams up with a mapmaker named Ellis to solve the mystery of the curse and destroy the bone houses forever"—Provided by publisher.
Identifiers: LCCN 2018054664| ISBN 9780316418416 (hardcover) | ISBN 9780316418409 (ebook) | ISBN 9780316418430 (library edition ebook)
Subjects: | CYAC: Dead—Fiction. | Blessing and cursing—Fiction. | Supernatural—Fiction. | Gravediggers—Fiction. | Brothers and sisters—Fiction. | Fantasy.
Classification: LCC PZ7.L77877 Bon 2019 | DDC [Fic]—dc23
LC record available at https://lccn.loc.gov/2018054664

ISBNs: 978-0-316-41842-3 (pbk.), 978-0-316-41840-9 (ebook)

Printed in the United States of America

LSC-C

10 9 8 7 6 5 4 3 2 1

To my grandmothers

The Living

THE GRAVEDIGGER'S CHILDREN *were troublemakers.*

They chased chickens through the neighbors' yards, brandishing sticks like swords, claiming that the fowl were monsters in disguise. They went to the fields and returned with berry-stained lips, crunching seeds between their teeth. They tumbled through the house, slamming into walls and breaking one of the wooden love spoons their father had carved. And once they'd tied a small wagon to a pig and raced through the village, screaming with mingled fear and joy. It was widely thought that the eldest, the only daughter at that time, was filled with mischief, and her younger brother trailed in her wake.

They would settle down, said Enid, the innkeeper. Children raised so close to Annwvyn were bound to have a spark of wildness in them. Their parents were both considered decent folk. The children would follow.

And if they didn't, said Hywel, the girl would make a fine recruit for the cantref's armies.

Their father dug graves and when he came home at night, his fingernails were stained with dirt and his boots were muddy. When there were no deaths in the village, he would vanish into the woods, reemerging with plump mushrooms, wood sorrel, and all sorts of berries. They were never rich, but their table was laden with good food. Their mother kept account of their bookkeeping, talked with the mourners, and planted fresh gorse along the edges of their graveyard as a protection against magic.

For all their freedoms, the children had one rule: They were not to follow their father into the forest. They would trail after him until the shadows of the trees fell over the rocky ground—and then the father would lift his hand, fingers splayed: "farewell" and "no farther," conveyed in a single gesture.

The children obeyed—at first.

"What are you doing?" asked the brother, when the girl stepped beneath the tree boughs.

"I want to see the forest."

The brother tugged at her arm, but she shook him off. "You can't," he said. "We aren't allowed."

But the girl ignored him.

The forest was beautiful—lush with ferns and thick with moss. At first, all was well. She picked wildflowers and wove them into her tangled hair. She tried to catch small fish from a stream. She laughed and played until evening fell.

With the creeping darkness, things came awake.

A figure stood nearby, watching her. For one moment, she thought it was her father. The man was tall and broad-shouldered, but too thin around the waist and wrists.

And when the man walked closer, she realized it was not a man at all.

It could not be. Not with a face of raw bone, with bared teeth and hollow eye sockets. She had seen bodies before, but they were always gently wrapped in clean cloths and then lowered into the ground. They were peaceful. This thing moved slowly under the weight of armor, and a sword jutted from a belt. And it stank.

The girl had a vague idea of picking up a fallen branch to defend herself, but she was frozen with fear.

The dead creature came so close that she could see the fine pockmarks and cracks in its bones, and the places where its teeth had fallen out. It knelt before her, its empty gaze fixed on her face. It pulled her close.

And then it inhaled. Sucked a rattling breath through its teeth, as if it were trying to taste the very air.

She quaked with terror. Every gasp was raw with it.

The dead thing drew back, tilting its head in a silent question. Then it rose to its feet and looked beyond her. Heartbeat hammering, the girl glanced over her shoulder.

Her father stood a few strides away. In one hand, he held a basket of forest greens, and in the other he wielded an axe. The threat was unspoken but heard nonetheless.

The dead thing retreated, and the girl shook so hard she could not speak. The father knelt beside her, checking her for injuries. "I told you not to follow."

Tears welled in her eyes.

"Death is not to be feared," he said. "But nor can it be forsaken. One must be mindful."

"What was that?" she asked. "Was it truly death?"

The father placed his hand on her shoulder. "A bone house," he replied. "They linger beyond death. It is why the villagers do not disturb the forest."

"But you come here," she said.

"Yes," he replied. "Those of us who deal in the trade of death are familiar with it. I don't fear them—and as long as you know how to navigate the forest, nor should you."

She looked at the trees—their tangled branches wreathed in fog, the chill of the night settling all around them. And she was not afraid—rather, something like excitement unfurled within her.

"Teach me?" she asked.

Her father smiled. He took her hand. "I'll show you. But hold on, and do not let go."

For two years, he showed her how to find paths through the trees, where rabbits made their warrens, how to tell between the sweet berries and the poisonous ones. And always, he carried his axe with him. On the days when they did not go to the forest, he brought her to the graveyard. She learned how to break up rocky topsoil, how to wrap a body, and how to pay last respects to the dead.

Winters came harsh and cold, and their provisions of food dwindled. Soup was watered down, and the memory of plump blackberries and buttered greens kept the children awake at night. The village became smaller; farmers packed up their families and went elsewhere, leaving empty homes and barren fields. And fewer people required the services of a gravedigger.

The mother became pregnant a third time, and when the father was offered a job as a scout, he accepted. The local cantref lord wished to investigate a collapsed mine, and the only way to get there was through the forest. And so he asked the man who did not fear the woods.

The daughter begged to go with him, but the father refused. When she protested, he gave her half of a wooden love spoon. He had carved several for their mother during their courtship—and this one had been broken when the sister and brother were tussling in the kitchen. The whorls of dark wood were smooth against her fingers, and she traced the overlapping hearts and flowers. "Here," he said, cupping his larger hands around hers, pressing the spoon gently. "You take this half, and I'll take the other. So long as you have it, you'll know I'll find you."

She clutched it to her chest and nodded. The father kissed his children and his pregnant wife, and he went into the forest.

He never returned.

By night, the daughter slept with her half of the spoon beneath her pillow, and by day, she carried it in her pocket. He will come back, she said, when anyone asked.

Some days, the daughter went back to the woods. She stood in the forest, beneath the shadow of the mountains and waited. She waited to see another dead man.

The forest did not scare her; rather, she wanted to be like it: ageless and impervious, cruel and beautiful.

Death could not touch it.

CHAPTER 1

THE EVENING AIR smelled pleasantly of a fresh grave.

Ryn breathed it in—the sweetness of overturned sod, mists rising from the green grass, and the woodsmoke drifting from the village. The spade felt comfortable in her hands, slotted in amidst familiar calluses. She hacked at the damp earth, dislodging rocks and thin roots. She'd marked the outline of the grave with twine and nails, and now it was just a matter of cutting through greenery and topsoil.

Her spade glanced off the edge of a rock, ringing high in her ears. She grimaced, grasped at the rock with her bare hands, and yanked it free. A worm came with it, squirming with the discomfort of a creature unused to sunlight. She picked it up between thumb and forefinger, and then she tossed it over her shoulder.

Someone made a noise behind her.

Ryn looked up.

Her brother stood over her, the worm caught in his ink-stained fingers.

"Sorry," said Ryn. "I didn't hear you coming."

Gareth gave her a flat stare, walked a few steps to her left, and dropped the worm into the grass. "It never occurred to you to put the worm back, did it?"

"Usually if something crawls out of a grave, I take an axe to it," said Ryn. "That worm should be grateful."

His frown cut fresh lines around his mouth. Despite being the younger of the two, he carried the weariness of an old man. "You needn't bother with the digging, Ryn."

A snort escaped her. "Because you're going to do it?"

Gareth's clothes were impeccable. Not a smudge of dirt upon his tunic, nor a stray blade of grass on his boots.

"Because," he said, and his voice was heavier, "Master Turner came by this morning and informed us that our services will not be needed for Mistress Turner. They've decided to burn the body."

For a heartbeat, she remained in place—caught between her task and the knowledge that it was no longer necessary. Her hands yearned to return to the digging.

She rocked back on her heels and began rubbing her dirty hands on her leggings. Gareth made a pained noise at the streaks of grime, but she didn't pay him any mind. "Well, that's unfortunate."

"That grave was our last hope." Gareth took a step back. "We were counting on Turner's ball-penny to get us through the winter." A breath rattled through his clenched teeth. "Come on. Ceridwen will be finished making supper by now."

Ryn rose to her full height. She was as tall as her brother, something that had always made her smile and him frown. Tall and lanky as a sapling, her mam had once said. And as graceful as a drunken colt, her father had added fondly. "I saw a bone house this morning," she said. "Caught a glimpse of it. I went for my axe, but the sun was up before I returned. It must have fallen in the tall grass, because I couldn't find it." She shrugged. "I'll wait for nightfall. Let it find me."

"A bone house?" A crease appeared between Gareth's heavy brows.

"Yes," she said. "I know, I know. You're going to tell me that bone houses don't leave the forest. That I'll probably just scare a vagrant half to death."

Gareth frowned. "No," he said. "I—I believe you. It's just that's the second one." He had their mother's eyes—the brown of healthy earth. And he had a way of looking through a person that made Ryn want to hold her secrets tightly to her chest. "They never used to leave the forest," he said.

It had the ring of an accusation and Ryn crossed her arms. "I haven't gone into the forest." The words were sharp. "Well, only the outskirts." Part of her wanted to remind him that the reason they still had food in their larder was because of her willingness to flirt with the edges of the forest.

"All right," he said. "Take care of the bone house. But when Ceri cries because I'm not good at telling her bedtime stories, that's on you."

"Just read her your accounts ledger," said Ryn. "That'll put her right to sleep." She softened the words with a grin and a clap on the arm.

Gareth winced, his eyes on where she had dirtied his shirt. "Just don't get yourself killed, all right?" He began to walk away, but he called over his shoulder: "And if you do die, that's still no excuse to be late for breakfast."

Colbren's graveyard was set outside the village proper. When Ryn was young, she'd asked her father why they buried the dead so far from the living. She still remembered his broad fingers carding through her hair, a smile on his mouth as he answered. "Death's something of a frightening thing to most people. They like a bit of distance between them and eternity. And besides, the dead deserve a spot of privacy."

The graveyard had been built before the Otherking fled the isles. As such, the old protections remained: Gorse grew at the edges of the graveyard, thick with yellow flowers. The thorny shrubs hid iron rods that had been driven into the ground. Gorse and iron. It would not stop a human from entering the graveyard, but it would stop *other* things.

The light faded from the sky, falling behind mist-shrouded mountains.

Ryn saw the familiar form of a man walking along the road leading from the village. His shoulders were bent by years of hard labor, and he carried a rusty sword. The damp, overgrown grass brushed at her fingertips as she approached him. "That looks a bit heavy for you, Mr. Hywel."

Old Hywel snorted. "Been carrying heavier things than this since before your parents were born, Ryn. Leave well enough alone." He spoke with a gruff fondness.

"Why does a miller need a sword?" she asked.

He grunted, and there was a shrewd edge to his words. "You know why."

She grimaced. "They haven't been at your chickens, have they?"

"No, no." Hywel huffed. "My chickens can fend for themselves." He slid her a look. "Your brother went past here a few minutes ago," he said. "Looked a bit out of sorts, if you don't mind me saying."

"If Gareth weren't worrying about something, he wouldn't be my brother."

Hywel nodded. "Any word from your uncle?"

It was a question folded into another question, a worry that neither of them would say aloud.

Ryn shook her head. "We haven't heard from Uncle. But you know how travel is from here to the city."

The loose skin around Hywel's mouth sagged in disapproval. "Never been, myself. Don't trust those city types."

There were those in Colbren who had never left the village. They might as well have grown up from the rocky soil like trees; they seemed to draw their lifeblood from the land, and they would not be uprooted.

"How is your sister?" Hywel asked.

"Likely baking something that would shame the finest cooks." When she'd left the house that morning, Ceri had already been up to her elbows in flour.

Hywel smiled, showing a missing tooth. "Those rowanberry preserves she made... there wouldn't happen to be any of those left, would there?"

There were, in fact. Ryn thought of the berries spread over sweet grilled cakes, and her stomach cramped with hunger.

"Our roof has a leak," she said. "Would be a shame to see all my sister's fine baking go to waste the next time it rains."

Hywel's grin widened. "Ah, that's how it is. You're a sharp one, Ryn. All right—two jars of preserves for the roof repairs and you've got yourself a deal."

She nodded, not precisely pleased so much as satisfied. Trading food for favors had become something rather common of late. She let out a breath and pressed her fingers to her temple. She could feel a headache building, stress forming a knot behind her jaw.

"You should be getting back," said Hywel, breaking into Ryn's thoughts.

Ryn inclined her head toward the fields of tall grasses. "I saw one of them. I need to take care of it before I return home."

Hywel gave her a despairing sort of look. "Listen, girl. How about we *both* head back to the village, stop by the Red Mare. I can spare an hour before returning to the mill. A drink on me."

"No." A hesitation, then, "Thank you. You shouldn't walk home in the dark, not tonight."

"Your family needs you," he said, more gently than she expected.

She stood a little straighter. The sun was all but set, casting a golden glow across the fields. Shadows crept in along the trees, and a cool breeze whispered through Ryn's loose shirt.

She thought of the grave mounds. Of the sleeping bones warm and safe beneath the earth.

"I know," she said. Hywel shook his head, but he didn't protest. He gave her one last nod before walking away from the village, toward the nearby creek and mill. The sword dragged, a little too heavy for the old man.

The village would be preparing for nightfall. Latches on all the doors locked. Gareth would blow out the candles, and the scent of burnt tallow would linger in the kitchen. Ceri would be getting ready for bed.

Ryn reached into her pack. She'd brought a bundle of hard bread and cheese and, lastly, her axe. She liked eating out here, amid the wilds and the graves. She felt more comfortable here than she did in the village. When she returned home, the weight of her life would settle upon her once again. There would be unpaid rent, food stores that should be filled for winter, an anxious brother, and a future that needed sorting out. The other young women of Colbren were finding spouses, joining the cantref armies, or taking up a socially acceptable trade. When she tried to imagine doing the same, she could not. She was a half-wild creature that loved a graveyard, the first taste of misty night air, and the heft of a shovel.

She knew how things died.

And in her darkest moments, she feared she did not know how to live.

So she sat at the edge of the graveyard and watched as the sun vanished behind the trees. A silvery half-light fell across the fields, and Ryn's heartbeat quickened. It was not truly dark, but it was dark enough for magic.

The sound of shuffling feet made her stand up. It was not the gait of an animal—but of a two-legged creature, one who could not walk properly.

Ryn rose and gripped her axe in one hand.

"Come on," she murmured. "I know you're out there."

And she did know. She'd seen the figure in the wee hours of the morning: a half-broken thing that had vanished into the tall grasses.

She heard the approach. It was slow—a staggering gait.

Thump. Shuffle. Thump.

The creature rose with the night.

It looked like something out of the tales that her father used to tell—a spindly creature of rotted flesh and tattered clothing. It was having trouble walking and every other step made the figure stagger.

Shuffle. Thump.

It had been a woman: A long dress trailed behind it, dragging in the dirt. Ryn didn't recognize her, but she must have died recently. Perhaps a traveler. A turned ankle could kill a person in the wilds, if they were alone.

"Good evening," said Ryn.

The creature went still. Its neck gave a sickening pop as it turned to look at her. Ryn wasn't sure how it could see—the eyes were always the first bits to go.

The bone house did not speak. They never did.

But still, Ryn felt obligated to say something.

"Sorry about this," said Ryn. And then she swung the axe at the dead woman's knees.

The first time, she'd gone for the head. Turned out, the dead were like chickens. They didn't need heads to blunder about. Knees were a much more practical target.

The blade bit into bone.

The woman staggered, reaching out for Ryn. Ryn ducked back, but the woman's brittle fingers caught her on the shoulder. She felt the rake of nails, the fingers stiffened in death. Ryn tore the axe free, and there was another nauseating wrenching sound, like tissues being rent apart. The dead woman fell to the ground. It rolled over, dug its bony fingers into the earth, and began to crawl toward Colbren.

"Would you please stop that?" Ryn brought the axe down a second time, and then a third. Finally, the creature went still.

Ryn pulled on a pair of leather gloves and set about searching the body. No coin purse, no valuables. She exhaled sharply, trying to hold back a sinking disappointment. She wasn't a grave robber—and she didn't take coin from the dead she was paid to bury. But these creatures that haunted the forest were fair game. After all, the cursed dead cared little for money. Only the living had need of it.

And Ryn did have need.

She'd gather up what was left of the woman, place the parts in a burlap sack, and bring them into the village for burning. Only the forge burned hot enough for bone.

It was the only peace she could offer the woman.

Ryn clenched her teeth as she hauled the burlap sack to the graveyard. She tied it shut, just to make sure no parts escaped. Her muscles burned with exertion. Despite the chill of the night, a sweat had soaked through her shirt.

The sack gave a twitch. "Stop that," said Ryn.

Another twitch.

Ryn crouched, settling on the ground beside the sack. She gave it an awkward sort of pat, the way she might try to calm her little sister. "If you'd stayed in the forest, you would have been fine. Want to tell me why death suddenly has an urge to wander?"

The sack went still.

Ryn pulled her gloves off and ate a few mouthfuls of bara brith. The dark bread was sweet and studded with dried fruit. The food eased the hollow feeling in her stomach. She looked at the sack and had the sudden urge to offer it a piece of bread. She tilted her head back and closed her eyes.

This was the problem with being a gravedigger in Colbren.

Nothing stayed buried forever.

CHAPTER 2

ELLIS HAD A fondness for travel.

When he first left the castle of Caer Aberhen, he had spent some time in the southern port cities. He had considered sailing to the continent on one of the sleek vessels brimming with freshly caught pollock and eels. He worked on a map of the docks for a harbormaster while he contemplated the course his life should take. He'd enjoyed a comfortable bed in the manor house, far from the bustle and noise of the city, and thought himself worldly for leaving Caer Aberhen so far behind.

But now he stood at the edge of a forest, utterly alone, and realized his own mistake.

He loved new places—but the travel involved was a nightmare.

His tent was sunken.

Strung between two small trees, it should have looked sturdy and warm, but instead appeared like a loaf of fallen bread. He frowned, tried to adjust the way the canvas draped, but pain flared beneath his left collarbone.

The cold night air aggravated his old injury. He was always leaning toward fires, hovering near wood stoves, and seeking out stray patches of sunlight. It was only when he was tucked amid the library stacks at Caer Aberhen that he'd forced himself to endure the chill that would settle into his joints. Even so, his hands remained deft. They had to be, if he were to make a living as a mapmaker.

With a resigned sigh, he reached for his pack. Rolls of parchment peeked out of the top. He plucked one from the cluster. The maps were old friends, speaking to him in lines and etchings as clearly as people spoke with words. He looked down at this particular map; it was smaller than the others, smudged with dirt and fingerprints. Yet there were flourishes of whimsy—small, shadowed creatures peeked through the branches of a forest, and a dragon perched atop a mountain. It reminded him of the maps he'd seen sailors use, where the edges of the parchment were marked with serpents. *Here be dragons.*

Ellis had never believed in monsters. And even if he had, this map wouldn't have made him turn back. For one thing, whomever had crafted it had done a laughable job with the distance markers. If this map were accurate, he would have arrived at Colbren in the afternoon and been cozily asleep under some tavern's roof.

Instead of spending the night on the fringes of a forest, under a crooked tent.

He balled up his cloak as a pillow and closed his eyes. Insects chirped and the wind whispered through the trees. He tried to focus on each sound, directing his mind away from his own discomfort.

And then everything went silent. There were no animal sounds, no rustling of wind through the trees.

The change kindled to life some instinct he had not known he had—an animal reaction of raw fear, of pounding pulse and shortened breath.

In the flickering light of his lantern, it took him a heartbeat to see the man. He knelt over Ellis, having entered the tent in perfect silence.

Cold fingers wrapped around Ellis's throat, so lightly at first it was almost a caress. The man's hand was as slick as a freshly landed fish, as cold as rainwater. And then the grip went tight.

Panic burned through Ellis. He reached for the only weapon he possessed: a walking stick. He jabbed it toward the man, trying to hit him around the shoulders and head. But it was little use. His heartbeat throbbed with an ever-rising pressure and his sight blurred at the edges.

Ellis could do little more than flail his arms and legs when the man began dragging him out of his tent. It took a moment for Ellis to realize that he was being pulled away from his camp, away from the cheery lantern light and the few trappings of civilization.

He was being dragged into the shadow of the forest.

Ellis was going to die. He was going to die alone, outside a village he could not find because *someone had put incorrect distance markers on their map.*

Desperation gave him new strength, and he threw a punch at the man's face. A cut opened up on the man's forehead, but there was no blood. He seemed more startled than injured; his fingers went slack. The man's wounded forehead sagged oddly, and revulsion crawled up Ellis's throat even as he broke free and skittered back into the circle of his small camp. The lantern light cast odd shadows upon the man's face—there were hollows where cheeks should have been, and his eyes were strangely blank.

He took a step toward Ellis, his fingers outstretched.

That was when the young woman appeared.

She looked at Ellis, then to the man. She was dressed in a loose tunic, her leggings worn and dirty at the knees. Her dark hair was bound in a tangled braid, and in one hand she carried an axe.

"Get out of here!" Ellis rasped, unsure if he was speaking to himself or the girl.

She didn't listen. When the man staggered toward her, she whirled once, as if to pick up speed, and then she swung the axe with more strength than Ellis could have mustered. The blade sank into the man's chest, collapsing part of his rib cage. The man fell, twitching, to the ground.

The girl placed her foot on the man's hip, holding him steady as she pulled the axe free.

Silence fell upon the small camp. Ellis breathed raggedly, his gaze fixed on the dead man. He didn't look like a bandit—or at least, not like any bandit Ellis had read about. His clothes were too fine, albeit soaked through with muddy water. His skin was too pale, and there was an odd bluish cast to his fingertips.

"Sorry about that," said the girl.

"No need to apologize to me," said Ellis, startled.

The girl's gaze flicked up, then went back to the man. "I wasn't."

The man twitched again. Ellis choked back a shout as the man began to sit up. He couldn't still be alive, not after taking a blow like that. But how—

The girl brought her axe down again. There was a thud and the next thing Ellis knew, there was an arm on the ground. Ellis found himself staring at it. He'd never been in battle before, but surely the removal of a limb would involve more blood.

"Listen," the girl said, as if speaking to an unruly child. The man rolled over, reached for her with the other, still-attached arm. "You need to stop that." A swing—a thud.

The man tried to move toward her, using his legs to push himself across the dirt.

"By all the fallen kings," said Ellis, sickened by the sight. "How is he not dead yet?"

The girl grimaced and slammed the axe into the man's knee. "He is. That's the problem."

"What?"

Finally, the man stopped trying to move. But still his eyes rolled about like those of an enraged animal.

"Do you have a sack?" asked the girl.

For a heartbeat, Ellis stood could only stand there. With a shake of his head, he ducked into the woefully crooked tent and began pulling the canvas free. "Will this work?"

The girl nodded. And without a trace of squeamishness, she reached down and began picking up the pieces of the man she'd just dismembered.

Ellis stared at her and wondered if he shouldn't cut his losses and run.

"Oh, sit down," she said. "You look like you're about to swoon."

He sank to his haunches. "Who—who are you?"

The girl began hauling the head and torso of the man onto the tent cloth. The dead man was still looking at her, mouth moving silently.

"Aderyn verch Gwyn," she said. "Gravedigger. And you are?"

Ah. No wonder a corpse did not disturb her.

"Ellis," he replied. "Of Caer Aberhen."

She waited for a family name—and he remained silent.

Aderyn looked down at the dead man. She began drawing in the edges of the canvas. A piece of twine appeared in her hand and she looped it around the bundle. "What did you do to him?"

Ellis frowned. "What?"

"Well, you must have done something." She finished tying off the canvas. "You wearing any iron?"

"What?" he said again. "No."

"Well, you should. Did you speak the name of the Otherking three times?"

"I—no, of course not."

"Dabble in magic?"

"Magic doesn't exist anymore," he said, some of his fear hardening into irritation. But if there was no magic, how could this man be—

"Dead," he said softly. He felt as if all his wits had been scattered about the camp, and he was scrambling for them. "He was *dead* and walking around—that can't happen."

Aderyn studied her handiwork. "Outside the forest, no. Inside the forest, yes." She gave his bedroll a dubious look. "Perhaps he just wanted to share your camp."

Ellis smiled thinly. "He probably could have found better lodging elsewhere, if he'd bothered to look." Aderyn laughed. Her gaze came up to meet his and she did not look away. It was the kind of look that held on a little too long. But it was not the same flirtatious glance that some young ladies gave him—rather, it felt like he was being picked apart, dismantled as easily as Aderyn had taken apart the dead man.

He glanced down, eyes on his hands. "Thank you," he said, realizing he had not said it yet. "For saving my life."

She let out a breath. "Well, to be honest, if I'd found that the bone house had already killed you, I was going to steal your coin."

He blinked. "Does that happen often?" He held up a hand, trying to buy a moment's time. "I mean, dead people coming out of the forest. Not you looting corpses."

"Never," said Aderyn. "Not until last week. Some dead bloke stumbled out of the forest and into the miller's yard. I was walking back to the village after picking berries, heard the shouting, and helped bring the bone house down." She gave a little shrug.

"The dead have the forest. I don't know why they're coming out of it, not now that magic has waned."

She spoke matter-of-factly. As if the risen dead were an infestation of plague rats she were trying to keep from her home.

"And what are you doing out here?" She nodded at his camp—at the overturned belongings, the maps scattered across the dirt, and the remnants of the fire he'd tried to make. "What brings a city lad into the wilds?"

He crossed his arms. "How do you know I'm from the city?"

"Because you tried to make a fire with green wood," she replied. "Because you have more parchment than food. Because you can afford enough oil to leave a lantern burning all night. Am I wrong?"

He gave her a shallow nod. "You're not wrong. And as for what I'm doing out here..." He reached down, picked up one of the scrolls. "I'm a mapmaker."

She frowned at him. "Why aren't you spending the night in the village?"

He looked around, groping for an explanation. "I—I meant to."

"You're lost," she said.

"I am not."

"You're a mapmaker who cannot find a village."

"I was using someone else's map," he said. "If I'd drawn it, this never would have happened." He rubbed at his forehead. "Can you bring me to the village? I have coin, if that's what it takes."

He saw the flicker of eagerness in her eyes. It was quickly quashed, and her neutral expression slid back into place. "All right. But I'm waiting to return until morning—just in case any more of these creatures decide to venture out of the woods. You all right with that?"

"I survived an attack of the risen dead," he replied. "I think I can spend a night without a tent."

Her eyes drifted toward the dark smudge of the trees only a few strides away. "We'll see, I suppose."

CHAPTER 3

THE ROAD TO Colbren was little more than packed earth. Sunlight reflected off the golden dead grasses that would revive with the autumn rainfall. Evidence of the village could be seen from here: Trees had been cut for firewood and the earthy scent of horse manure wafted from nearby fields.

Ryn carried one and a half of the bone houses. She considered it one and a half since she hauled the man—the heavier one—in her right hand, and she helped Ellis drag the woman with her left. For all that Ellis was taller than her and seemed like he should be able to carry a sack of flour with ease, he had winced when he first tried to pick up the bone house. Perhaps he'd been badly bruised in his tussle with the dead man.

Even this early, there was smoke in the air. Smoke from

stoves, from the tavern, from bakers lighting their ovens. It was always a welcoming smell to her—home.

Colbren's iron fence encircled the village. It was simple, rungs of old metal set wide enough that a child or slender adult could slip through. The fence was rusted a bloody red, and several lines of drying clothes were strung from it. Ryn caught Ellis's look of surprise when he saw the barrier. "Do you get many thieves?" he asked.

She shook her head. "The cities took down their iron protections after the otherfolk left. But you'll find us countryfolk a little more wary."

Ellis made a sound that might have been a suppressed laugh. "You still worry about the tylwyth teg?"

She did not smile. "Not them. Their leavings." She nodded down at the sacks.

"You mean magic."

"What's left of it."

"And what are we to do with these?" His voice had a pleasant rasp to it, low and a little hoarse. As if he'd need to lean in to say something important.

"Burn them," she replied. "I know the blacksmith—she'll help."

The smithy was on the southern edge of the village, where the winds could carry off the scents of burning metal. Ryn did not bother to knock, but rather headed around back to the forge.

Morwenna could have been anywhere from thirty to forty. With her darker skin and wiry hair, she clearly was not from

Colbren—which was usually an unforgivable offense. But Morwenna had simply shown up five years ago, taken over the abandoned smithy, and after only a few weeks it had seemed as if she'd always been there.

At this moment, she wore a heavy leather apron and work gloves. She went still when Ryn and Ellis walked into view, dragging the sacks beside them. Morwenna nodded at the bundle. "Ryn." She said the name with a bit of exasperation. "Please tell me wolves got a few of Hywel's sheep."

"No," said Ryn. "Another bone house—well, two of them."

Morwenna slipped her leather gloves off, then knelt beside the sacks. She rested one work-worn hand on them, as if trying to feel for life. "I'm not sure whether to believe you or not. You sure this wasn't some dead vagrant you found on the road?"

Of course she wouldn't believe Ryn—Morwenna was not of Colbren. She hadn't grown up listening to the old tales, standing at half-cracked doors as the candles burned to nubs while the elders murmured stories of the old days. But then again, even most of the younger villagers would have agreed with Morwenna. The Otherking had left the isles in the days of Ryn's great-grandfather, and the memories had faded into myth. Ryn's generation had little belief in magic. Which should have been a reassurance to her—even with these strange sightings of bone houses, they might have gone on using her burial services instead of burning the dead.

But the elders remembered. And they were the ones who, more often than not, needed the services of a gravedigger.

Her empty coin purse rested against her hip; Ryn ran her fingers over one leather edge before saying, "Believe me or don't. The bodies are real enough, and I need to burn them before nightfall. If you want proof, keep a hand for yourself and see what comes when the sun goes down."

Morwenna flashed her a smile. "Mayhap I'll do that—and perhaps slip it through Eynon's window the next time he comes to collect the rent."

Ryn tried not to smile, but she didn't try very hard.

"Who's this?" said Morwenna, with a look at Ellis.

"Traveler," replied Ryn. "Looking for a place to stay."

Morwenna's eyes raked over Ellis. "It'll be the Red Mare for him. Unless one of these houses pinched his coin." She gave the words a mocking little twist, a smile on her lips.

Ryn let out a sharp breath. "Just burn them, please?"

For all her amusement, Morwenna inclined her head. With a snap of her fingers, she summoned her apprentice—a lad who looked to be about ten or eleven. Ryn turned to leave, but Morwenna called after.

"Wait."

Ryn turned.

"You've got iron, right?" asked Morwenna. "At your home?"

"Of course," said Ryn. There was a horseshoe nailed beside her home's door frame, just like all the older village houses.

"Well, if you need more, come here. I've always got scraps."

It was a gesture of good will. Even if Morwenna didn't believe, even if she mocked and smiled, she'd offer Ryn what she could. Ryn gave her a deeper nod this time—an acknowledgment of the offer. "Thank you."

Just before she turned to go, she saw the apprentice begin to shove the canvas wrappings and their contents into the forge. Sparks flew into the air and Ryn hastened out of the room before the flames could truly catch. Burning the cursed dead was a kindness—but it also smelled rank.

The Red Mare was a large home that had been turned into a tavern. The upstairs rooms were for rent, and the downstairs consisted of an eatery and a tavern. Mostly, people went to hear the town's gossip.

"Go on in." Ryn nodded to the door. "Ask for Enid—tell her that I sent you and she'll charge you a reasonable fee."

Enid had always been at the Red Mare. She had always been red-cheeked and smiling, always widowed, always with frizzy gray hair. She would probably take one look at Ellis and decide the lad needed fattening up.

"Thank you," said Ellis. "I appreciate you bringing me here—and, again, for saving me from that... thing."

Ryn held out her hand, palm up.

Ellis smiled, took her hand, and shook it. His fingers were colder and softer than hers, lacking the calluses that creased her palm. When he released her, Ryn's hand remained in place. Ellis stared, then understanding lit behind his eyes.

"Ah, right." He fished about in his pack and came up with several coins. He dropped them into her palm.

She nodded, pocketed the coins, and walked away. "I'd keep to the roads, if I were you. At least until you find better maps."

She heard his snort—and she smiled to herself. But then she picked up her pace, and as she strode through the village, all thoughts of Ellis faded away.

Her home was on the edge of Colbren. It looked like the other old houses—wooden walls, thatched roof, and smoke rising from the chimney. There was a large yard where they kept the chickens and the single goat they could afford. The chickens were merrily strolling about the house, searching for food in the tangled grasses.

It felt as if a fist loosened around her heart when she pushed the door open and stepped inside. She savored the small familiarities: Woodsmoke, clean clothes hanging up to dry, the elaborate wooden spoons her father had carved for her mother hanging on the wall, and the goat—

The goat.

There was a goat standing in the hallway.

She looked at Ryn, opened her mouth, and bleated a greeting.

"Ceri," said Ryn, her voice rising. "Why is your goat in the house?"

There came the clatter of metal, a curse, and then Gareth stumbled out of the kitchen. He wore an apron and carried a cooking spoon in one hand. He waved the spoon at the goat. "Oh, not again. Shoo! Get out!"

The goat gave him a flat stare.

"Ceri, your goat's in the house again," called Gareth.

No answer.

"Ceridwen!" This time Gareth bellowed so loudly that both Ryn and the goat jumped. "Get your goat out of the house!"

Footsteps thudded across the floor, and Ceri came rushing into the room, hair ribbons streaming out behind her. "Good morning," said Ryn, a trifle drily. "I see things have gone well in my absence."

Ceri took gentle hold of the goat and began ushering her toward the front door. "Good morning!"

"How come Ryn gets a 'good morning' and I get a 'what's for breakfast,'" Gareth said. He still held the cooking spoon, and for the first time, Ryn noticed the batter that clung to his fingers. He must have been making griddle cakes.

"Because your idea of telling me a story last night was to get out your accounts ledger," said Ceri, grinning. As she strode by, tugging the goat, she rose to tiptoe and dropped a kiss on her brother's cheek. He sighed, waving her off as he retreated toward the kitchen.

There was an ease to Ceri's affection that Ryn envied. She kissed everything from the chickens to freshly baked loaves of bread. For Ryn, kisses were—

A press of lips against the braided crown of her hair. The dry rasp of her mam's cough when she pressed a handkerchief to her mouth, blood staining the folds.

—farewells.

Trying to push her thoughts aside, Ryn followed her little sister into the yard. The goat was tugging restlessly at the rope lead, staring hungrily at a patch of vetch near the iron fence.

"The goat should go in the pen," she said. "Letting her wander about is bound to get us in—"

Her voice faded.

A man stood in the yard. He could not have looked more out of place amid the overgrown grass and the chickens. He wore the crisp, clean clothes of a nobleman. His hair was silver, and he held himself rigidly straight.

"—trouble," said Ryn. "Ah. Hello there, Master Eynon."

She had never liked Lord Eynon. He was the sort who would run over a person's cat with his cart, then coolly deliver the body with a warning that should such an incident happen again, he would take it up with the cantref court.

Ryn should know. She'd been ten and she'd loved that cat.

"I suppose you know why I'm here." His voice had a silky tone, and it set Ryn's teeth on edge. She thought of her axe and decided it was likely a good thing she wasn't still carrying it.

"I do," Ryn replied, unwavering. "And I'm afraid we'll have to postpone payment."

Eynon's fingers slid down his spotless sleeve. He straightened it, studying the fine material with studious care. "I am not sure what you mean, my dear girl."

Ryn resisted the urge to tell him that she was not his dear girl. "The Turners decided not to use our services. And if we give you payment now, with no certainty that we'll bury anyone else before winter, we might not be able to feed ourselves." She was half aware of the door opening behind her, of Gareth walking into the yard. Ceri moved closer, the goat's lead still in hand. Ryn wondered if it was a show of strength, or if her siblings felt better with their elder sister between them and the irritable noble.

"I see." Eynon gave her a cool look, and he sighed. "That is a pity. You see, your uncle was already late in returning payment to me. I fear that if I'm not paid in full soon . . . I will have to take the coin from elsewhere." He stepped back, his gaze sweeping over the house. "Perhaps by selling this place."

Ryn's fingers clenched. "You can't just—"

"I can," he said. "And if I'm not paid within the fortnight, I will."

Anger rose within her; it was the kind of anger that came from helplessness, that made wild animals snarl and bite. She wanted to threaten Eynon the way he had threatened her, and the words slipped out before she could stop them. "Surely you skim enough coin from the coffers that you should be giving to the prince. Our uncle's debts won't inconvenience you."

Eynon's expression went flat and his gaze fixed on her.

She heard Gareth's sharp intake of breath. He stepped forward, placing himself between Eynon and Ryn. "Debts cancel each other out," he said quickly. "If you were to forgive our uncle's debts, we would no longer hold a claim on you."

Eynon gave him a cold look. "What?"

"The coin you owe our family," said Gareth. "For the scouting job our father took." If Ryn did not know him so well, she would not have heard the slight hitch in his voice. "From which he did not return."

"He did not complete the job," said Eynon, voice silkier than ever. "I paid those who did."

"He died," snarled Ryn.

"His companions cannot confirm that." Eynon flicked a piece of dried grass from his sleeve. "According to them, your father went into the mine and did not come out. Perhaps he tired of your family and decided to wait until the cover of night to slip away."

"He would never have—"

"And it is all moot," said Eynon. "Without a body, you can't prove his death. And I am under no obligation to give you coin for a never-completed expedition. As for your uncle…he does owe me. He never was a good gambler. You *are* obligated to pay that debt."

He gave them a smile and turned to go. Ryn breathed in, held that breath like her mother used to tell her to, and then exhaled slowly. She had to be calm. She had to handle this like a proper adult. She had to—

"Release the goat," she said quietly.

Ceri looked up at her, confused. Then she loosened her hold on the goat's lead. The goat blinked at her sudden freedom, looking about. Goats were rather opinionated creatures. Once they got it in their mind to do something, dissuading them could be a battle. As for Ceri's goat, she had long ago decided that the yard was hers—as were the people within it. Intruders were not to be tolerated.

The goat took one look at Eynon and lowered her head. Hooves thumped on the packed earth, and Eynon heard the approach just in time. He turned to see the goat barreling down on him, and surprise flashed across his face. He tore into a run, fine coat billowing behind him. Chickens scattered out of his path as he sprinted away, enraged goat on his heels. Eynon snarled, scrabbled for something to defend himself with, and ended up tossing a handful of dead grass at the goat.

The goat was not deterred. She chased him from the yard, and the two vanished around a corner.

"Oh no," said Ceri, in an utterly neutral voice. "The goat got loose."

"You should get her back before she wanders to the baker and begins begging for scraps," said Ryn.

Ceri grinned and skipped away, her hair ribbons still drifting over her shoulders.

Ryn stood there, shaking with anger, until Gareth came up behind her. "I'm not sure that was wise," he said softly.

"Which part? Mentioning that he steals from the prince or sending the goat after him?"

"Both," he replied. "But the first one worries me more."

Ryn turned on her heel, stalked back into the house, Gareth still behind her. "Everyone knows he lines his pockets with the coin he should be sending to the castle."

"Yes," said Gareth, "but there is a difference between knowing a thing and threatening someone with that knowledge."

She went to the kitchen and found several griddle cakes smoking ominously. She scraped them from the hot stone, her eyes watering from the sour smoke.

It was just the smoke.

And nothing else.

Gareth leaned against the wall, watching her work. He

twirled the cooking spoon between his fingers. "We could do it, you know."

"Do what?" She reached for the spoon, plucking it from his hand. She scooped a fresh dollop of batter onto the griddle. A stray droplet skittered across the hot stone.

"Sell this place."

Ryn's head jerked up. "What?"

Gareth shrugged. "It's always been a possibility and you know that. Uncle's debts mean we need the coin. And with the strange behavior of the bone houses—I don't know. I would feel better starting over somewhere else." His tone became gentler. "Ceri could apprentice to a baker. I could work for a merchant. And I'm sure graveyards near the cities could use a gravedigger."

"We are not selling our home." The words jerked out of her, each one painful. "Mam lived here—she died here. Da loved this place. And—"

"And none of that matters right now." Gareth took a deep breath. "I understand you don't want to leave. But if we can't feed ourselves come winter..."

"We'll find a way." She turned the cakes. Perfectly golden on one side.

"But what if we can't—"

"I can."

"You're not an adult yet, and I'm a year younger than you." He ran a hand through his hair, streaking the dark locks with flour. "You can't legally run the graveyard for another year. I know people have been letting us, but Eynon's a bad enemy to have. What if—"

Ryn slammed her hand against the wall. It hurt, but it was better than listening to him. She pushed past him, walked out of the kitchen and to her bedroom. There was a window cut into the wooden wall, and she looked through it.

Ceri was in the yard, stroking a brush along the goat's back. She was talking to the animal, saying that it was wrong to chase strangers, even though she couldn't truly blame her for wanting to chase Master Eynon.

Ryn watched her younger sister. Ceri was comfortable here—with her goat and her friends, in a home built by their great-grandfather. She slept beneath a quilt crafted by their mother and ate on a table hewn from a slab of wood that their father had cut from a nearby oak tree. This place wasn't just their home—it was their history.

They weren't leaving.

CHAPTER 4

YEARS AGO, RYN'S mother would tell her stories of how Colbren came to be.

The village was founded in the roots of the Annwvyn mountains before the Otherking fled the isles. In those early days, it was not uncommon to hear strange noises in the night. In the morning, the damp earth was marred by clawed footprints, and livestock would often have vanished, leaving only tufts of bloodied fur behind.

One day, a woman had ventured into the mountain forests with a basket of her finest wares. She carried golden churned butter, and fresh loaves of bread studded with dried fruits, and apples that tasted of autumn sunlight.

She placed the basket on the mossy ground and waited

until she heard the bushes rustle. Then the woman spoke to the empty air.

If you let us be, she said, *we will bring offerings again.*

She turned and left the forest, never glancing behind. But the next day, the basket was placed on the woman's doorstep, emptied of its contents.

The disappearances of livestock ceased after that. There were no more strange tracks or noises, and Colbren was left alone. And every autumn, one of the farmers would leave a basket of their finest foods in the woods.

Even after magic fled the rest of the isles, Colbren still prospered.

When a vein of copper was discovered in the nearby mountains, the village flourished. Eynon, a distant relative of the cantref prince, came to reside in Colbren, and he took control of the mine. It was a source of wealth for all—sons of farmers became miners, and homes that were once crafted of wood were built in stone. Sentinels guarded the village at night, for fear of bandits who might try to rob the stores of copper.

It was said that in these fruitful times, the people of Colbren grew forgetful. With full bellies and heavy purses, they did not think to send the yearly offerings into the forest. After all, magic had gone. Why should gifts be left for the forest?

But then one of the mine shafts collapsed.

Eighteen men were buried, and for fear of losing more, the mine was closed down. The wealth that had once streamed into the village slowed to a trickle. Fields yielded fewer crops; livestock wandered away with alarming frequency; the roads that led to the village fell into disrepair.

Ryn remembered the touch of her mother's fingers weaving through her hair, steady and sure, twining her unruly locks into a braided crown. *It's just a story*, her uncle would say. *A morality tale to scare the children.* He was their mother's brother, and had come to live with them after their father vanished. He had been a man who had only grown more brittle with every year. He rarely left his rocking chair but for the promise of drink or a fresh grilled cake. And he always scoffed at the tales.

The autumn after her father had vanished, Ryn took a few late-harvest apples. She did not have a basket, so she bundled the fruit into a worn cloth, clumsily knotting it closed. She walked into the forest, where the shadows were deep and the frosts lingered. She left the small offering on a fallen log.

The next week, Ryn found a young goat in their yard. It was a scrappy little thing, chewing on one of her uncle's old boots. Ryn hastily took the goat out of sight, tied her to a fence post, and went into the village to see if anyone had lost a goat.

But no one claimed it. Ceri took to the goat as if she were a favorite new toy, braiding grasses around her neck and taking naps between her hooves.

"We are not naming it," said her uncle, when he discovered Ceri's fondness for the animal. "It is livestock, not a pet. And if we have a harsh winter, it'll be the first thing we eat."

"Hush," Ryn's mother had told him, and she allowed Ceri to keep the goat.

Every autumn, Ryn left apples in the forest.

Her uncle complained of the missing food and her brother looked on in quiet disapproval, but Ryn ignored them both.

They might have forgotten the old magic, but she had not.

And perhaps, if she left enough gifts, the forest might give her father back.

In the dawn light, Ryn slipped from her room.

Her bare feet were silent on the floor, and moved unerringly even in the dimness. A sack in one hand and her boots in the other, Ryn carefully nudged the door shut behind her.

The chill morning air was clotted with fog and Ryn breathed in the familiar smell. The cold was bracing but pleasant, and she smiled as she pulled on her boots. A heavy wool cloak was wrapped around her shoulders, and she strode away from the house. The goat was nowhere to be seen, Ryn reflected, and she wondered vaguely if the animal was off stealing turnips from a neighbor's garden.

She loved this time of the morning, when everything was lush and quiet. The damp grasses brushed her fingertips as she veered left and cut through a field.

She retreated to the forest the way some people took refuge in chapels. It was soothing in a way she could not wholly describe: The stillness and the vibrant greens, the sense of life all around her—hidden, yet still thriving. The call of birds high up in the trees, the earth freshly tilled by moles and gophers, the soft mosses.

This was the truth of the forest—it was life and death in equal measure. Brimming with acorns and berries, yet beneath the fallen leaves were the bodies of animals that had not survived.

"You took your time getting here."

Ryn cursed, startled, then glared at the speaker.

"Sorry." Ceri stood a short distance away, leaning against an oak. Her hair was braided back, her face freshly scrubbed. "I didn't mean to frighten you."

"Why did you follow me?" Ryn crossed her arms.

Ceri held up a basket. "You're going to look for berries, are you not? Because you don't want to sell the house."

She should have expected this; for all that Ceridwen played at being the innocent younger sister, that was all it was—an act. She was a sharp-eyed little thing, and she concealed her shrewdness behind her sweet smiles. "You shouldn't listen at windows," Ryn told her.

"You and Gareth never tell me anything." Ceri was unabashed. "Now come on. I brought a basket—and I'd like to be home before noon."

"All right," she said. "Come on. But if Gareth asks, you followed me without my say-so."

"That's true." Ceri pushed away from the oak and whistled. A small white animal came lumbering toward them.

The *goat*. "If she eats all our berries—" said Ryn, with a groan.

The goat lowered her head, allowing Ceri to scratch between her horns. "She's not so bad," said Ceri. "Just a little protective. Sort of bristly. I don't know who she reminds me of."

Ryn did not dignify that with a response.

"What are we looking for?" asked Ceri. The goat was pulling oak leaves from a low branch, chewing with the slow contentedness of an animal that knew it would never go hungry.

"There are blackberries on the western edge of the creek," Ryn pushed aside a branch and walked ahead.

Ceri gave a gentle tug on the goat's horn and she tottered after them, still eating everything she could grab along the way. "I'm not sure we can make enough preserves to pay off Uncle's debts," said Ceri. "Or were you hoping to find nightshade?"

Ryn let out a startled laugh. "Ceridwen!"

"No one would miss Master Eynon," she said. "A few poisonous berries slipped into a jar of blackberry preserves…"

"I don't understand how someone with such a sweet face can come up with such terrible ideas."

"That's why no one would suspect me." Ceri grinned, but then her smile faded. "All right, all right. So we need something less drastic than murder."

"Preferably."

A lone vine stretched out, blocking their access to the berries, its leaves like extended fingers, and Ryn pulled a knife from her pocket and cut it away before the thorns could snag. The bushes smelled wonderful—the sweetness of the berries and the green of the forest warmed by morning sunlight. The goat began to tear into the blackberry leaves, uncaring about the brambles.

"It's the bone houses that are the problem," said Ceri. She looked at the forest all around. "You know most young people don't believe in them."

"We do," said Ryn.

Ceri gave a little shrug. "I remember Mam talking about them—and you've said you've seen them. But most people—they think they're *stories*, Ryn."

"Hywel doesn't," said Ryn. "And even though the graveyard is protected, the Turners thought there was enough truth to the stories to burn their dead rather than bury them. Enid keeps planting gorse about the Red Mare."

"Right, and they're all old," said Ceri.

"Everyone is old compared to you," said Ryn, a corner of her mouth lifting. "What does this have to do with selling the house?"

"Because our lives depend on people dying." Ceri dropped a handful of blackberries into her basket; her fingers were stained crimson. "And old people tend to die more quickly than young ones. But they won't be paying for your services, not so long as they think the dead will rise."

"So I'm a gravedigger being put out of business by the risen dead. Which means we can't pay off Uncle's gambling debts." Ryn's fingers slipped and a thorn snagged on her knuckle. She popped the finger into her mouth, the coppery taste of blood on her tongue. "We'll have to find another way."

Gareth's words still rang in her mind: *Debts cancel each other out.* If she could prove to Eynon that her father had not fled from his job, if she could find proof that he had indeed perished in the mine—

She closed her eyes. Her other hand slipped into her pocket, caressing the worn surface of a wooden love spoon. Broken in two, edges still a little sharp. Half for her, and half for her father. A silent promise to return.

The living had a tendency to make promises they could not keep.

CHAPTER 5

ELLIS SPENT THE night recovering at the Red Mare.

He felt as if he'd been hit by a hammer on the left side of his body; his muscles clenched and spasmed, spiking pains through his ribs, down his spine, across his lower back. This was the problem with pain, he thought. It refused to be quieted. It devoured, the way flame consumed wood. It took and it took, and all he could do was lie on a mattress of straw, torn between boredom and fear. Fear that this time the injury would not let up. That this time the pain would finally conquer him.

He chewed willow bark, the sinew caught between his back teeth. It helped, but it only kept the agony at bay for a few hours. When he felt well enough, he worked on preliminary sketches of his maps. And then he would close his eyes and wait. For the throbbing to pass, for his control over his own body to reassert itself.

Finally, the next morning, he walked down the stairs, each step a little soft and careful, until he stood in the tavern proper. The tables were planks of wood set atop wine barrels, and the floor was uneven, but the food smelled good. Despite the early hour, there was a bearded man asleep in a corner, slumped against a barrel.

Enid beamed at Ellis. "You're feeling better, then?" she asked, sliding a plate of sausages to him. He nodded in answer and thanks, and picked up a fork. As he ate, he listened to the conversation two tables over.

"—chickens gone missing," a woman was saying. "It's either thieves or a fox that's gotten too brazen."

"Or maybe Eynon's decided to start collecting fowl instead of rent."

There was a snort, and then someone else said, "He's taken more iron. Can't be right—not the way he's pulling it off. If it were free to take—"

"Then you'd already have pinched it, Rhys." A laugh. "It's cantref property. 'Course he can take it. And if anyone makes a fuss, they'll have to face him in the courts. No one's going to protest."

"I heard he was going to sell it," said the woman. "Use it to shore up the granaries for winter."

"Well, we'll never see any of that food, so eat up, girl. Before there's frost on the ground."

Ellis listened and ate—all the while keeping his gaze down. He could feel the weight of eyes upon him, and while it wasn't an unfamiliar sensation, it also wasn't comfortable.

"Who's that?" This time the voice was lowered to a whisper.

"Traveler," came another murmur.

"Trader?"

"Too young."

"Trapper?"

"Look at his boots—that stitching. Only worn by nobles. He must be a relative of Eynon."

People could never place him: Half of them saw his clothes and manners and thought he must be a wayward noble; some thought he was a thief who'd stolen his clothes. Either way, merchants always overcharged him.

Perhaps the most galling thing—Ellis could not contradict any of them.

He was all of those things and none of them at all.

When he was finished with his meal, Ellis went out to take his first true look at Colbren.

Mapmaking was about details. Specifically, what details to include and what to leave out. Ellis remembered his first lesson how his teacher had said mapmaking was a profession of responsibility. Wars could be won or lost with a map; travelers could lose their way; entire villages could vanish.

On most maps, Colbren existed as a dot beside the forest. Half the time, it was not even labeled—and he could see how such an oversight had affected the town. Several homes were abandoned. Clothes were mended and worn soft with age, and several of the youths traipsed about with muddy knees and no shoes.

As for the mountains, they appeared on paper—but never as more than a few rough sketches. They were a place no mapmaker had managed to capture—and as he walked, he drew a leather-bound journal from his pack and began to sketch. A rough grid of the town appeared on the parchment, and his gaze flicked back and forth between the village before him and the one taking form on the paper.

A bleat drew his attention.

A goat stood beside a cart, half an apple wedged in its mouth. It stared flatly at a villager, who appeared to be gesticulating wildly at the apple. The goat's eyes never left the villager as it crunched the treat.

"She's sorry," said a girl, who was trying to drag the goat by the horns. "Come on. Let's go find food elsewhere." She glanced over her shoulder and said to the villager, "I'll pay for the apple tomorrow, I promise!"

Ellis watched the girl go, then he strode up to the villager and offered her a coin. "For the girl's apple," he said. She blinked, then pocketed the coin.

"You don't have to do that," said a voice behind him. Aderyn stood there; her hair was bound in a braid and her face was scrubbed clean—and this time, she carried a basketful of berries rather than an axe. But she appeared no less formidable.

"Good morning, Aderyn."

She slid the basket of berries onto the villager's cart.

The villager held up a blackberry between thumb and forefinger. "From the forest?" she asked.

Aderyn nodded. "We have too many for preserves—I thought you might be interested in a few."

The villager named a sum. It was lower than what Ellis might have expected. Aderyn took her empty basket and began to walk away. "You needn't have paid for my sister's apple," Aderyn said. "I can do that."

"I didn't mind," he said. He fell into step beside her, unsure where she was going, but glad for a moment's conversation. "And you seemed fine with taking my coin before."

"That was for services rendered," she said.

"Do you know of a good cloth merchant?" he asked. "I need to buy a new tent."

She narrowed her eyes. "First the apple, now a tent. If you think you can bribe your way into Colbren's good graces... well, you're probably right."

That made him laugh.

"If you remember," he said, "my tent was destroyed helping carry a dead man to the village."

She seemed to relent, but only a little. "You'll want Dafyd. He's the only one who won't overcharge you. Come on." She tucked the basket into the crook of her arm and her step quickened. "How are you finding the Red Mare?"

"Comfortable," he replied. "Thank you."

His gaze swept west toward the mountains; he could just make out peaks through the low-hanging clouds. "Do you know of any villagers who might be willing to take me into the mountains? It would be a week's journey, I think."

"Into the mountains," she repeated. "Into the—you do remember, right?" She waved her arms vaguely. "Dead man tried to drag you in that direction?"

A shiver ran through him. But he managed to keep his voice steady when he answered, "I do remember, yes."

She pointed at the mountains. "Annwvyn," she said. "The land of the otherfolk. The birthplace of monsters, of magic, and where Arawn used to rule."

"If it's so dangerous, why did you venture near the forest the night we met?" he asked.

"I grew up here," she said. "I saw my first bone house when I was six."

"Well," he said. "It looks as if I've found my guide."

"No." Aderyn gave a sharp shake of her head. "I have a job. And a family. I can't go blundering about in the woods, not even for—" Her protests died away. "How much *would* you be willing to pay?"

He named a sum.

She doubled it.

He winced. "I—I am not sure I could pay that."

Aderyn's gaze swept deliberately over his finely embroidered cloak, then back to his face. Her mouth was set in a disbelieving line.

He didn't know how to tell her that while he might have grown up among the nobles, he wasn't one of them. Finally, he shook his head. "I can pay you half now, and half when we return."

It would take some doing, but he'd manage it. And if he did map those mountains, he could sell that knowledge for a pretty sum.

"It's a deal," she said, smiling. "We can't go right away, as I'll need to prepare. But..."

Her voice drifted at the same moment her attention did. Ellis watched as her gaze swept to the side, hooked on something beyond him.

A man stood beside the iron fence. He wore the heavy leathers of someone used to working with metals, and he bore tools that flashed in the sunlight. He was pounding a chisel into the place where one bar met another, and with a yank, he pulled it free.

He was dismantling it.

Ellis felt a whisper of air as Aderyn ran past him, toward the fence. Her face was utterly pale, making her freckles stand out in stark contrast. She reached for the iron pole, trying to yank it from the man's hand. *"What are you doing?"*

"Eynon's orders," said the man. He wasn't much older than Ellis, perhaps only in his mid-twenties. He had a heavy jaw and he spoke with the kind of assurance that was not reassuring at all. "We're going to sell the iron."

Aderyn's mouth worked. She seemed to be reaching for words. "You—can't!"

"I assure you, we can," said the man.

"If you do this—" She threw an arm out toward the mountains. "Cold iron. That's our protection. If you take it away—"

"Protection against what?" The man laughed, and Aderyn visibly bristled. "Against those corpses you keep dragging to the village?"

"The bone houses are real!" Her hands fisted. "I've seen them. Hywel has seen them. Ask anyone who's gone into the forest, ventured near the mountains—"

"That forest drives people mad," said the man, with the tolerate arrogance of someone sure he was right. "It's turned your mind—and it took your father. Thought you'd know enough to leave it be."

She raised a hand as if to slap him. But the man reached out, caught her wrist. "Now, now, Aderyn. None of that. You don't want to be brought into the courts for assaulting a man—you can't afford it."

Her teeth bared in a snarl of utter fury.

"Release her," said Ellis. Where Aderyn's anger burned hot, Ellis felt his temper like a chill running through his bones.

The man looked at him, seemingly aware of Ellis for the first time. "What?"

"Release her," said Ellis again. "Or I will see *you* in the courts. And I *can* afford it."

Or, he could until he paid Aderyn to take him into the mountains. But if she were arrested, she couldn't be his guide.

The man let go of Aderyn's arm. She jerked away.

"Come on," said Ellis, tugging on her sleeve. Aderyn remained rooted in place.

He pulled a little more insistently, and she relented, taking several steps back, even as her gaze never left the man.

"Come on," said Ellis again, and this time, Aderyn allowed him to pull her away.

She seemed to be moving on instinct alone; her feet knew

the way. She took him to a merchant from whom he bought a new tent—and a crossbow, for good measure. It took too much coin, but he knew better than to buy a longbow with his shoulder. When the money had exchanged hands, Aderyn walked him back to the Red Mare. She still held her empty basket, and her gaze seemed unfocused, awash in thoughts that he could not fathom.

He took her gently by the elbow and her eyes snapped up to him. "One drink?" he said. "I hear this place makes a fine barley tea."

Her mouth crooked up at the corner. "Tea? You want to drink tea at a tavern?"

He smiled back, but his was a little more restrained. "Yes," he said simply.

Enid was serving the midday meal to a few older men. She beamed at Ellis, said, "Well, well, I see you've made a friend. Ryn, don't you go scaring off this young man like you do all the others."

They took a corner table, and Ellis said mildly, "Is she trying to find you a spouse?"

"No," said Aderyn. "She just doesn't want me scaring you off because then she'd have no one to rent that upstairs room."

They sat in silence until the tea arrived, and Ellis took a sip. Aderyn's attention seemed to be drifting again; her tea sat untouched on the table.

"I believe," said Ellis, "it's time you told me what exactly a bone house is."

Aderyn looked at him. It was a flat look, the kind his teachers had given him when they were sure he should know an answer.

"It's a dead person," she said, taking a swig. "A risen corpse. You saw one. I shouldn't have to explain it to you."

He considered his words more carefully. "I mean, if there truly are risen dead wandering around, then why have I never heard of them?"

She fixed him with a look. "Tell me. When you go back to the city, and someone asks you about your journey—are you going to tell them that you were attacked by a dead bandit?"

He shook his head. "Of course not."

"Why?"

"Because they'd think I was mad." The words came out before he'd even considered them.

She nodded.

"Because most people don't believe in magic," said Aderyn flatly. "Even here, at the edge of the tamed lands, the younger ones have begun to think it's all tales. And those who do believe keep their mouths shut, for fear of being called mad or liars. Except me. And a few others who don't give a damn what the village thinks of us."

Ellis frowned. "But... you've brought bodies to the smithy for burning. Is that not proof enough?"

"I suppose it's easier to think that people have just been dragging corpses back to the village to scare people."

He wrinkled his nose. "Where do they think you get the bodies?"

Her anger was all fire and sparks. "I suppose they think I dig them up from the graveyard. As if I *would*." She closed her eyes, breathing hard through her nose.

"Did the bone houses always bother folk who go into the forest?" He considered. "Surely, when the mine was in working order, the miners would have noticed."

"The mine closed twenty-five years ago," she said. "The bone houses appeared…I don't know. I was too young to remember. Fifteen years ago? Eighteen?"

"Eighteen years," said Ellis. It seemed a long time to live in the presence of such creeping danger. Perhaps a person could grow used to it. "Does anyone know how it started?"

Aderyn laced her fingers on the table. "You want to hear the story?"

Ellis nodded.

CHAPTER 6

THE MOUNTAINS OF Annwvyn have never welcomed humans.

They began with fire. With hills that spewed ash and flame until they rose to jagged peaks. People rarely went into them—the mountains were little more than sharp-edged slate and wind-torn trees.

It was the king of the otherfolk, Arawn, who made his home there. Castell Sidi, a fortress of granite and enchantment, rose up beside a clear mountain lake, the Llyn Mawr. It is said he brought the magic with him—for he was immortal and lovely, and he could weave enchantments as easily as we spin wool. And where he went, other magical creatures followed.

There were the afanc, who lurked beneath the surface of rivers, watching for unwary travelers; the pwca, shape-changers and creatures of fortune that might bestow luck or bring a person to ruin; and, of course, the tylwyth teg—the immortals, who held revels that would last decades.

It was said Arawn rode with crimson-eyed hounds, and he would wreak terrible retribution on anyone who interrupted a hunt. But he was not a monster. Those he favored found themselves with gold and health and magical trinkets. For many years, all was well.

But those gifts drew attention.

There was a man called Gwydion of the house of Dôn. He had some talent for magic and mischief—and he loved both. When his brother yearned for a maiden the king favored, Gwydion began a war between the north and south kingdoms so that his brother had time enough to seize her. And that was the least of his crimes.

Gwydion slew kings, taunted enchantresses, and befriended enough poets that tales of his exploits became known throughout the isles.

And then he turned his gaze toward Annwvyn.

He had heard of the Otherking's wealth, of the magic and monsters that dwelt within the mountains. But rather than frighten him, those tales made him greedy.

So he slipped into Annwvyn and stole from Arawn.

Perhaps the ensuing war might have been averted if Gwydion had offered some kind of apology. Most men would have cowered before the rage of the Otherking; he had those red-eyed hounds, as well as great knights, a cauldron said to raise the dead, and an undefeated champion.

Gwydion should have retreated, but he had spent years gathering power and an ego to match. He called the trees to fight for him, and in the ensuing chaos, he met Arawn's champion.

If Gwydion had fought fairly, he would have perished. But he was a clever, wicked sort, and he did not fight.

Rather, he spoke the champion's true name.

And broke his power.

"Wait, wait," said Ellis, holding up his hand for silence. His elbow knocked into his cup. Ryn grabbed for it, saving the tea. "Sorry—but how does speaking a name defeat Arawn's greatest champion?"

Ryn scowled and dragged the cup to the middle of the table. "Because names have power. Always have."

"Enough power to defeat a champion? Why not simply lop his head off?"

"Creatures of magic," she said, "are creatures of will. Their name is often . . . I don't know. A part of that. If you could name them, if you could pin down exactly what they were, then you might be able to bend that will to your own."

Ellis appeared unimpressed. "So if you were one of the otherfolk, I could say 'Aderyn' and you'd be powerless against me?"

She pointed a finger at him. "My name means 'bird,' so probably not. But if my name were Farmer, and I was a farmer, and my whole life was farming, then perhaps."

"So it's not just a name," said Ellis. "You have to pin down their role, their identity." He tilted his head in thought. "Maybe that's why so many surnames have to do with occupations."

"It wouldn't work on humans, though," said Ryn. "We're too stubborn. And not magical enough." She took a sip of her own tea, wetting her dry tongue. "Now do you want to hear the rest?"

Ellis placed a finger against his lips. "I'll be silent as the grave."

Furious and disgusted at the greed of men, King Arawn withdrew from Annwvyn. He took his court and his magic, and he sailed to where no human could follow. Castell Sidi was abandoned.

As the years passed, people stopped believing in magic. The rivers were dragged, and the afanc slain. The pwca starved, as the farmers who had once believed in luck no longer laid out offerings for them.

All that was left of magic were a few traditions: copper coins tossed over the prow of a boat, a sprig of rowan tucked into a pocket, and always the right stocking pulled on before the left. Such small magics were repeated until their original purposes were mostly forgotten.

But there were some who did not forget.

It's said that perhaps twenty or so years ago, a man ventured into the mountains of Annwvyn. He had heard of great treasures left in the Otherking's fortress. He knew something of magic, so he brought gifts for the last of the monsters: fresh kills to distract the afanc and small sweets to appease the pwca.

The man went to Castell Sidi, hoping to find treasure or jewels. But what he found was far more valuable: a cauldron crafted of the darkest iron, its edges stained with rust.

Most men would have scoffed at such a find, but this one recognized the worth of the cauldron, sensed the power wrought within the iron.

He took it and returned home.

When the man said the cauldron would make his fortune, people laughed at him.

The man was right.

Terribly, horribly right.

For that night, he boiled water within the cauldron. He took a cup of it to the graveyard; a young woman resided there, beneath blankets of soil and moss. He had courted her, but a sickness claimed her before he could. He dug up the grave, opened the coffin, and trickled the water into the dead woman's mouth. In a heartbeat, her eyes flickered open. Her skin brightened and became new. She drew one breath, and then another, and when she could speak, she said the man's name and smiled. She took his hand, and he pulled her from her grave.

The man brought the woman home, and her family recoiled

with terror. She should have been dead—they knew that. But the man hastily explained: He had found the cauldron of rebirth within Annwvyn.

Word spread. People flocked to the man, begged him to save their lost loved ones. And he did—for a price. The man and the woman dwelt in wealth and happiness, and she bore him a child.

But word of this reached several kingdoms. When the princes learned of the cauldron, they imagined wars won before a single arrow was fired. No one would dare attack a kingdom if its armies could not fall.

At first, the cantref princes were kind to the man. They sent gifts for his child, sacks of gold, promises of land and titles. The man smiled and rejected them all.

When kindness did not achieve their ends, the princes began to bargain. It was simply too dangerous to have such a magic, they insisted. If the cauldron fell into the wrong hands, it would be a weapon. Surely the man wanted it to be protected?

The man said he could protect it.

And then the soldiers arrived.

For if they could not cajole or bargain for the cauldron, the princes would simply take it.

The village was put to flame. Many perished in the fires, including the man. His wife stole a horse, took their young son and the cauldron, and fled. There would be no safe place for them—at least, not in the tamed lands.

In desperation, she recalled her husband's tales of how he

had found Castell Sidi and used those memories to retrace his path. She took refuge in the old fortress, hoping that the forest and the mountains would keep her small family safe.

However, the cantref princes did not give up. They sent knights and soldiers into the mountains. Those who did not perish in the wilds found their death when they tried to cross the lake Llyn Mawr. After the knights and soldiers failed, the princes sent spies—and their corpses joined the knights' and soldiers' in the lake.

But one of the princes was shrewd. He did not send a knight, or a soldier, nor a spy.

He hired a thief. A man with quick fingers and an even quicker mind. The thief looked at those wilds like they were just another house to break into, and he made a plan. He covered himself in dirt and leaves, made a coat of animal pelts so that the beasts would let him pass. He crossed the wilds unseen and unheard, and when he approached Llyn Mawr, he did so with care.

He waited for twilight, when the evening could trick the eye, and then he pushed a log into the lake and swam alongside it.

When his bare feet touched the graveled shore, the thief remained low. There was someone walking outside the fortress. He notched an arrow, raised his bow.

The man was a thief—so he did what all thieves do. He took.

Only this time, what he took was a life.

The figure fell, arms flailing as if unsure what had happened, and it was then the thief realized that the form was too small to be the woman.

Dread filled his heart as he approached and saw what he had slain. It was a child.

The woman rushed from Castell Sidi. When she saw what had happened, she hit the thief over the head with a rock and carried her child inside.

The child was dead; she could save him.

She had never used the cauldron, but she knew how it was done—boiling water within its depths.

But the thief awoke. He followed the woman into the castle and saw the cauldron. The woman tried to stop him, but as he seized it, the hot iron scalded his hands and he recoiled with a snarl of pain.

The magical cauldron slipped from his burned fingers, falling to the stone floor.

Then it *cracked*.

Water spilled across the floor—the last water the cauldron would ever hold. The woman fell to her knees, trying to scoop the water into her hands, but it slipped through her fingers and through the cracks in the stone floor.

No one knows what became of her after that. Perhaps she wasted away inside the fortress, her body resting by that of her son. Perhaps she wandered away, to take refuge in a nearby village.

As for the thief—he ran. The magical water had soaked into the hem of his cloak and the soles of his boots. When he slipped into the lake, the power seeped into the Llyn Mawr—the lake that fed those creeks and rivers trickling toward Colbren. The once-contained magic began to bleed into the soil, trickled into the mountains, and crept into the forest creeks.

The next time night fell, the surface of the lake quivered. A bone-tipped hand emerged from its waters. Figures draped in tattered clothing and rusted armor dragged themselves ashore.

The things that crawled from the lake were sinew and rotting flesh. They were silent, with hollow eyes and bodies that caved in.

They were called bone houses.

CHAPTER 7

THE NEXT MORNING, an eviction letter was nailed to the door.

Ryn stared at it. It was written in the familiar hand that decried all official notices in Colbren. She recognized the flourishes without even having to see the signature. She tore the page free, felt its edges crumple in her hard grip.

For one terrible moment, she wanted to burn it. To see its embers float into the wind, to be scattered among the rocky soil. It would be as if this message were never delivered—and perhaps she could go on with her life. If she pretended all was right with the world, perhaps the world would do so as well.

Tucking the parchment into her tunic, Ryn strode into her home.

And it would *remain* her home if she had anything to say about it.

Even if it meant she had to lead some lordling into the mountains.

Gareth was sitting at the kitchen table. It had been carved from a fallen tree—each leg a branch, and she could still see the knotholes and whorls of the wood. He looked up, unsmiling. When he was a child, he'd laughed and grinned. Perhaps he had never been as boisterous as she, but he had regarded the world with merriment. It had drained away over the years.

He gave her a nod. "You saw?"

"The notice?" she replied. "Eynon broke his word again. Said we'd have two weeks."

"Well, perhaps you shouldn't have set the goat on him."

A fair point, and she conceded it with a small nod. "You saw he's also taking down the iron fence? Fallen kings, he's a fool."

"He's a bastard, but he's no fool," replied Gareth. There was a weary acceptance in his voice, and it made Ryn bristle. "He'll sell the iron, use the coin to stock up the village's granaries. If the winter is a harsh one, it will save lives."

"And the bone houses will be able to enter the village," she said. "Which I'm sure will save so many lives."

Gareth gave a little shrug. "Perhaps the ones you've seen outside the forest were stragglers. Either way, it doesn't matter. We're leaving," he said, and the words settled between them. It felt as if the ground had split, and she was gazing at some uncrossable distance. "We'll give the house to Eynon to settle Uncle's debts and use any leftover coin to make our way south. There are other small villages, Aderyn. You could apprentice to another grave-digger, if you wanted. And I..." His voice drifted off. His thumb stroked the edge of his accounts ledger.

The longing in his voice—it hurt more than his words. She knew part of him wanted to leave, to have a fresh start some-where else.

She could not leave. Colbren was as much a part of her as the memories she carried. This house was hers—and she belonged to it, as well. She could not imagine living elsewhere. She could not leave home—not with its carved wooden love spoons made by her father's hands, nor the places on the walls where their mother had marked her children's growth, nor the mounds of earth and rock in the graveyard. Her mother was buried there, along with her grandparents. She loved everything about Colbren: the blue-bells that grew along the forest floor, the gorse that had to be cut back every spring, and the rocky soil, the neighbors who had known her family for generations, the taste of wild blackberries and sharp river water.

To leave, she would have to cut the memories out of her heart—and she imagined her grief spilling forth like blood.

Gareth must have read some of the panic in her face, for he said, "Ryn, I understand you want to stay here. But we can't. And I don't understand why you're so attached when you're never at home. You're always at the graveyard or the forest, or in the village—"

"Trying to make a living!" She threw up her hands. "Trying

to make enough coin so we don't have to abandon this place. Not that you care. You *want* to leave, don't you? Because you don't care about this place. You've never cared—"

"I care about our family *now*," said Gareth, "not about preserving what *was*. There's a difference, not that you're willing to see it."

Ryn turned on her heel and began to walk out of the kitchen.

"Oh yes, go to the forest," said Gareth bitterly. "Much better than talking things out with your family."

A muscle in her jaw twitched. "I'm going to talk to Eynon, you ass."

She did not slam the door behind her, but it was a close thing.

Eynon's home was a place of beauty.

The cantref had long had a noble living within the village, ever since the mine opened. There were rumors that it was an undesirable placement, that the noble sent here was often one in disgrace. Which would explain much about how Eynon treated his neighbors, Ryn thought. Not as people, but as burdens.

Eynon's manservant answered the door. His face was set in lines of arrogant indolence, as if being Eynon's servant gave him some sort of status.

"What is it, Aderyn?" he asked.

She considered all sorts of rude answers, then decided not to test her luck. "I need to speak to Eynon."

"He's not here."

Ryn crossed her arms. "Where is he, then?"

He did not answer, not at first. It was that hesitation that gave her certainty. He was constructing a lie. She pushed past him, her shoulder jostling his as she walked into the house. His surprise slowed his steps, so that by the time he caught up, she was already in the sitting room.

Eynon was in a chair, a cup of tea beside him and a book in his lap. He looked like a spider sitting at the center of its web. His clothes had neat, even stitches and his hair was bound at the nape of his neck.

His gaze slid up from his book and came to rest on her. "Aderyn," he said. "What can I do for you?" He exhaled slowly. "Are you here to plead your case? Because as much as it pains me to do this, I must have repayment from your uncle."

She forced her face to stillness. "He is not here, sir."

"I know." He spoke as one did to a child, and it rankled her. "Which is why I must have your house. And it isn't right, three children living alone like that. You should have gone to one of the workhouses in the city once it was clear your uncle had abandoned you. And your younger sister would be better served in an orphanage. At least then she wouldn't look half-starved and ragged."

He did not abandon us. The words rose to her lips, but she bit them down. He might as well have. Uncle had been a gambler and a drunk, too fond of his own pleasures to give them up for his family's sake.

"I can pay off Uncle's debts," she said.

He leaned back in his chair, a faint smile on his mouth. He

gestured to the table beside him with a roll of his wrist. "You can leave the coin there."

Ryn did not move. Nor did Eynon; the smile remained fixed on his mouth.

"You don't have the coin, do you?" he said. He shook his head with the air of a benevolent ruler bestowing wisdom upon an unruly citizen. "Let me tell you something, Aderyn. Empty promises—and empty threats—hold little value."

"They're not empty," she said. "The newcomer—Ellis. He's hired me as a guide. Once he's paid me, you'll have your coin."

His smile froze in place. "He has that kind of coin?"

"Yes." Ryn shrugged. "He said he's from Caer Aberhen."

The name of the prince's fortress seemed to make Eynon's jaw flex. "And what is his surname?"

"He didn't give one." Ryn shrugged. "What does it matter?"

"It matters," Eynon said, his smile iced over, "because some of us do have business with the prince. If he is keeping wards, they should be welcomed."

If anyone had offered to welcome her with that tone of voice, Ryn would have run the other way. But the politics of the nobles mattered little to her. "I can pay you—but it will take a little time."

Eynon hesitated—and for a moment, Ryn's heart leapt into her throat. Maybe, just maybe, this would work.

Then he shook his head. "No, no. I need the coin—as does the rest of the village. The winter promises to be a harsh one, which is why I'm seeing to stocking the granaries. It is why the iron fence must be sold—and why I shall call in the debts I'm owed. It is for the good of the village, you see."

For a moment, Ryn felt unsteady with disappointment. And then it hardened into anger, burning hot as coals low in her belly. He sounded so smug, so confident; it was as if he had blown upon those coals.

They caught fire.

"But not all our coin will go to the granaries, will it?" she said.

The false geniality slid from Eynon's face. "I don't know what you're talking about," he said.

Ryn looked about the room.

The rugs were brilliant reds and blues—the dyes would have come from far away. His table was polished so brightly it shone, and the teacup was made of delicate porcelain. A tapestry hung from the wall, stitched to give the likeness of a long-dead king.

It was a beautiful room. And it was far more than Eynon should have been able to afford.

"The taxes we pay you," said Ryn. "They should go to the cantref prince, right? Do they all make it to his coffers? It would be a shame for the prince to find out," she said. "Perhaps if a ward of his carried word back..."

It was the worst kind of threat—one that held little weight. She didn't even know if Ellis was truly nobility, or if he were someone's bastard, or perhaps just a well-dressed tradesman. But then again, Eynon didn't know, either.

Eynon rose from his chair. His eyes were flinty and his mouth was pressed into a thin line. He stood a head taller than her, and she hated that she had to look up to meet his gaze. "You tread a very dangerous path, Aderyn." He spoke in a soft voice, so quiet that the servant would not hear. "Take care what rumors you listen to, my dear girl."

A headache throbbed behind her jaw, tight muscles pulling at her neck. She tried to steady her breathing, to will herself to calm. Helplessness was something she hated, and it made her want to pick up every expensive trinket in this house and smash it against a wall until Eynon understood what loss felt like.

"At the very least," she said, "leave the iron fence be."

"Or what?" He let out an incredulous laugh. "You'll drop a dead body on my doorstep?"

She closed her eyes. He would not listen to her, but she spoke the words regardless.

"No," she said. "I won't have to. Any dead that appear in the village will come of their own accord."

Several emotions chased themselves across Eynon's thin face: surprise, fear, and then anger. As if the threat came from her, not from the mountains. And as if he might deal with it by silencing a single young woman.

She turned and strode from the house.

CHAPTER 8

FOR ELLIS, MEALTIMES were time for work.

One of the women who'd raised him, a cook, had long ago despaired of keeping him from his sketches. No matter how often he blotted a page with porridge or cheese, he kept working—fingers moving over the parchment, constructing landscapes of nothing but lines and measurements.

He ate an early supper in the Red Mare, one hand holding a spoon and the other cradling paper-wrapped lead. His sketches of Colbren were coming together; if his map was circulated, at least travelers wouldn't find themselves sleeping under crooked canvas in the forest. He had walked the village twice, charting buildings and measuring distances with footsteps. Now he could have walked the village blindfolded, so long as he knew his starting point.

Perhaps this was what had drawn him to maps in the first place: He liked seeing whorls of ink and reading landscapes. Maps held no secrets, no intricacies that he could not parse. He could know a place far better than he could know a person.

The tavern bustled around him, but he paid it little mind.

The mutton stew had the tang of rosemary and mint, and he ate as he worked, placing the final measurements on the town's outskirts.

A cup thudded down before him. Ellis glanced up, expecting to see Enid trying to coax him into eating more, but a man stood before him. He had a rather pinched expression, and he gazed at Ellis as if the young man were a smudge on the side of his boot.

His clothes were finely wrought and his boots were in fact untouched by mud. Only one man would wear such clothing.

"Master Eynon," Ellis said, with a polite bow of his head. He knew of the lord; he'd been made to memorize all of the cantref's nobility when he was twelve. But Eynon must have despised court or simply declined invitations to Caer Aberhen, because this was the first time Ellis had met him.

Eynon sat down across from him without responding. Ellis felt his brows draw together; it was a minor slip of courtesy, to join without being asked.

"Who are you?" said Eynon. There was a frosty chill to his words.

Ellis's spoon stilled halfway to his mouth. A chunk of mutton slipped back into the tureen. "Ellis of Caer Aberhen. In such a small village, I had assumed my presence was well known."

Eynon's eyes swept over him. "There are rumors. My servants have a tendency to talk when they think I can't hear them. They spoke of a noble."

Ellis tapped a finger against his parchment. "I'm a mapmaker."

Eynon made a sound low in his throat. He was too well-mannered to snort, but it was a close thing. "Don't be coy. The prince sent you," he said. "To report on me."

Ellis's smile was not kind. Nor was the laugh he uttered. "I've been called many things," he said lightly. "A stranger, an outcast, a cripple, and a nuisance—but I've never been accused of being a spy before. Tell me, what gave it away? That I've told everyone my name or that I'm walking about in broad daylight?"

Color spilled across Eynon's face. "Half a name," he said in a low voice. "I notice you've given no one your family name."

There were some pains so old they were almost a comfort. "No," said Ellis, "I have not."

"Is there a reason?"

"My lord," said Ellis. He made sure to keep his voice smooth. "I do not owe you answers. Not when you have interrupted my meal. Now I'd like to get back to my work."

Eynon's gaze fell to the sketchbook.

"It is a rather good story," he said quietly. "Perhaps you trained in mapmaking, perhaps you did not. But I know why an agent of Caer Aberhen has come. Why you have spoken to that damned gravedigger. She would put stories in your head, ones you will bring back to the cantref prince. I know there are those at court who would like to replace me here."

Ellis's good manners gave way to irritation. "I can't see why," he said. "Those nobles have estates in far better condition."

Eynon's mouth went pale and tight. "The mine," he said, jaw barely moving. "It belongs to me."

"The mine collapsed long ago," said Ellis. "Seems a rather fitting metaphor for this place."

"The mine would be worth more than your head, should it be reopened," said Eynon coldly. "More than any of these people's lives. There is a king's fortune in those mountains, and someday I will reopen them."

"Then why wait?" He wondered if Eynon would mention the risen dead.

"Because," said Eynon, "too many yet fear a further collapse. They say that we should never have pushed so deeply into the mountain. And the last group I sent to scout the mine was not successful after one of them vanished and the rest lost their nerve." His mouth twisted with irritation. "But once the village is hungry enough, I believe there will be... sufficient volunteers to scout the mine again."

Ellis thought of the run-down homes, the clothing worn thin, and the eagerness with which Ryn had taken his coin. Perhaps Eynon was right—in a few more years, the villagers might be desperate enough to return to a collapsed mine.

"And in the meantime," Eynon said, very quietly, "I'll not have spies spreading rumors that I've not done my duty for our prince. I know what Aderyn's been telling you, and I won't have it."

Ellis swallowed a curse. Of *course* he found himself caught up in petty village politics. Because attempting to map the unknown, sneak past the risen dead, and merely survive weren't enough. Ellis slanted a glare toward the ceiling. "Just for once," he said, more to himself than to Eynon, "why can't things be simple?"

Eynon rose from his seat; the chair squeaked against the wooden floor. "Enid!"

The woman appeared as she always did—rosy-cheeked and hair tumbling from its knot. But her smile was a little too rigid, and her hands clasped. "Master Eynon?"

"I believe our guest is ready to leave," said Eynon, his gaze steady on Ellis. "He won't be staying the night."

A flash of panic crossed Enid's face. Her glance darted between Eynon and Ellis, seemingly torn. If Eynon was the kind of lord Ellis thought he was, then if Enid did not agree, her rent would be raised without so much as a word.

Ellis bit back his anger, held it in his belly. With no family name to protect him, he could not afford anger.

He closed his eyes for a heartbeat, breathing evenly. He stood, picked up his things, and nodded to Enid. "Thank you for your hospitality," he murmured, and walked past Eynon. He'd gather his things, then be on his way.

It was time to find his guide and leave this place.

CHAPTER 9

THAT EVENING, RYN went out to the forest.

The trees were still damp with yesterday's rain. It dripped down the trunks of oak trees, sent acorns tumbling to the ground. Ryn began gathering them, scooping up handfuls. It was slow work filling her basket, but she didn't mind it. There was a peace to be found in the forest, in the shadow of the mountains, where so few people dared to come. She did not have to worry about the mud spatter on her leggings or her wind-tangled hair.

This was the only place she felt unburdened.

At least until she heard a familiar *"Bah."*

Ryn turned and saw the goat standing some distance away. The animal flicked one ear, then bent down to crunch an acorn.

"What are you doing here?" said Ryn. The goat's only reply was to nudge another acorn. She blinked at Ryn, as if the two were mere acquaintances who had happened upon each other. "You got out of the pen again."

"Bah."

Ryn walked forward, took the goat by one horn, and gave a gentle tug. "Come on, you."

If a goat could look affronted, this one did. "No," said Ryn. "You're not going to forage with me. You'll eat everything."

"Talking to the goat?"

A new voice made her jump.

Ellis stood a distance away. He looked like the noble he claimed not to be—at least, he was dressed as one. She felt the grime beneath her nails all the more keenly.

"She's a good listener," said Ryn. The goat, as if determined to prove her wrong, turned her head away and began nipping at low-hanging leaves. "What are you doing here?"

"It seems I have worn out my welcome in Colbren. The fields might prove a safer place to sleep." He slid a pack from his shoulder, setting it between his feet. "If you've made preparations, could we leave in the morning?"

She frowned. For all that Colbren was small, it had never been unwelcoming. Or at least it had never been unwelcoming to those with coin to spend. "What happened? Did Enid's chickens get into your room? They won't hurt you, you know. Just throw them some grain and they'll leave off."

He huffed out a breath that was half amusement, half scoff. "Has that happened before?"

"More times than I can count."

He laughed—and the sound had the resonance of true

mirth. Warmth kindled in her chest, and she found herself smiling back, charmed by her ability to charm him.

"Master Eynon paid me a visit," he said, and at once she sobered. "He seems to think Caer Aberhen sent me as a spy. And that you've been feeding me stories."

A curse caught between her teeth. She grimaced, shifting on her feet, irritated with both Eynon and herself. "Sorry, sorry. My fault," she said. "I... may have paid him a visit this morning to talk about my family's debts to him. I told him I'd be able to pay him, if he could just wait. And when that didn't work, I may have implied that he's been lining his pockets with the tax money meant for the prince... and that you could carry word back to Caer Aberhen."

"Truly?" Ellis sounded exasperated. "Why did you have to drag me into this?"

"Because I was angry," Ryn said, "and because I didn't think he'd chase you out of town, and... all right, it was an ill-advised plan. But all I have are rumors, and if I want to keep my house, I needed him to believe that he could lose his."

The answer seemed to satisfy him. "Has he?" asked Ellis, interested. "Been lining his pockets?"

"Well, would he react this way if he wasn't?" She shrugged. "People know you're from Caer Aberhen. You're dressed like a noble. You haven't given me a surname—and obviously you didn't give Eynon one, or he wouldn't be in such a state. And a mapmaker goes all sorts of places, so it would be a perfect cover. It's not a leap to think you might be a spy. Perhaps Eynon thinks I sent a letter to the prince in hopes of getting him sacked. Then I wouldn't have to worry about my uncle's debts."

"You didn't, though," he said.

Her answering smile had a wicked edge. "Only because I didn't think of it. It's a good plan, but a little too complicated for my tastes. If I come across a problem, I take my axe to it. Or bury it. I'm good at burying things."

His eyes swept over her. "I think you're capable of more."

It was the kind of statement that might have drawn her ire if Gareth had said it. She would have taken it to mean that she was not trying hard enough, that she should have been doing more. But there was no judgment in his eyes or voice—only gentleness.

She did not know how to reply, and part of her was nettled by her own silence. She was not one to be befuddled by a beautiful boy and a few well-spoken words. Beautiful things were often poisonous or useless—a handful of glossy berries that could kill with a taste, or a carved wooden spoon with no other purpose than to be admired. She should have had little use for them. But her fingers found the carving in her pocket, and she softened.

"Come on," she said. She reached out and picked up his pack. It was surprisingly light; she thought he would have brought more with him. She slung it over her shoulder and hooked her basket full of acorns around one elbow.

"You're stealing my pack," said Ellis mildly.

"You can have my bed." She glanced over her shoulder. "I've slept on the floor before—I can do it again."

His brow creased, and for a moment he looked baffled. "I can't—you're already doing more than enough for me."

"Consider it room and board in addition to my services as a guide."

He shook his head, seemingly more amused than concerned that she was walking away with his belongings. Evening cast the sky in hues of gold and red, and their own shadows preceded them across the grass.

"Thank you for this," he said. "If you don't mind me asking, how did your family tangle with Master Eynon? You said your family is indebted to him?"

She frowned. "Yes. Our uncle has a taste for drink and cards—and he does neither very well. He borrowed money from Eynon, coin we couldn't afford to pay back. A few months ago, he went to the city to sell some goods. He has yet to return."

"So your missing uncle owes Eynon coin," he said.

"Yes. And the worst part is, Eynon should be paying *us*."

"How so?"

Her gaze was drawn back toward the shadow of the mountains. They were rimmed by sharp sunlight, jagged peaks against the horizon. "My father was part of the last expedition to see if the mine could be reopened. Eynon promised them all payment—but Da never returned."

His breath caught. "I—I'm sorry."

She shrugged. "We never found him," she said tonelessly. "And Eynon said since the job had never been done, and there was no proof he died in the mine, we would receive no payment."

Ellis seemed to consider. "He's a right bastard," he said.

She forced herself to smile. "You're not wrong."

Sunset and autumn burnished the forest into something strange and beautiful. The faltering light turned the bark of the Scots pines a bloody crimson. The undergrowth was all shadows, ferns and moss and tangled weeds. They would come out near Old Hywel's farm; he wouldn't mind them cutting across his sheep pens to reach the village.

Behind her, Ellis made a startled sound. She turned and saw that his foot had caught in something. He reached for the only thing he could—a small sapling—but it broke beneath his weight and he crashed into the undergrowth. She extended a hand to help him up, but then her eyes fell to his foot.

At first she thought it was a hunter's trap. Sharp edges gleamed in the dim light, snagged on his boot.

But it was not a snare.

He had stepped into a rib cage. It had belonged to a man; farther along the skeleton, she saw thick leather boots and clothes in tatters.

Ellis reached down, trying to pry apart the ribs. His foot remained caught, and there was a tightness to his mouth that spoke of restrained disgust. Ryn knelt beside him and took hold of the thickest ribs. One sharp yank and the sinew gave. Ellis pulled his leg free.

Ryn rocked back on her heels, rubbing the dirt from her fingers. She half expected Ellis to put some distance between himself and the dead man, but he squatted beside her. His eyes raked over the body. "Is it . . . ?"

She shook her head. "I don't know. It's—not dark enough yet. There's half an hour until true night, and then we'd know."

It could just be a man. They were on the fringes of the forest—the magic might never have reached him.

"Either way," said Ellis, "we should bag him up and bring him to the smithy."

Ryn felt her jaw clench. "No."

"No?"

"If it's a bone house, it goes to the forge," she said. "But if it's just a dead man, I'll bury him in the graveyard. It's a courtesy."

A confused line appeared between Ellis's brows.

"The dead deserve something," she said, trying to explain in a way a layman might understand. "A remembrance, a marker, a place to rest. Death should be peaceful—the dead have earned that much. The bone houses—they're a mockery of death. Burning them... it's a last resort, not a way out."

Ellis inclined his head. "I understand." He reached for his pack, now resting beside Ryn. "We should gather him up, either way."

"Agreed."

Ellis pulled a pair of gloves from his pack and slipped them on. Together, they tried to free what was left of the man from the undergrowth. The grasses had tangled with his bones, grown up and through his rib cage and skull. Ryn yanked at the vines of vetch and pulled the grasses away, trying to keep him at least a little intact as they placed the pieces of the man into a small burlap sack.

The sun sank behind the horizon, leaching warmth from the air. Ryn shivered, but continued to work. By the time they had finished, dusk had settled into the corners of the forest: into the nooks beneath tree roots and under the thick leaves of the bushes.

For a moment, Ryn and Ellis gazed down at the burlap sack.

It remained resolutely still.

"All right," she said. "I'll carry it back. If it doesn't twitch on the way home, I'll bury him come morning."

Ellis nodded. His fingers pulled at the mouth of the sack, ready to tie it shut.

A branch snapped. The sound cracked through the quiet forest—and it was only then that Ryn realized how silent the forest had become. There was no chirp of insects, no rustle of small creatures finding places to sleep.

A strange chill settled at the base of her spine. "Ellis," she said slowly. She was not sure why she spoke his name: perhaps as a warning—or to remind herself that she was not alone.

Something moved in the evening dim. It stood taller than Ryn—and her eyes strained in the dusk light, trying to see the shape of the thing. It was only when it stepped through the bushes that she saw it was a soldier.

A very dead soldier.

"Stay still," she said out of the corner of her mouth. "We're on the edges of the forest. Perhaps it will return to the deeper woods."

The bone house tilted its head back and forth, gazing at the two living creatures before it. She could almost see the consideration in its hollow eyes.

Go on, she thought, as if she might will it away. *For your own sake, just go back into the forest.*

And then she saw more movement. Her heart thudded so hard against her rib cage.

Another bone house emerged from the trees—this one dressed in a mail coat and holding a crossbow. It still had tendrils of hair snagged in its collarbones.

"Aderyn?" said Ellis. He made her name into a question.

Two bone houses. And they weren't lost travelers or trappers; dressed in armor that would cost a family a year's salary, these were cantref soldiers. She had not heard of such soldiers being sent into the woods, not since—

Not since the princes sent doomed troops to try to find Castell Sidi and the cauldron of rebirth.

"Fallen kings," she cursed. "All right. Ellis, we're going to leave. Slowly—very slowly, stand up."

Ellis nodded and placed a palm on the ground. He started to rise.

A hand surged from the burlap sack, quick as a striking snake, and seized Ellis by the shirt. He gave a hoarse cry of surprise, falling sideways.

The bone houses' heads snapped toward him.

She heard them inhale—that slow, rattling breath that slid across rotted teeth. And then the hiss of a sword being drawn from it sheath. A blade glinted, and Ryn's fingers settled on her axe.

Above them, the last vestiges of sunlight drained from the sky.

CHAPTER 10

A BONE HOUSE lunged, raising the bright edge of a sword. Ryn skittered to one side, twisting away.

She heard the hiss and the ghostly touch of wind. The bone house whirled, raising its sword again. Ryn caught the blow on the curve of her axe. A painful jolt ran up both her arms.

Out of the corner of her eye, Ryn saw Ellis struggling with the third bone house—the one they had bagged up. It was in pieces, its fingers locked around Ellis's shirt collar while the rest of it thrashed inside the sack. It looked like a bag of rats trying to escape—and it might have been amusing another time. But not now.

The second bone house raised the crossbow, and Ryn felt as if time slowed. She saw the rusty tip of the arrow glint in the moonlight.

She threw the axe. It flung wildly through the air, and only its handle hit the bone house in the chest. The chain mail slowed the blow, but could not halt it. Ryn rushed the creature, seizing her axe from the ground and aiming another blow at the bone house's unprotected throat. Its head dropped to the undergrowth. The creature's jaw clacked, as if in rebuke.

Then the second bone house hit her with its armored elbow. Pain flared in her skull and she fell. One of the bony hands wrapped around her ankle, dragging her closer. Ryn scrabbled at the forest floor, trying to find purchase as the creature leaned over her.

With a scream, Ryn clawed at that hand, trying to free herself. But her effort was as fruitless as that of a rodent caught in the grasp of a snake; she was squeezed even harder, and the bone house bent over her, mouth wide. She heard that terrible breath again, and she wondered if this was its attempt to speak.

A crossbow bolt slammed into the creature.

Ryn glanced up; Ellis stood beside her. His mouth was pulled back in a snarl as he aimed his crossbow a second time. He fired and the bolt struck the first bone house through a gap in its armor.

It jerked backward, looked down at the shaft of wood emerging from where a heart should have been. It tilted its head, studying the weapon. More confused than injured.

Ryn gritted her teeth, a curse caught in her throat as she reached for the fallen axe. It was trapped beneath her, and she struggled to roll over, to pry the weapon free.

The bone house reached into its own chest. It pried its ribs apart, rummaging about for the bolt. The creature looked down at Ryn, and she caught a glimpse of yellowed teeth. The axe was still beneath her, and she couldn't bring it up fast enough—

Its mouth widened farther and a sound emerged from its hollow throat. It was not speaking words, not truly, but perhaps the *remembrance* of words twisted into a dry screech.

Ryn's blood turned to ice. She hit it at the knee, where the armor was hinged. The axe lodged in the joint and stuck, and the bone house fell to one side. She scrambled backward, and then there were hands on her shoulders, dragging her upright. The world was shaking, and she realized that she trembled hard, and Ellis was just as unsteady.

The bone house reached out, its yellowed fingers feeling the wood of the axe's handle. Its grip tightened and it pulled the axe free. But the blade must have done damage, for the creature could not rise.

It was enough. Ryn darted forward and picked up the axe.

She swung around, gathered her strength, and loosed a wild cry. It was not one of fear, but of challenge.

The axe came down, singing through the air, and slammed into the creature's spine.

She took it apart.

Piece by piece, bone by bone. She dismantled the creature, pulled bones free of armor, broke everything until she realized that she was panting, sweat rolling down her brow and stinging her eyes, and she was making a terrible noise, a snarl of defiance that went unanswered.

Her heart kept lurching, her body trembling with unspent fear. Her breath came too heavily, fogging the cool night air.

Her fingers were bleeding, she realized. One of her nails was cracked and oozed sluggishly. Other injuries asserted themselves into her awareness—her forearms would likely be bruised and she ached between her shoulder blades.

"Where'd the other one go?" she said.

"Don't know." Ellis spun in a circle, his finger resting against the crossbow's trigger. "Think it might have gone back into the woods. You all right?"

"Think so."

"What—what happened?" Ellis finally said. His voice was frayed, as if he had been screaming. Perhaps he had been.

Ryn looked down at what remained of the creature. Shards of old bones, rusted armor, and a splintered bow. "They attacked."

"I figured that much." The thinnest of smiles flashed across Ellis's mouth. "But the way you made the bone houses sound—like they were stragglers, not a dead army."

It felt as if the world had been upended and she was struggling to right herself. "They're not an army. They're not supposed to be."

Ellis knelt beside one of the bone houses. "Well, he's armored. It's the good kind—I've seen this at Caer Aberhen. This man would have been marching to war, dressed like this." He lifted his gaze to Ryn. "Have any armies ever marched through the forest? Could they be deserters?"

A quick shake of her head. "No one would send an army into the forest," she said haltingly. "Well—not since..."

He caught on quickly. "When the princes were seeking the cauldron of rebirth. They sent soldiers into the mountains.

None of them came back." He touched the soldier's breastplate, running fingertips over the rusted metal. "I suppose this is what became of them." He looked up sharply. "So it wasn't just a story."

A deep sense of unease made her glance about. "We should get back to the village. We'll be safe there. There's the—"

Iron fence. The words caught on her lips.

She remembered the iron bars hefted into a cart, the clang of metal on metal as they were loaded together. Eynon would sell them, and when winter came and people were starving, he would show the world how generous he could be as he sold them grain.

She thought of her family, sitting down for the evening meal.

And she thought of the half threat she'd given Eynon: *Any dead that appear in the village will come of their own accord.* Careless words, spoken when she was confident it wouldn't happen.

Now she wasn't so sure.

CHAPTER 11

THERE WAS A chicken missing.

Old Hywel's finger moved through the air as he counted and recounted. Sure enough—there were eleven of the birds perched along the stable walls. They liked to roost high, out of the reach of foxes and stray dogs. One of the hens cocked her head at him, beady dark eyes sharp and observant. Hywel walked through the barn, muttering to himself as he strode by the sheep pen. The sheep were in for the night—they had all come running when he shook a bucket of grain. It was easy to bring them home.

Chickens, though. Chickens liked to roam. More than once he'd found a hen in the trees or even atop the house. He'd once had a rooster that enjoyed sitting on the village wall and crowing every few hours, dawn or no. One of the inn's patrons finally took issue with the noise, and the Red Mare's soup tasted distinctly of chicken for a few nights.

Hywel latched the barn door, striding back toward the house. The sun was low in the sky, light skimming over the fields and casting long shadows. There wasn't much time to look for the fool bird, but with winter coming, he had little choice.

He picked up the feed bucket and shook it, hoping the familiar noise might lure the creature out.

"Come on, you bloody thing," he muttered. Were his wife alive, she might have scolded him for his language. But she'd taken ill some years ago, leaving him with a house that felt too big and a village that felt too small. No matter how many times his friends urged him to move into Colbren proper, he waved them off.

His farm and his mill were where he belonged. And besides, there was too much work for a man to be truly lonely.

He shook the bucket a second time, his gaze scouring the bushes.

Something moved.

"Oh, there you are." Hywel set the bucket down and stepped closer. He walked into the shadow of the trees. A strange scent wafted through the air: rot and metal, and something about it made the hairs on his arms stand on end.

Some instinct told him to go still.

A creature emerged from the undergrowth.

The bones were stained brown, the wide jaw gaping in a skull's grin. In its hands was a rusted sword.

Hywel was one of Colbren's old blood, whose family had

dwelt there since the beginning. He knew of the wild magics, of the lush beauty and dangers of the mountains. And he knew that such creatures did not speak the language of mercy. So he did not beg. Nor did he raise an arm to defend himself when the bone house brought the sword down across his throat.

Atop the barn's roof, a lone chicken sat watching as figures began to emerge from the forest.

CHAPTER 12

RYN HEARD THE clamor before they reached the village.

The night's silence was broken by the high-pitched clucks of startled chickens, the cries of restless sheep, and the clatter of a barn door as its occupants tried to paw their way out. Ryn turned away from the path, veering left toward Hywel's farm.

"What is it?" said Ellis. His pack bounced from his elbow, and he held the crossbow in both hands. "Shouldn't we keep going?"

Ryn shook her head. "Something's wrong."

Ellis gave her a look as if to convey that *of course* something was wrong, things had been going wrong since nightfall. She jerked her head toward the barn. "Hear that?"

"It's a farm," he said. "I thought they were supposed to have sheep."

"Sheep don't panic at night," she replied. "Nor do chickens or goats. Not unless something startles them."

She took two steps and hopped over the short wooden fence. Ellis followed.

Hywel's farm was a familiar place for Ryn—he had been friends with her grandfather. She remembered the smell of freshly ground barley and the rich butter churned from sheep's milk that he used to give them.

She rounded the corner of the barn and came to an abrupt halt.

Before Ellis could follow, she threw up her arm, catching him in the chest. He grunted, startled. "What is it?"

"The bone house with the sword," she said, turning. "I think it came here."

Ryn was familiar with the sight of corpses, but the bodies she'd seen had been claimed by illness, by a wound that had sickened, or by old age.

Blood spread across the grass and the old man lay in a crumpled heap, his head half torn from his body. She felt Ellis step around her, heard his quiet curse.

There was no time for grieving; that would have to come later.

"Aderyn," said Ellis. He hesitated, then continued. "In the stories—those soldiers that were sent into the mountains to retrieve the cauldron. How many were there?"

It took several heartbeats to answer. Her thoughts felt oddly sluggish. "I—I don't know. Tens? Hundreds? The tales weren't specific. Why?"

Ellis nodded at the fields beyond.

She didn't see it right away—the darkness helped cover the sight of trampled grass, of fresh mud churned up. The fields looked like they did on the days when the sheep were herded from one pasture to another. But there was no familiar pattern of cloven hooves: Rather, she saw boot prints.

There were so many—too many.

Ryn bolted, full tilt, up the hill toward the village. The world swam, jolted with every step, as her lungs burned for more air.

Ellis followed her to the smithy, and Ryn slammed her fist against the door several times. If she could ensure that the occupants were awake, they might have a chance.

Morwenna's lad came tumbling from the house, all lanky arms and legs. He gazed at Ryn with sleepy confusion. "What's—"

"Wake everyone up," she snarled, and he jumped. "Morwenna. Tell her Hywel's dead."

The lad gaped at her.

There was no explaining, not to him. It would take too much time. "Wake everyone in town," she snapped. He gave a jerky nod and sprinted for the next house over.

She hoped it was enough to rouse the others. Her feet carried her west, to the house where she knew her family was sleeping. Ellis was at her back; she could hear boots slamming against the hard-packed earth.

She tore through the front yard, her feet finding the familiar spaces between rocks and grass. The door would be locked, but she knew all it took was a slight upward jiggle and the latch would come loose—she'd been talking about fixing it for years, but it had never been done. Now she was glad for it. The door swung open and she stepped inside.

She hit something. Something as tall as her—with clothes and hair—and she raised her axe. A shout rang out and she stumbled. A hiss, and one of the few oil lanterns came alight. Gareth stood in the hallway, shadows cast along his face, his brows drawn together. "Fallen kings, Ryn. Where have you been? Who—who is this?"

She didn't answer. Reaching for the door, she slammed it shut behind Ellis and re-latched it. "Is the house safe?"

To his credit, he didn't question her. "Yes. Why—"

"Get the table," she said to Ellis. He nodded, slipping past Gareth. Gareth watched him go, bewildered. "Who is that?"

"Hywel is dead," she said.

The words hit him like a blow. "What?" he asked, incredulous.

A grunt came from the kitchen, and then she heard the screech of table legs against the wooden floor. She hastened over and took the other end of the table. Ellis seemed to be holding most of the weight with his right arm; perhaps he'd injured the left. "Get the other end, Gareth."

Gareth didn't move. "What's going on?"

"Bone houses," she said. "Attacked us. I think they got Hywel, too. I mean—I suppose it could have been bandits or maybe one of his chickens got hold of a blade, but I don't think so."

"What?" That would be Ceri, coming out of her room and rubbing the sleep from her eyes.

"Gareth, get the other side of the table," snapped Ryn.

He did, but he wasn't steady; the edges of the table jounced off the walls. "So we're blocking the doors?" asked Ellis. "What about windows? Are there any other ways inside?"

Ryn's jaw ached; she had to unclench her teeth to answer. "Pantry," she said, glancing over her left shoulder. "There's a door into the pantry beneath the house—it leads outside."

"Hywel's gone?" asked Ceri, her face pale as moonlight.

"Yes," said Ellis. "I'm sorry." The table was just a little too wide, but they managed to angle it up and over, the flat surface pressed to the door.

"We need something else heavy," said Ryn, panting. "Gareth, grab some of the chairs. Ceridwen—can you lock the pantry door?"

She nodded and whirled, vanishing around the corner. Gareth hastened toward the kitchen. Ryn leaned against the wall; for a moment, all her exhaustion and aches and cuts seemed to crowd in on her. *Fallen kings.* All she wanted was to curl up in her own bed, to smell the familiar scents of wool and fire smoke, to close her eyes and pretend that none of this was real.

"Adcryn."

When she opened her eyes, Ellis stood beside her. His hand was half-extended—it fell back to his side. Part of her was selfishly glad for his presence: She didn't have to be scared alone.

"I bet you're glad you came to Colbren now," she said with a shaky little laugh.

He cast about for words, but none seemed to come to him. "I—yes. I'm still glad."

"I don't know if you're foolish or just a bit mad," she replied, but she was smiling.

He opened his mouth to reply, but something slammed into the door.

The house reverberated with the blow: Jars rattled on shelves, a wooden spoon dropped from its hook, dust slipped free of the rafters and fell into Ryn's hair. Before she realized she was doing it, she had thrown her weight against the overturned table, bracing it.

Gareth half ran, half staggered into the entryway, dragging two chairs. His face was pale as bone, pale as—

Something crashed into the door a second time. Ryn's mouth formed a silent curse as she felt the table move a fraction. The latch was old, meant to keep neighbor children from wandering inside, not to stop an invasion of the dead.

"Here," said Gareth, and wedged one of the chairs against the table. Ryn pressed her forehead to one of the table's legs, trying to brace herself for another impact. "Where's Ceri?"

"She went down to the pantry," said Ryn, still holding the door.

"I can check," said Ellis quickly. "Three of us barely fit here—I'll go." She gave him a short nod and watched as he turned and strode out of sight.

Ryn's house was . . . nice.

It was a strange thought to have during a siege, but Ellis couldn't help thinking it. The sturdy wooden walls, the scuffs along the floor, the flowers drying in a clay jar—it all looked comfortable and lived in. Caer Aberhen had been made of stone that grew uncomfortably cold in winter, and while it had always been beautiful, it had never truly been his home.

But this house seemed to emanate warmth, and it had the comfort of an old garment: lived in and soft.

At least, when it wasn't being attacked. He heard another crash from the front door and quickened his steps. He found the pantry easily enough: There was a door in the kitchen. It was slightly open, and he could smell the damp, cool air from beneath the home. A lantern rested on the narrow stairs.

"Ceridwen," he said. He'd heard Aderyn use the name. "Are you there?"

A sound came from below—it was an animal noise, choked and wordless.

His feet moved before his mind did; he clattered down the stairs in a rush, heart hammering against his ribs.

The pantry was made of hard-packed earth and shelves, little more than a cool place to store food. There was a small door that led outside—and it was half off its hinges.

The younger girl, Ceridwen, was in the grip of a dead man.

This bone house stank of rotted flesh, and his white hair trailed from his skull. He did not speak, but a terrible noise emanated from his chest—a rusty groan. His fingers were blackened with rot, and they were tangled in Ceridwen's hair. And in his other hand was a dirty knife.

Ellis charged, and then he was grasping at the young girl, trying to free her from the creature's grip. Her hair was tangled in the bony knuckles, but she wasn't screaming. Somehow her silence was even more terrifying.

A *child*. This bone house had attacked a *child*—and Ellis realized he wanted to pull it apart, bone by bone, for attempting such a thing.

He slammed his good shoulder into the bone house, breaking its hold on Ceridwen. The corpse staggered back, taking several of her long hairs with it—and then the girl was scrambling away on hands and knees.

The bone house reached for Ellis, and he felt the touch of its fingers against his throat. Cold and damp, like fallen leaves after a long rain. Ellis lashed out with a forearm, striking that hand away before it could close around his neck. The creature tried to push itself forward, its jaw working in a silent snarl.

Ellis threw a punch at the creature's cheek. The blow connected, but it seemed to hurt Ellis far more than it did the bone house. Pain flared up his arm, while the creature remained undeterred.

A jar shattered against the bone house's skull. Something thick and dark slid down its face, and glass shards were embedded deeply within its cheek. The bone house retreated.

Ellis turned and saw Ceridwen standing beside a row of glass jars, another one clutched in her hands. Her lips were bloodless, pressed into a thin line, but she did not run. Rather she raised the second jar as if to throw it.

Distracted, Ellis did not see the bone house's other hand. It lashed out, seized Ellis by the hair, and bent his neck to a painful angle. And then it slammed his head into the wall.

Stars kindled behind his eyelids. He blinked, once, twice, several times, and found he was staring up at the ceiling. It was dirty—the undersides of the floorboards of the house, and they spun for one wild moment. His left shoulder was throbbing in time with his heart, and it was this old pain that called him back. This pain was as familiar as a lullaby, as much a part of him as his name. He rolled, coughing as air crept back into his lungs.

He smelled the bone house as it stepped over him. Pungent and heavy, sharp and foul. He choked on his inhale, chest spasming, and he had to cough several more times, hoping he would not be sick.

Ellis twisted, saw the creature reaching for Ceridwen again. She raised her jar.

Ellis grabbed for the bone house's ankle and *pulled.* It was a strength born of fury, and it made him feel weightless and strangely untouchable. He would not let this thing hurt a child. It was as simple as that—he cared not for his own pain, for the possibility that he might die in the attempt. He did not matter.

The bone house crashed to the floor and kicked out, catching Ellis in the shoulder. He bit back a cry, but he did not let go. The creature's boots were heavy leather, and he saw the brand burned into the ankle—a mark of craftsmanship. It was easier to focus on these small details, to take in the pieces rather than look at the whole picture.

"Get away from him!" The cry came from above; Ellis looked up, and to his utter relief he saw the familiar form of Aderyn. The blade of her axe bit into the ground; the bone house darted beneath the blow. Aderyn wrenched the blade free and pulled back for another swing.

The bone house kicked at Ellis, who clung on. The creature gazed at Aderyn, and its half-rotted face contorted. Its mouth opened, as if to speak.

"I'm sorry," she said. "I'm so sorry."

And then she took the creature's head off.

Ellis heard the thump as the bone house collapsed, twitching, to the hard earth. But it was not the dead man he couldn't look away from—it was Aderyn. The expression on her face was terrible: crumpled with fear and horror and something he could not put a name to. She pressed one hand to her lips, and her chest jerked, as if she were holding back a retch.

"Ryn, what—" Gareth strode around a corner, a cooking knife in hand.

When he saw the head of the dead man, that knife clattered to the floor. He jerked violently, staggering to one side as if the dead man might attack a second time. Gareth's gaze went from the bone house to Aderyn, to the axe clutched in her pale-knuckled hand. And then he spat out a vicious curse.

"He came back," said Ceridwen, her voice shaking. "He came back."

Aderyn's voice was ragged. "Gareth! The front door!"

For a moment, he appeared torn—his gaze jerking between his sister and the upstairs. Then Gareth gave a tight nod and hurried away.

"Go with him, Ceri," said Aderyn. Then sharper, "Ceri!"

Ceridwen seemed to remember herself. She threw a look at her sister before hastening up the stairs.

"That man," Ellis said. "Ceri said, 'He came back.'" Aderyn's eyes met his, and she looked exhausted and pale—and for the first time since they met, a little defeated.

Aderyn glanced to the beheaded man.

"That was," she said, and the words seemed to catch in her throat. She swallowed. "That was our uncle."

He was past the point of surprise; there had been too many shocks, and numbness seemed to have taken hold of him. Aderyn gave him a quick look before her gaze darted toward the dead man again. "Come on," he said. "We should try to put the door back on its hinges."

Aderyn's eyes remained on the man, even as she picked up the fallen door. He went to help her; panic had seared all thoughts of pain away, but he knew he'd be dealing with his shoulder in the morning. If they lived that long. Together, they hefted the wood upright and dragged it toward the frame.

Distantly, he heard the sounds of shouting and the clash of metal upon metal.

The bone houses weren't only attacking this house. They must be everywhere.

As they tried to angle the door, Ellis glanced outside. Moonlight illuminated the yard beyond, and movement drew his attention.

And then he saw the goat.

The last time he'd glimpsed her, she had been meandering back home, grazing along the way. She would have done better to remain in the wilds.

Three bone houses stood before her, weapons raised. And the goat did not retreat.

Aderyn jerked. "Oh no." She raised her voice. "Goat! Goat!"

The goat did not turn, but her ears flicked toward the sound. Her head lowered in a threat, and one hoof slammed into the ground.

"She's defending the house." Aderyn's voice shook. "Damn it."

"We can't go out there." Ellis gave the door a little nudge, and Aderyn had to help or risk dropping it. "I'm sorry, but we have to get this into place."

The goat charged the dead men, her horns gouging one's hip. It would have been excruciating, had the man been alive. But the man was not truly a man, was not truly alive, and it felt no pain. Rather, it held on to the horns, keeping itself close to the animal. It threw her to the ground, holding her there.

Ellis turned away, shoving the door into the frame. The wood creaked and protested—and the sound helped to block out the noise of weapons hitting flesh.

CHAPTER 13

WITH SUNLIGHT, THE sounds of battle died away.

It was abrupt. One moment, there were fists pounding on the walls and jagged screeches at the windows, and then all Ellis could hear was the rasp of his own breath.

He had spent the rest of the night in the pantry, his back to the broken door, his crossbow at hand. Aderyn came down a few times to check, but most of her attention was on the front door and her family.

When morning came, his legs finally gave out. He sat on the dirt floor, eyes slipping shut.

He might have fallen asleep like that, if not for the voices. They were audible from upstairs.

"—cannot believe it."

"Well, it happened." That voice was Aderyn's, and it was brittle. With exhaustion or anger, or perhaps both.

"It was too close." That would be Gareth. "We can't stay here, Ryn. People will have seen him. People *will* see him. We'll have to burn the body—it can't stay down in the pantry."

"Where are we supposed to go?" Aderyn sounded impatient. "We can't outrun this, Gareth. And if we leave, we'll be worse off than if we stay. Here we have land, we have jobs—"

"Not anymore!" Gareth's voice lashed out. "We don't even have a house! Eynon might have waited a few more weeks, to see if Uncle would return, but now that there's proof Uncle's dead—"

Ellis let the argument slip away into background noise as he leaned his head against the wall, eyes closed. The squabbling felt almost comforting after the night they'd had.

The sound of footsteps made Ellis blink his eyes open. It was the young girl, Ceridwen. She came down the stairs, then she slid to the floor, folding her legs beneath her. "You all right?" he asked. His voice sounded even more hoarse than it usually did.

Ceridwen nodded. "Thanks to you."

He shrugged. Her gratitude made him feel unaccountably awkward. "Anyone would have done it."

She looked at him, far older than a young girl should look. "No. Not just anyone would have helped us."

They sat there in a strangely companionable silence for several minutes. The lack of danger felt as potent as a strong swig of ale, and his limbs were too heavy, his head fogged with exhaustion.

"Your uncle is dead." The words left his mouth in a tumble, before he even realized he had said them.

Ceridwen nodded, and her voice was dry. "You noticed that?"

"I'm sorry."

The body was covered; Ellis had taken one of the canvas sheets from a cupboard and tossed it over the dead man.

"I'm not." Ceridwen gazed at the far wall. "He wasn't very nice," she said tonelessly. "Threatened to send us to the city—to workhouses or orphanages if we annoyed him." She spoke with the kind of honesty that seemed to come from shock—divulging truths that would otherwise have remained silent. Ellis nodded, hoping the gesture conveyed sympathy.

Ceridwen added, "My goat is dead, too. I found her body in the yard."

"I met her once," he said. "She seemed like a fine goat."

Ceridwen nodded. She had the faraway look of someone who had lost too much in too short a time. "She was."

"What was her name?"

A choked little laugh, and the girl shook her head. "We—we never named her." Another laugh. "Uncle said we might have to eat her someday—and naming her would make it harder. So we just called her Goat. Now she'll never have a name."

Perhaps, on another day, Ellis might have deemed it odd to mourn a goat. But having spent the night fending off hordes of risen dead, this grief seemed perfectly normal. "My sympathies," he said, with utter sincerity.

Ceridwen nodded again. Then she rose and said, "Are you hungry?"

He shrugged. He was too wearied to tell.

"I'll make breakfast," said the young girl. And then, decisively, "You'll help me."

Ellis pushed himself upright. "First we fend off bone houses, and then we eat porridge?"

"Yes."

Colbren smelled of death and burning.

There would be much to fix—the doors, the broken latches—not to mention several dead chickens, and the goat, to be handled. Just looking at the house made Ryn want to retreat to her room to take a nap. But there was no time.

She dealt with her uncle first.

She hoped no one would see.

It was a vain hope. Colbren was a small village, and if there was one thing she knew about small villages, it was that they were sustained by sharp eyes and gossip.

Several of the villagers saw her heave the cart across town. "One of the bone houses or one of us?" asked an older woman, her hair bound in a knot, her knuckles spotted with age. Her face was all worry and concern.

"Bone house," said Ryn quickly, giving the cart a tug. The old woman reached down before Ryn could stop her, and twitched the old sheet aside.

When she glimpsed the desiccated flesh and familiar half-bald pate, the older woman's hand jerked, the sheet slipping.

Ryn closed her eyes and swayed in place. *Should have left the head at home,* she thought. And that single thought was so morbid and terrible that she almost laughed.

"I'm sorry," the old woman said, her expression pained. "We'd hoped—we'd hoped he would come back."

People always offered platitudes to the grieving; they were always just as meaningless.

"Thank you," said Ryn. It was the correct response, but she couldn't put much emotion into the words. Knowledge of her uncle would spread quickly.

Uncle was dead—and debts had to be repaid.

She heaved Uncle into the forge, skin crawling when she touched him. He was damp and heavy, too still, and smelled of forest dirt. She had not felt unease around a body for years, yet she yearned to run from this one. She forced herself to watch the flames consume him, to watch as the sparks caught on his clothes.

An emptiness yawned wide within her. She did not dare look too closely at her own reactions, for fear of what she would find.

There were too many bone houses to place them all in the forge. Ryn helped the other villagers pile up the corpses onto several carts and they were dragged out of the village, downwind of the houses, and gathered in a heap. With the damp grasses and sodden earth, it was difficult to get a flame to catch, but several men kept at it. Finally, a billowing fire caught, and smoke began to stream into the sky.

It was hard work; there were too many bodies—mostly bone houses, but a few villagers—and too few able hands. Those who had thought the bone houses a mere story stood amid the wreckage and looked blankly at one another—at least until Enid snapped at them to get moving. But no one spoke a word of complaint—neither about the work nor the smell.

Not a single body—bone house or villager—could be left in the village, lest it rise again with nightfall. Those who grieved did so quietly; the traditions of bringing food to the bereaved would have to wait until after the village was safe again.

Ryn spotted Morwenna tearing the old boards from an abandoned house to repair the door to the forge. It was the same attitude most of them held: Those who lived in the wilds were as stubborn as they were loyal. Colbren would devour its own homes before it would surrender.

Eynon emerged from his house at midday. He was more unkempt than Ryn could ever remember, with red-veined eyes and hair uncombed. A cooking knife was strapped to his belt.

Ryn was moving toward him before she realized her own intentions. Her hand slammed into the older man's chest, holding him in place. Anger born of helplessness was the worst kind—it made her want to snarl, to lash out, to take her axe to something she could break. The truth was, she had almost lost the last fragments of her family last night, and she wasn't sure she could defend them a second time. The bone houses were simply too numerous, and they would not fall to pain nor to exhaustion.

Eynon had put them all in this position. And she yearned to make him feel what she did: that gnawing dread and biting fury.

"I told you," she said, making no effort to remain quiet. "I told you not to tamper with the iron fence."

"Don't touch me," he snapped. Flickers of anger sparked at the corners of his eyes, drawing old lines taut.

"This is your doing!" She gestured at the body she and Morwenna had been carrying.

"My doing?" His mouth twisted into an ugly snarl. "*My* doing? I'm not the one who ventures into the woods every day! I'm not the one who led them here!"

"I didn't—" Her protest faded into silence.

Fallen kings. She had been out in the forest last night. She had flirted with the edges of Annwvyn, as she had always done. But the terrible magic had never followed her home before. This wasn't her fault. Even those three stragglers that Ryn had seen outside the forest in the past couple of weeks hadn't been armed; they were lonely and forgotten bodies, unburied and unremembered. They were each their own small tragedy. These bone houses had come with armor and swords. They had come to make an end of Colbren—and perhaps it had been because the iron fence was half gone.

Or perhaps something else had changed. She did not know.

Eynon knocked her arm away with all the care of someone brushing at an unruly fly. "I know what came to your door," he said, his voice harsh. "People talk."

She swallowed hard.

"Your mother is dead," said Eynon. "Your uncle is dead. Your father is missing—and I have everything I need to ruin your family. The graveyard is mine. The house is mine." He lowered his voice, so that only she could hear. "You'll learn that there's a high cost to threatening me."

He turned and strode away, servant at his heels. The younger man gave Ryn a narrow-eyed glare before hastening after his master.

A chill crept over Ryn's bare arms. Her sleeves were rolled, since she'd spent all morning hauling bodies. A heavy mist fell from the iron-gray sky, and she felt the moisture settle in her hair, on her hands, in her mouth. The cold threatened to seep into her bones and freeze her in place. She should have been moving, but she could not.

"Come on," said Morwenna, giving her a gentle nudge. "There's no point in worrying when there may not even be a village tomorrow."

The words hit home—because Morwenna was right. If another attack came tonight, she wasn't sure Colbren could withstand it. They were a small village, and their fighters were retired soldiers and young farmhands.

If this happened again...

Ryn found herself standing by the fire, feeling the scorch along her bare skin. She watched the flames devour bone and sinew.

This would be the end of Colbren.

This would be the end of her family.

This would be the end of home, of the only place she had ever felt safe.

Unless—

Ryn thought of a bundle of apples on a mossy log. She thought of the quiet spaces between shadow and tree, the moments when she was sure something watched her, something she wasn't frightened by.

She thought of her father, his fingers tangling in her hair as he kissed the crown of her head. And a broken love spoon in her pocket.

No warrior could stop the dead.

But perhaps a gravedigger could.

The Dead

IT BEGAN WITH *a hunt.*

The fortress of Caer Aberhen did not need the food, but its prince was a skittish sort. He was young, having lost his father and mother to the blighted cough. He chafed at the constraints of his new position, and when the endless meetings and paperwork became too much, he declared he would ride out.

The hunt should have stayed within the boundaries of his cantref, but the prince rode farther. He loved the wind on his face, the smells of the trees and mountains, and before he knew it, his horse was restless, skittering away from the trees.

They had ridden to the borders of Annwvyn.

The prince knew all the stories of the mountains. He remembered being frightened of them as a child, hiding beneath his covers lest one of the pwca creep into his room and steal him away. The remembered fear made him reckless now, eager to prove his courage. So he kicked his horse into a trot and went into the forest.

He did not find game, nor did he find monsters. He laughed, because he proved that the stories had no hold on him. But then a branch cracked behind him, and the prince saw the creature emerge from the undergrowth. At first, his heartbeat stuttered with fear—then he saw it was not a creature at all.

It was a wraith of a boy. Hollow-cheeked and silent—perhaps three or four years of age. The prince slid from his horse and went to the child, asking where his parents were, but the boy could not answer. So the prince picked the boy up, placed him in front of him on the horse, and rode back to Caer Aberhen. Every step the horse took made the boy cry out in pain, and he clutched at his left shoulder. The prince checked him for injury, but found only an old scar. "How were you injured?" he asked, but the boy did not answer.

It took a warm bath and a hot meal before the boy uttered a word. "Ellis," he said, when the prince asked his name.

He did not know where his parents were, or if they even lived at all. "You will stay here," said the prince, and gave him to the keeping of the servants. The prince saw Ellis as proof of his own charity and goodwill. He would introduce the boy to visiting nobles, tell the story of how Ellis had been found, parentless and alone, and allow praise to be heaped upon himself for giving the lad such a fine home.

Ellis kept his gaze downward, speaking only when asked a question. He rather liked Caer Aberhen, with its thick stone walls and winding corridors. He liked sitting on the roof and watching the people come and go. He liked the thick slices of dark bread clotted with dried cranberries that the cook would save for him. He liked the tutors and the learning, even if he was too fearful to ask questions.

The cook took a liking to him and heaped his porridge with dried berries and honey, and bought tinctures of willow bark when his shoulder ached. Slowly he grew into himself. He smiled and spoke and tried to make friends, but the other children shied away from him. They did not know what to make of him, and Ellis spent most of his time in the courtyard, under the broad leaves of an old wych elm. He was ill-suited to climbing—his left arm could not bear his weight—but he liked to sit with his back to the tree, a book cradled between his knees.

He did not like being a token of the prince's goodwill. It made him feel as out of place as a stray dog at a noble's table. And despite the tutors and the fine food, Ellis never made the mistake of thinking he could ever be a noble. The other children made sure of that. One day, a girl, two years older than Ellis, with eyes as blue as a winter's sky and just as warm, kicked him to the ground and kept him there with a foot on his left shoulder. His eyes watered with hurt and humiliation, and one of the servants chastised the girl for her behavior—calling it unworthy. But the same servant did not so much as glance at Ellis, nor offer him a hand. He rose, red-cheeked and shoulder smarting, all on his own.

When Ellis asked to be and then became apprenticed to a mapmaker, he found friends. He never told them of his past, so they assumed he was the illegitimate son of some noble. It was a common enough story, and he endured a bit of good-natured ribbing over his lack of a family name. And he loved the maps—oh, how he loved the maps. He loved the feel of parchment in his hands, the pins and the string he would use to make straight lines. He even loved the numbers, the way he had to use his thumb to measure distances and to plot paths. There was a logic to it, and a nobility. After all, a town might go hungry if there were no maps to mark its existence. Travelers could vanish and landmarks go unseen.

Part of him wondered if he liked maps because they were a reassurance. A promise that he would never again be without a path.

But in his dreams, he wandered through an endless forest—and he could never find his way home.

CHAPTER 14

ELLIS STRODE THROUGH Colbren. He walked past the torn gardens and collapsed doorways. Some villagers were gathering at the Red Mare; he could see movement through the cracks in the boarded windows. All this destruction had taken place in the course of a single night and another night was coming on.

When he entered the yard, Ceridwen was at the front door. She had two chickens with her—one under each arm.

"Did they get into the house?" he asked.

The younger girl shook her head. "No, no. I'm *bringing* them into the house." Her chin lifted, and he saw a bit of Aderyn's steel in her eyes when she said, "The bone houses may have killed my goat, but I won't let them have the chickens, too."

Ellis nodded. "Do you need help?"

"These are the last ones. I'll keep them in my room. And hopefully Gareth won't notice."

"Where is your brother?" asked Ellis.

"Boarding up the pantry door."

Sure enough, there was the distant thud of a hammer on wood.

Aderyn strode around the side of the house; she carried a shovel in one hand and another chicken in the other. "Gareth doing manual labor," she said. "Things have truly gone awry." She held up the chicken—she had it upside down by the legs, and the bird had its wings extended, but it did not flap nor try to escape; rather, it looked as resigned as a bird could. "You forgot one."

Ceridwen hastened into the house. "Just—hold on to her for a moment, please!"

Aderyn's gaze went to Ellis. For a few heartbeats, neither said a word. And then she said, "You still want to pay me to take you into the mountains?"

Surprise made him stumble over the words. "Yes, but... you can't mean..."

"That I'm still willing to be your guide?" she said. "Well, I am. And we'll leave tonight."

"Tonight?" She couldn't have shocked him more if she'd handed him the chicken and asked him to dance with it. "You wish to leave at night?"

"Yes," she said. "We've boarded up the windows and secured the front door and the pantry door. Save for the doors, this place is as sturdy as anything. My home will be safe—at least, unless the bone houses bring a battering ram. As for Eynon…well, he probably won't have time to evict us while the bone houses are banging on his door." Her eyes flicked eastward, in the direction of Eynon's estate. "And if the bone houses are focusing on the village, perhaps they won't notice two travelers slip into the forest."

"You want to use the battle as a distraction so we can get into the forest?" He half expected her to deny it, but she nodded.

"Why?" he said. "You're not doing this merely for coin."

Her gaze swept over him—and it felt like that night they'd first met, when she had watched him impassively, picking apart every small detail. "Nor are you," she said. "For all that you claim to be a mapmaker, there's another reason you wish to enter Annwvyn."

He could have denied it—but there was no point. "Yes," he said. "I do have my reasons. What are yours?"

Before Aderyn could answer, Ceridwen barreled out of the house. "All right, give her to me," she said, taking the last chicken from Aderyn. The creature glanced about, as if glad to be held upright again. Ceridwen kept her hands carefully around its wings as she returned indoors.

Aderyn watched her go—and her face was softer than Ellis had ever seen it.

Oh.

So this was why she'd go into the mountains. He should have realized—but then again, he didn't know what it was like to have a family. He couldn't guess to what lengths he would go to protect them.

Aderyn said, "I want to make sure nothing like last night

happens ever again." Her throat moved in a little swallow. "I'm going to end this."

There was a moment's quiet.

Ellis opened his mouth, faltered, and had to try a second time. "You—you think you can destroy the bone houses?"

"Yes."

For a moment, his mind simply would not cooperate. He was exhausted, likely in shock, and here was a young woman claiming she was going to stop the monsters. If he could strip the situation down to angles and distances, perhaps he could consider it rationally. "Castell Sidi," he said. "The cauldron. That's what began all of this—if the stories are to be believed."

"I think we've established the stories are true," said Aderyn, with a grim little smile. "All of this began when the cauldron of rebirth was cracked. It must have made the magic go awry—I thought, if I could destroy the cauldron altogether, the magic would vanish.

"As for getting to Castell Sidi . . . well. The mine leads into the mountains. If I can get through that, I could cut a week from the journey."

"The collapsed mine?"

"One shaft collapsed," she answered. "Not the whole thing."

"So you are going to go into a forest teeming with the risen dead, venture through a mine, and journey into the mountains of Annwvyn to find the cauldron of rebirth."

"Yes."

"You do realize how mad that sounds, right?"

"They attacked my home," said Aderyn. Her hands fisted at her sides. "If the dead beyond the forest start to rise, nowhere will be safe. And if you're still eager to get yourself into the mountains… then at least I'll have enough coin to buy Eynon off."

"And if we both die in the forest?"

"Maybe I'll still find the cauldron." She gave him the barest of smiles. "Death doesn't seem to slow people down much these days."

Or perhaps they would each become one of those mindless creatures, weapons in hand, happy to attack a village.

Ellis knew what he should do—he should pack his things, bid these people farewell, and return to Caer Aberhen. He could draft a report and give it to the prince, ask that the nobles send reinforcements, and hope that they did not come too late.

But if last night's attack was anything to judge by, the bone houses would lay siege to Colbren again and again, and the chances of getting a letter to the prince in time were slim. And that was if the prince would even believe there were armies of the risen dead attacking a remote village.

But even if he sent soldiers, what could they do? Defend Colbren, of course. But none of them had studied maps of the forest like he had—none had spent nights with their fingers tracing inked edges, eyes taking in the lines and empty spaces. "One of my maps might help us. The one that led me to Colbren—"

"The one that got you lost?"

"Yes. It contains the very edges of the mountains—mostly pictures of wild beasts. But it does contain a few sketches of the mine." He returned her thin-lipped smile with his own. "It might prove useful to you. Even if I do not accompany you all the way to Castell Sidi, you may have it. Along with whatever coin I have."

He had few illusions about finding Castell Sidi—he was not on this journey to recover lost magic nor to find monsters.

He was going for himself. But if he could help these people, all the better.

Aderyn gave him a little bow of her head—a silent acceptance.

The decision was made. For better or for worse, he would be going into a forest teeming with monsters.

Footsteps clattered, and then Ceridwen appeared a third time—arms empty. "All right," she said. "Now for the goat."

Aderyn made a pained sound. "Ceri, the goat is—"

"Dead, I know." Ceridwen crossed her arms. "I'm not a fool. But nor am I going to just leave her to rot in the backyard."

"Tomorrow," said Aderyn, "you should take her to the graveyard. There's still a half-ready grave for Mistress Turner. Use that. But it's getting dark, Ceri. You should go inside."

Ceridwen's face tightened, and she walked stiffly toward the backyard.

Aderyn heaved a sigh, pressing her hand to her eyes. "Damn goat," she murmured, as if to herself. She strode after her sister.

Ellis waited, unsure whether to follow. Then he shook his head and trailed after.

The goat had been laid out on the ground. Ceridwen crouched beside it, eyes downcast. She touched a hand to the creature's head, murmured a few quiet words. She looked at the goat with a weary sadness, but there was no raw grief.

Ellis remembered that she had lost her parents—and seen her uncle's corpse the previous night. Perhaps one could become used to loss. Or perhaps the grief went so deep that he could not see it.

"You seem a bit uneasy," Aderyn said, glancing toward him. "You've not spent much time around dead things, have you?"

He shook his head. "People passed away at Caer Aberhen, of course," he said. "But I didn't see them. I've lost no one close to me. Even dead animals were the servants' responsibilities." He knelt beside the goat. Not knowing what else to do, he picked a small wildflower and laid it upon the goat's neck. His fingers brushed the soft fur—once, accidentally. The second time, it was deliberate. He smoothed one of the stray tufts of hair out of the creature's closed eyes.

Aderyn rose to her feet, brushing dirt from her knees. "All right. We've all said our farewells to the goat. We'll go inside—Ceri, you should get ready for bed—"

She never did finish that sentence.

Because at that moment, the goat lifted its head.

Ellis cried out. He reached for Aderyn, pulling her behind him as he lurched away. She made her own startled sound, and then she nearly tripped over a root. They both staggered, clinging to each other.

Ceridwen fell over sideways, gaping at the creature.

The goat looked at them.

Ellis choked back a curse. "By all the fallen kings. What is—"

"Ceri, get over here," Aderyn choked out. "Ceri, come on!"

The goat shifted, struggling to its feet. For one moment, Ellis wondered if perhaps it had been asleep this whole time. But that couldn't be—it had a gaping wound in its side. It had died. They had all heard it being killed.

It was dead.

And yet it wasn't.

"Goat?" said Ceridwen, and her voice quavered.

Ellis remained still, barely daring to breathe. His chest burned, but he feared the moment they moved, the creature would attack.

The goat blinked. Then it laid its head gently on Ceridwen's leg, gazing up at her with something like adoration.

"What is this?" said Ellis, barely moving his lips.

"It's a goat," said Aderyn.

"It's *dead*." He felt foolish pointing out the obvious but someone had to say it.

"I can see that."

There was a heartbeat of silence. Then the goat took a step forward, and then another. Ellis fumbled for his crossbow, but he couldn't reach it soon enough. The goat was in front of them, lowering its head and—

It nudged Aderyn's thigh gently.

As if out of habit, Aderyn reached down and scratched the creature between the horns.

Ellis stood there, crossbow in hand, frozen by the sheer impossibility of the situation. "Don't shoot her," said Ceridwen, lunging to her feet. She put her arms around the goat and held on.

"The goat is dead," he said.

"That has been well established," said Aderyn.

"The goat is dead and you're both petting it."

"What else are we supposed to do?" she said helplessly.

"Kill it!"

"It's already dead!" Her gaze fell to the creature. "And it's—not attacking. It's . . . she's acting like she always does."

He threw up his hands. His left shoulder gave a twinge and he lowered that arm at once. "Just when I thought things could not be any stranger. A goat comes back to life. I thought—do animals do this?"

"No." She gave a sharp shake of her head. "Otherwise, Colbren would be overrun by dead gophers and mice. This . . . this has never happened before. Perhaps the soldiers carried some of the magic with them. I don't know."

Aderyn's fingers smoothed the goat's tufts of fur behind one horn. Ellis's hand twitched; he was not sure if he wanted to pet the creature or run from it. He felt a kind of twisted fascination with the animal, even as it repulsed him. The goat closed its eyes in pleasure and leaned into Aderyn.

Well, at least it did not seem to mean them any harm. "Something's changed," said Aderyn quietly. "The lack of iron, perhaps."

"What do you mean?" asked Ellis.

She gestured at the goat. "This doesn't happen. It just doesn't. Animals don't become bone houses—and bone houses don't rise beyond the forest. Do you know what this means? Because I don't."

Ceridwen rested her cheek against the goat's side and said, "It means Gareth will *never* be able to sell her now."

Ryn tied the dead goat to a fence post.

It was all she could think to do—what was a person supposed to do with an undead goat?

"We'll deal with it later," said Ryn wearily. That was becoming a common phrase of hers. "Right now, you're going to bed."

Ceri gave her a flat look. "Truly?"

"Yes. You're a child and you still need some rest."

"But what if the bone houses—"

"Come on," said Ryn, giving her nudge toward the bedroom. "I'll tuck you in, and then you're staying in bed."

Ceri's room was small and cluttered with drying herbs and jars of preserves. She must have taken them from the pantry; the air smelled of mint and rosemary.

Working as a gravedigger, Ryn had seen many people after they'd witnessed a death. Sometimes they became attached to a chair or a table that had belonged to the deceased. Sometimes they turned to a friend. And some just wrapped their arms around themselves. Ceri reached for an old quilt. It had been stitched together by their mother and given to Ceri when she was born. "What are you going to do?" Ceri asked.

In that moment, Ryn felt as if she might be able to take on all of Annwvyn. For her sister, for her brother, for their home. She would do anything to keep this, all of this.

She put her hand over Ceri's cold fingers and squeezed. "What I must," she said simply, dropping a kiss on Ceri's hair. "Now, get some rest."

Ceri nodded, pulling the quilt up to her chin. Ryn rose, walked to the door, and gave her sister one last smile before pulling it shut behind her. Ellis was outside, and she didn't want to keep him waiting.

She packed quickly—mostly food, and a change of clothes. A few tools: firesteel and a small knife, a canteen, and twine to hold her hair in a braid.

And half of a wooden love spoon. She slipped her fingers into her trouser pocket, felt the familiar edges.

She could not say good-bye. It would be too hard; she moved like a ghost through the house, finally heading toward the front door.

Before she reached it, Gareth strode out of the pantry into view. He still had a nail tucked behind one ear and a hammer in his left hand. He looked exhausted and dirty, but no less sharp for it.

His gaze swept over her: the traveler's cloak upon her shoulders, the pack at her feet, and the axe strapped to her belt.

"You going out to hunt them?" he asked.

There was something about siblings—a language that was half memory and half glance. Jests and jibes. They were a tangle of love and resentment, and despite their differences, Ryn knew he would defend her to the death.

But he could not come with her.

As a child, he, too, had loved stories of afanc and pwca, of bargains and magic, of corpses that could never quite die. But when she had ventured into that forest, he had kept to the outskirts. He remained with their mother, learning how to use her ledger and balance their coin. He loved the stories—but only as stories. He had never wished to reach out and touch them.

When she did not answer, the silence seemed to speak for her.

"No," said Gareth heavily. "That pack is far too heavy for a single night." He let the hammer slip from his fingers and he pressed a hand to his eyes. "Fallen kings, Ryn. I remember when we were young, and you ventured into the forest on your own. You were always fearless. And I have never forgotten how frightening that could be." He ground the heel of one hand against his eyes. "You're going to do this, aren't you? Regardless of what I say."

She gave the smallest of shrugs. He knew her well enough to see it as a yes.

"Then come back," said Gareth. There was a strain in his voice she'd only ever heard once—after Mam died. *Where is she?* Gareth had asked. His grief had been caged behind decorum and the tasks that surrounded death. He'd lost himself in numbers and paper, but in that moment his voice had cracked. *Where is she?*

He would sound the same if Ryn did not come back.

Ryn would come back. One way or another. Heart beating or no, she would come back. Of that, she was sure.

He stepped forward and pulled her into a tight embrace. He smelled of dust and books and home—and she held on to that scent for just a moment.

"Protect the village," she said. "Make sure I have something to come back to. And if Eynon tries to send you to a workhouse, brain him."

She felt the hoarse laugh jerk through him. "Oh. That will be no trouble at all, I'm sure."

"Morwenna will help dispose of the body," she said, with her own small smile.

She stepped out of her brother's arms, gave him one last half smile, and reached down to pick up her pack. "Tell Ceri to save some of those rowanberry preserves for me."

She walked out the front door.

Ellis crouched a few paces away, his crossbow balanced on his knee. When he heard her, he rose and offered her a small smile. "Ready?"

"Almost."

Ryn went to the fence post. The dead-not-dead goat laid on the ground, absentmindedly chewing on some of the tall grasses. Ryn knelt beside her and untied the rope. Ellis made a small sound behind her, but she ignored him.

The goat was not trying to kill them. Perhaps it was some lingering loyalty or her animal nature that kept her safe. Either way, she did not deserve to be tied up when the bone houses returned. She should at least have the opportunity to run.

The goat rose and nudged Ryn's hand, seeking treats. Ryn gave her a little pat.

"Now," she said. "I'm ready."

CHAPTER 15

RYN LED THEM into the forest—beneath the bows of birch and rowan, over the moss and ferns, with only moonlight and memory to guide her. Her previous expeditions to the forest had been kept to the fringes, but now her path took her to the heart of the trees, farther than she had come in years.

They lit no torch, for fear of the bone houses finding them. Ryn worried over the sounds of their passage, of panting breath and twigs beneath boots. Only the dead goat moved silently—and no matter how many times Ryn threw a look over her shoulder, the animal continued to follow.

So goats were as loyal in death as they were in life. And Ryn did not have the heart to take her axe to her. The creature seemed harmless enough.

She welcomed the lassitude that crept into her body; exhaustion could be as potent as drink. And so long as she was exhausted, fear could not find a foothold within her. The undergrowth rustled with unseen creatures; wind made the trees shiver; a river flowed nearby, unseen but never unheard. Ellis paused a few times to take a knife to a tree, marking their passage. She wondered if he were trying to track their way in his own mind, mapping their passage with thought before he could do so with ink and parchment.

A few hours before dawn, they saw a bone house.

The grind of metal against bone caught her ears, and she threw her arm out, catching Ellis in the chest. She pressed him against a tree, their backs to the trunk so that she did not have worry about attacks from all sides.

The whisper of movement made every muscle in her body tense. The memories of the battle rose up to greet her: Hywel's blood cascading across the dirt path, the startled shouts, the smash of armored fists against unprepared doors.

It was a single figure. It moved with jerky little steps, limping like an old man. But it bore the armor of years past and a heavy cudgel rested in its spidery fingers.

She reached for her axe, but Ellis's hand fell on her arm. "If there are more," he whispered, his breath touching her ear. "If there are too many..." He trailed off, but she understood.

There was nowhere to hide in the wilds. There were no houses to fortify, no places in which they could take refuge. If there were more bone houses, if there were too many, they would overwhelm Ryn and Ellis before they could even make it to the mine.

But if she let them go, they could attack more people.

A memory seized her: the half-rotted corpse of Uncle, his teeth bared in a skull's smile as he reached for Ceri.

The monsters were no longer held by the confines of the forest.

Her body flinched with a shudder, and she clenched her muscles, trying to still her own thoughts.

The goat nuzzled at her, and she gripped one of her horns tightly, trying to keep the animal from stirring the brush. The three of them—young woman, young man, and dead animal—waited for a few breathless minutes. Only when Ryn could hear nothing, when the forest was silent and still, did they dare move again.

By the time dawn cast the sky into shades of pink and gold, they were deep into the forest—farther than Ryn had ever dared go. Her legs ached, but she kept moving. The forest was beautiful in the morning—with dew still clinging to the leaves and the air bright and clean. It smelled of juniper, of the sharp tang of mountains, and of—

Smoke.

That made her go still.

Smoke meant people—and she was not sure if that frightened or excited her. No one was supposed to live out here. The lure of copper was not enough for the villagers to risk their lives. At least, not yet. Ryn wondered if perhaps a few more years of lean summers and harsh winters would change that. Perhaps when people were as thin as bone houses they would willingly walk into the forest for coin.

A branch snapped behind her and she flinched. Ellis gave an apologetic shake of his head. "That was me," he said. "Sorry."

That was one thing she liked about him; he never hedged

or tried to shift blame. He simply apologized—and she had not realized how rare that was until she met him. "We should move more slowly," she replied. "Smell that smoke? I think there are people ahead."

His face had been sharpened by lack of sleep—his cheekbones cut across his face and his eyes were overbright. "People," he said, as if testing the word. "People in the forest." He placed his right hand on a tree, leaning against it. "What... kind of people live near Annwvyn?"

Something about the question made her hesitate. It reminded her of a starving man, one who sat at a table and asked with restraint if he might have a helping of food. There was hunger behind every word.

She should have asked for specifics earlier. When they were in the warmth of the Red Mare, surrounded by walls and people, when she had a cup of tea in her hand and the knowledge that she was safe. Perhaps then she would not have feared the answers.

"I think it's time you told me why you wished to come here," she said quietly.

Ellis's gaze lifted to hers. A corner of his mouth unfurled into a mocking smile—but all his recrimination seemed to be turned inward. "I want to map the mountains. This place is a mapmaker's dream—if one can survive long enough, of course." He took a breath, and his exhalation fogged the air around them. "But no. I am not here merely for the mountains." He closed his eyes, steadying himself.

"When I was a young boy, the prince of Caer Aberhen found me on the edges of this forest. Took me in. I had nothing—only the clothes on my back." Again, there was that mocking half smile. "Have you ever been to the other villages that border Annwvyn? Do you know what use they have for the woods?"

She shook her head.

"It's a dumping ground," said Ellis. "Well, not here. Colbren doesn't seem to have that much to get rid of. But if you went south, you'd see. Villagers send things into the forest—things they do not want. Sickly animals, people who've fallen ill with plague, and even unwanted children." His smile became so sharp it was nearly a grimace.

Unwanted children.

"You're looking for your parents," she said, understanding.

"For some sign of them," he said curtly. "I know it's unlikely. I've searched several other towns that border the forest. I've looked everywhere else—except *inside* the forest and the mountains. And I would like to try."

To venture into the mountains in search of his past... it was irrational and foolish—but she understood. There were some things that couldn't be laid to rest by time nor distance.

"And of course," Ellis added, as an afterthought, "mapping Annwvyn will ensure that I become the most sought-after mapmaker in the isles."

"Of course," she said.

"But," he continued, "if there are people in the mountains... I don't know. Maybe I wandered away or they didn't mean to lose me. Maybe my family still lives there." His voice quieted, as if even voicing the desire aloud was a show of weakness.

She bit back her reply: *Or they might be dead.*

Death was common in the wilds. Death from starvation, from cold, from sickness, from an animal bite. His parents might be rotting in the ground—or still walking above it. But she did not say that, because some things could not be said. Not when a person looked cracked open with pain and hope, when a single word might shatter them.

To most people, death was the worst thing.

After years of digging graves, Ryn had little fear of death. Death was quiet and stillness. It was fresh earth and wildflowers. It was coin in her purse and a hole in the ground.

No, the worst thing was uncertainty. When her father had vanished, it would have been a relief to have had a body, rather than just questions. For her family there had been none of the small rituals that surrounded death: no draping of white cloth, no placement of fresh flowers, no building a mound of stones.

Her fingers found the wooden love spoon in her pocket, traced the broken edge.

"We should keep moving," she said, glancing behind her.

The goat had curled up on the ground, as if she were sleeping. Eyes shut, nose gently brushing the leaves, hooves neatly tucked beneath her.

Ellis saw where she looked, then grimaced. "Is it dead?"

"She's been dead for a while," she said drily. "If you're asking if she's the unmoving sort of dead…well, it is daylight. I suppose if she's anything like the other bone houses, then she won't wake until nightfall."

Ellis shook his head. "A bone goat," he said. "Of all the things I thought I'd ever see, a bone goat was never one of them."

That made her laugh.

"What do you know of this place?" asked Ellis, nodding to the pillars of smoke.

Ryn began walking again; her steps were slower, more careful. "There would have been people here long ago," she replied. "All mines have them—small communities that crop up nearby. Families of the miners, those who sell food, tradesmen who deal in black powder and repair equipment, and those who cart the metals away." She pushed a branch from her path, holding it so that Ellis could pass. As he did, she saw the sketchbook in his hand. One eye seemed to be on their path, the other on the parchment. She caught a glimpse of lines and notes—measurements, she realized. He had been counting his footsteps.

"That was before the bone houses, though," she said. "After the dead appeared, reopening the mine must have proved impossible."

"The risen dead do seem to have an ill effect on commerce." Ellis nodded at the smoke. "So people still live out here?"

"I don't know," she said, her jaw tight. "Eynon would be furious if he knew this place was being used for something other than his coffers. They must be squatters—explains why they haven't been to Colbren. But I don't understand why they'd stay here. It can't be safe."

"Perhaps they did not come here for safety," said Ellis mildly.

It took another half hour before they arrived at the encampment. She stepped beneath a low-hanging branch and found herself in a clearing. The houses had been built of oak and cedar, and some had foundations of stone. They formed a circle and at the center was a building that likely served as a small eating house or tavern. Time had taken its toll; one roof sagged and another had fallen in entirely. Ivy crept up the walls, and moss across the paths.

One of the doors opened, and in the scant space, Ryn saw a small face watching her. The door slammed shut.

"Traditional country greeting?" asked Ellis mildly.

She opened her mouth to reply, but a voice called to them. Ryn's hand went to her belt. The old woman had a walking stick carved of an old tree branch, the whorls and knots polished smooth. She had been sitting on a chair beside one of the cabins, Ryn realized. And now she was making her way toward them, eyes as hard and beady as those of one of Hywel's chickens.

"Good morning," said Ellis. He touched his fingers to his heart in greeting. "I hope we've not disturbed you."

The woman's gaze narrowed as her attention settled on Ellis. "You speak like a southerner," she said, "but you've the accent of the north. What brings you to these parts?"

Behind the woman, Ryn glimpsed movement. Other doors were opening, and from the houses spilled more people. They were dressed in clothing that was patched but clean.

"We're looking for a place to rest," said Ryn. "We'll be no trouble to you, if you're no trouble to us."

Ellis threw her a sharp glance, his face taut. He did not seem to approve of the tacit threat.

Ryn merely smiled, her fingers resting lightly on her axe. She knew enough of hunger to be wary—these people looked as though they had little, and desperation might drive them to take what they could. Ryn wouldn't attack without cause, but nor would she allow them to rob her.

The old woman's eyes narrowed. Her gaze snapped from Ryn to Ellis. "No one else?"

The question made Ryn hesitate. She was not sure if the woman were ascertaining that they were alone, that they had no reinforcements, or if there were others who needed feeding. But it was Ellis who answered.

"There are no others."

If the answer put the woman at ease, she did not show it. Her gnarled fingers tightened on the walking stick, and she gave the sharpest of nods. "There's a spare house on the eastern side of the encampment," she said. "You can stay there, if you like."

It was as though she thought they wanted to live in the encampment. Ellis opened his mouth, but Ryn seized his sleeve, silencing him. He threw her a confused glance, and she shook her head.

"Thank you," she said to the woman. "I'm Ryn, and this is Ellis."

She half expected the woman to ask for their family names, but she did not. "Ah," the woman said. She turned on her heel and walked toward one of the houses, moving with surprising speed for a woman of her years.

For a heartbeat, Ellis and Ryn stared after her.

"What do we do?" he said, in an undertone.

"Eat breakfast," she replied.

"And then?"

"You can ask around. See if anyone here knows of a child

who was lost about fifteen years ago. I'm going to ask if anyone has visited the mine." She shifted on her feet, eyes drawn to the shadow of the mountain. Together, they set off in the direction of the aforementioned empty house. They walked slowly, taking in the sights and sounds of the encampment.

Ellis looked at the cabins. "How do they survive in a place like this? How have they kept the bone houses at bay?"

Ryn met his gaze and held it. "That is a good question. And it is another reason why I do not trust this place, nor its people."

"Hello there."

Ryn looked over her shoulder; a woman stood a few strides away. Her hair hung in a heavy braid over one shoulder, and she appeared only a few years older than Ryn. She gave Ryn a small smile. "Has anyone offered you breakfast yet?"

"No," Ryn replied.

The woman laughed, but it was a rueful sound. "I fear my neighbors are not great believers in offering hospitality to travelers." She drew a shawl more tightly around her shoulders. It was of fine make, and this woman was pleasantly rounded. She had not lived here long—or if she had, she'd brought better supplies than the others had. "Come in," she said. "I have a spare room and the kettle is on the fire. You look as if you could use it."

Ryn did not move.

The woman's friendly expression did not falter. "I'm Catrin," she said. "My mam lives here as well. I know—this place seems rather intimidating at first." She cocked her head. "I know what it's like to come here with little more than a few things on your back. Mother and I did the same a year ago—it wasn't easy. You can repay me. I have wood that needs chopping before winter, and another pair of hands wouldn't be unwelcome."

Ryn nodded. Kindness was not to be trusted in these lands, but a fair trade—she could depend on that.

Ellis looked to Ryn.

"I'll leave the two of you alone to decide," said Catrin, and took a few steps back. "I live two doors over—you can knock if you decide you want to stay with me." She gave them a little nod before retreating along the path.

"I don't like this encampment," said Ellis.

"Nor do I." Ryn shuffled a little in place; her calves ached from walking, and she yearned to sit down and close her eyes. The exhaustion of the last few days was seeping into her bones. "But at least we can not like it indoors. With a warm fire. We'll spend a night—we need the rest."

Ryn took a step, but Ellis remained in place. "Come on," she said. She nudged him with her elbow. "We've got your crossbow and my axe. She's no taller than you. If it came to a fight, we could bring her down."

"She did say she lives with another," Ellis pointed out.

"Her mother," said Ryn. "Likely a frail old woman."

"Clearly," said Ellis, "you have not spent time near older women. I've met ones who could bring down a dragon with a glare and a sharp word." He rubbed his left shoulder. "All right. Food and rest—and then we'll decide what to do after."

CHAPTER 16

CATRIN'S HOME WAS larger than Ellis expected. Catrin led them to a kitchen; a fireplace was lit and the heavy scent of burning peat made Ellis's eyes water. Iron skillets and a baking stone rested on a table, and a half-full cup of tea had been abandoned near a rocking chair.

"Here," said Catrin, and she gestured upward. There was a loft built above the room, and a wooden ladder leaned against the wall. "I don't have much in the way of beds, but I've blankets. It'll be better than the cold ground.

"Mam sleeps down the hall, but please leave her be. She'll wake when she's ready." She took a step back. "I'll be in the second room down the hall. If you need something, knock." She gave the two of them one more look before closing the door behind her.

"Come on," said Aderyn, reaching for the ladder. "We might as well get a little rest."

Ellis took a step back. The thought of climbing made his shoulder twinge; after a whole night of walking, he wasn't sure he could do it. "I think I'll take a short walk," he said. "Get a feel for the camp."

Aderyn shrugged. "Don't get bludgeoned over the head, please."

"Thank you for the advice." He gave a small bow of his head before slipping out of the house.

He did not know why, but he felt better the moment he walked outside. Perhaps it was the burning peat or the oppressive darkness. Such homes had the smallest slits for windows, and they let in so little sunlight.

The camp was awake and bustling. The communal stone oven was aflame, and a woman removed loaves of flat bread, loading them into a woven basket. Children strung damp clothes across a line, pausing every so often to use the sodden shirts and socks as playful weapons. A pen of sheep made themselves known with loud braying until a man unlatched the pen, herding the animals into the forest. A dog trotted alongside.

Ellis could feel eyes upon him. He stood out—with his fine clothes and neatly trimmed hair. The woman at the oven gave him a polite nod but the children shied away. He walked to the fringes of the camp, where he found an old yew tree. He sat among the roots, his back resting against the trunk. The sunlight warmed him, and he felt his body relaxing. He stayed there for some time, simply listening to the sounds of the forest.

A branch snapped.

He straightened, opened his eyes, and looked toward the circle of houses. A boy around twelve or thirteen approached Ellis, all the while keeping a wary eye on the others. He had the wiry build of a stray dog, and the keen eyes of the street children Ellis had seen in the cities.

"Hello, there," said Ellis, smiling.

He received no such warmth in return.

"You new to town?" said the boy. He gave a little jerk of the chin to indicate that he didn't truly care about the answer.

"Yes," said Ellis.

"You run off with that girl?" the boy asked. "Which one of you is it, then? Got to be you—all pale and skinny."

Ellis frowned. "Pale and skinny?"

"Maybe girls like that sort of thing," said the boy, as if trying to unravel a puzzle. "Don't know why, though."

Ellis tilted his head, and then he laughed. "You think—Aderyn and I—"

"Pretty name," said the boy with a shrug. "Pretty girl. You'd not be the first married against their family's wishes, nor even the first to come here when things don't work out."

Ellis smiled, just a little. It wasn't as if Aderyn was not attractive—she was, of course. She reminded him of an ocean—beautiful, with enough salt to kill a man. He suspected it would take a knight or a hero of legend to impress one such as her.

"No, I'm here looking for my parents," said Ellis.

The boy squinted at him. "You from here? You don't look like it."

"I grew up at Caer Aberhen. The prince took me in."

The boy's brows flew skyward. "You run away with a servant?"

Ellis snorted. "No. Aderyn verch Gwyn is a gravedigger from Colbren. I'm a mapmaker."

"And you came here?" said the boy, confused. "Why?"

Ellis smiled faintly. He knew what he looked like—a tall, thin young man in borrowed finery. "I was found near here. When I was a very young child—starving and alone. Surely my family must have been near." If they hadn't simply shoved him into the forest and walked away.

The boy eyed him with new interest. "When'd you go missing?"

The way he said it gave Ellis pause. Because he had never looked at his past in such a way: He had been *found*; he had never gone *missing*.

Or, most likely, *been unwanted*.

He shook away that thought. "About—fifteen years ago? I'm eighteen now, I think." He could never be sure, although the prince's physician had checked him over several times and made that his pronouncement.

"Fifteen years ago," the boy murmured, as if mulling over memories. "I wasn't born yet, but I can ask Mam. She's been here since just after the mine was shut up. She wasn't no miner, but these houses were all ripe for the taking... so she took."

"What about your father?"

The boy shook his head. "He don't speak now," he said. "One of the wordless."

Ellis was not quite sure what that meant, but he tried to look sympathetic. "Have most of you lived here since just after the mine was closed?"

The boy nodded. "I'll ask about your parents," he said. "What's your name?"

"Ellis."

"Your family name?"

"I don't know it."

The boy's face softened to something close to pity. This boy, with worn clothing and fingers chapped from work—and he pitied Ellis.

"The bone houses," Ellis said, changing the subject, hoping the words would distract. "How do you deal with them?"

The boy squinted. "What'd you mean?"

Had the bone houses not bothered these people? Surely that couldn't be the case. Ellis had seen no iron surrounding the encampment, and this place was closer to Annwvyn than Colbren was. Why wouldn't the settlement have been attacked?

"Ah, well," said Ellis, "never mind." The conversation felt as if it had veered far away from what he'd intended. "If you do find out anything, I'd be glad to know it. You can find me at Catrin's house."

The boy nodded. "I'll be 'round." He trotted back toward the other children. A boy and a girl were in a tussle, using damp tunics to swat at each other. The boy who Ellis had talked to barked at them, and the two scurried back to the clotheslines.

When Ellis returned to Catrin's home, he made the short climb to the loft, keeping his weight on his good arm. Aderyn was curled up on her side, with her pack as a pillow and her cloak as a blanket. Her red-brown hair had been loosened from its braid and it fell in waves around her face. Even in sleep her hand rested gently on the hilt of her axe. A gentle snore emerged from her parted lips.

He felt himself smile.

She was fearless—and part of him envied her for that. He had spent most of his life trying to anticipate the wishes of others, to conform to what was expected of him, to be the kind of person everyone liked. Sometimes it felt as if there were no true Ellis. He had been an obedient ward of the prince, a good student to his teachers, and polite to everyone he met. And if he were a little aloof—well, it was better to hold one's self back than to risk being hurt.

The air was thick with smoke from the fire below. It made his eyes water and his throat burn—and he wondered if he could sleep in such a place.

He didn't enjoy sleep; his dreams were of a never-ending forest, of fingers pushing aside branches, of bare feet numbed by cold ground, of a blazing fire in his shoulder and a hollow ache in his belly.

He never dreamed of his parents. But in the moments between waking and sleeping, he heard the whisper of a woman's voice: *My darling boy.*

He slept soundly. When he opened his eyes, the light had changed.

Aderyn was nowhere to be seen. The fire had died down, and the house smelled of cooked meat. He slipped a small strip of willow bark from his pack, placing it between his teeth so he could climb down to the first floor.

Catrin stood beside the fire. She glanced up, and a smile touched her lips. It was an odd smile—fond, but without any mirth. "Willow bark?" she asked quietly.

He took it from his mouth and said, "Yes."

"Ah." The woman's face softened with understanding. "I have a few herbs that help with pain. And a drink—it tastes foul and will burn any taste from your mouth, but it'll put you into a good sleep."

He huffed out a breath. "I'd rather not drink myself into a stupor. I prefer to be awake and in pain rather than unconscious and unfeeling."

She nodded. "Aye. My mam was the same when she was ill."

"You said she lives here?" Ellis glanced about, half expecting to see an old woman.

Catrin nodded. "She isn't awake yet. But she'll be glad to meet you."

Ellis knew enough of manners to give Catrin a courtly little bow. "I'm sure I will be glad to meet her, as well."

That same odd smile crossed Catrin's mouth. "You're a good sort," she said, and her voice was heavy with some unspoken emotion. "Your friend is outside—I think she wanted to look through the village, see if there's another place you can stay."

Ah. Then Aderyn had not told Catrin they did not intend to linger. Perhaps she wished to keep their journey to herself, for fear that these people would hinder them—or worse, would want to help by coming along.

"Should we be out after dark?" he asked. He still did not know how these people dealt with bone houses, and thought it only prudent to ask.

Catrin laughed. "It's fine. We've got plenty of people out at night. There's a fire going, and always company. Caradoc might play his crwth if you're lucky—and if his fingers aren't too stiff."

Ellis gave her one last nod and smile before slipping out the door and into the evening.

The encampment was settling in for the night: parents rounding up wayward children, a dog barking at a sheep that refused to get in its pen, and an old couple loudly arguing about whose turn it was to carry wood to the fire pit. Several people gawked at Ellis, someone even peering through a doorway to get a better look at him.

Ellis merely waved. One small girl raised her hand in reply, her other arm clutching a carved wooden horse. An older man—presumably her father—used the distraction to scoop the girl into his arms and toss her over his shoulder. She squealed with laughter and protest as he carried her toward the house.

Longing welled up in Ellis, like blood from a reopened wound. He wanted—well, he wasn't even sure what precisely he wanted. From a noble's view, there was nothing to be envied here: small houses, rotten roofs, and the smell of sheep and cook fires. But there was warmth, a sense of belonging that he'd never found.

Perhaps it was foolish, but he'd never stop looking for it.

He realized his gaze had lingered on the father and daughter too long when the older man gave him a wary nod as he passed. "If you're looking for your girl," he said, "she went to the northern reaches of the camp."

Ellis grimaced. Aderyn wouldn't appreciate being referred to in such a way, he was sure. "Thank you," he said.

He found Aderyn leaning against a tree, her gaze on the shape of the mountains. In the blaze of sunset, he could see only the outline of the peaks, in shades of flame-red and orange. The mountains themselves were a dark shadow.

"You're awake," she said, not looking at him. "You were sleeping like the dead when I left. You don't snore, at least."

"You do," he said, smiling.

That earned him a sharp glance. For a moment, her mouth remained rigid—then the frown splintered into a rueful grin. "All right."

The sound of footsteps drew his attention. He looked up to see the boy from earlier. His face was reddened, as if it had been freshly scrubbed, and his hair was damp. He looked a bit like a feral cat that had escaped from a bath. He nodded to Ellis. "Hello, princeling," he said, by way of greeting.

Ellis exhaled. "Mapmaker—not a prince." He threw a despairing look toward Aderyn. "Will anyone ever look at me and think *mapmaker*?"

"Probably not," said the lad.

"It's your boots," said Aderyn.

"And your way of speaking," said the boy, grinning.

"And your hair." Aderyn exchanged a smile with the lad. "It's far too neat."

Ellis's hand went to his hair. He forced his arm back down. "Did you find anything?"

The boy nodded. "I did some asking around."

Aderyn's forehead wrinkled as she gazed at the boy. "You?"

The boy stood a little taller. "If someone wants to know something in this village," he said with pride, "I'm the one to ask." He seemed to be trying to puff out his chest for Aderyn's benefit, but the display was in vain.

"You are?" said Aderyn drily. "What? Do you listen at closed doors?"

The boy's posturing faded, and he looked irritated. "No. But I know people, and older sorts don't notice when I'm around."

Aderyn seemed amused. "All right. I'll leave you two to it, then." She turned, but the boy held up his hand.

"Verch Gwyn, was it?" he asked. "You're not the first of them to come through here."

Ellis had once seen a boy get shot. It had been an archery accident—the slip of a trainee's fingers, and the arrow embedded itself in a boy's hip. The boy had come out of it all right, but Ellis had never forgotten the expression on his face.

Aderyn looked that way now.

Her freckles stood out against her skin, her body frozen midstep. "What did you say?"

The boy crossed his arms. "There was another gravedigger that came through here some years ago. Older chap—had red hair. Only remember him 'cause he left some food in the woods. Said it was for luck. We made off with it as soon as he was out of sight." He smiled. "I was young then. Wasn't allowed very far into the woods."

"We'd appreciate brevity," said Ellis.

"What?" said the boy.

Ellis made an impatient gesture. "Get on with it."

The boy frowned. "Not sure I will now. Not with you being all cross."

Ellis sighed. He reached into his pocket and withdrew a coin. He balanced it on his index finger, then snapped his thumb forward. The coin spun into the air, glinting in the moonlight as the boy grabbed for it. His round-cheeked face was ruddy with excitement.

"Now," said Ellis. "Tell us what you've found."

The boy's gaze was drawn to the coin. It was a mere copper, but it must have seemed like gold to the boy. "Nothing about you," he said bluntly. "No child named Ellis was ever known in these parts. Any lost child—either their parents went missing as well, or they found bits later. Fingers or scraps of clothing."

The disappointment was an old one; it settled like a familiar weight on his shoulders.

Aderyn gazed at the boy as if she wished to shake him for answers. "My father—did he—"

"He went into the mine," said the boy. "We never saw him again."

Ellis hesitated; part of him wanted to reach out, to place a hand on her shoulder or arm. He knew that touch could be a lifeline—but it could also be an imposition.

"Thank you," he told the boy.

The boy did not move.

Ellis made to cross his arms, but a warning twinge kept his hands at his sides. "We'd like privacy now."

The boy smirked. "Sure you would." He skittered back a few steps, as if he expected Ellis might swat at him. He flashed Ellis a grin before hastening away. Ellis watched him until the boy vanished into one of the smaller cabins.

"What was he on about?" asked Aderyn, but not as if the answer mattered.

"Oh," said Ellis, "I'm pretty sure he thinks we're having some illicit romance and your family disapproves of me."

She scoffed.

"It's true," he said. "Although I think that rumor does me more favors than you."

A flicker of movement caught his eye. He whirled, heart beating quickly, wondering if the boy had returned.

A creature stepped into the moonlight.

It was a goat.

It was a goat with curling horns, tufts of fur around its ears, and a gaping wound in its side.

"Bone goat," said Aderyn, with a shake of her head. "You're awake."

"It found us," said Ellis. At least the creature still didn't seem dangerous. It trotted toward them, tail swishing from side to side.

Aderyn reached down and absentmindedly scratched the

goat's ears. It leaned against her, eyelids drooping. "You have never spent much time around goats before, have you?" she asked.

He shook his head. "One summer I helped with the chickens," he said.

"Goats are two things chickens are not," she replied. "Very, very loyal. And incredibly stubborn."

"I can see why you're so attached to it, then." The words slipped out without his meaning them to. He winced. "Apologies."

She shook her head. "No apologizing for that one. I know what I am. And there's worse things to be than loyal and stubborn."

He watched her as she petted the bone goat, treating it as anyone might treat a favored animal. When everyone else would run, Aderyn remained firmly still. When everyone else would recoil, she merely shrugged.

She met his gaze, and her mouth softened into something near a smile. "Doesn't mean I'm going to let anyone else see the goat, though. We'll have to keep her out here. Don't want to stir up a panic." She took hold of one horn and led the creature into the woods. "I'll tie her to a tree for the night until we leave. She'll try to find us again, I'm sure, but she won't be able to follow me through the mine. I hope she'll just wander into the woods. I don't want anyone else hurting her again."

He noted her use of the singular. "You don't intend to uphold your end of our bargain?" he asked mildly.

She slid him a sharp glance. "It's dangerous in the mountains," she said. "You sure you want to come along?"

"It's pretty dangerous out of the mountains, too," he replied.

And there was the part of him that burned to push beyond the edges of the map. To make his own path, rather than follow another's. To see what so few had witnessed.

And to make his own map, of course.

"I'm going with you," he said.

She nodded. "All right. But if you die, I'm going through your things to find the coin you owe me."

He barked out a startled laugh. "Fair enough."

Aderyn finished tying the rope. The goat looked at her with a flat stare, as if to indicate disapproval. "You're fine," she told the creature.

The goat looked as if it wanted to heave a sigh but did not have the breath.

"Come on," said Aderyn, walking toward the camp. "We should get inside. If the goat's awake, it means other dead things will be, too. We don't want to be caught unawares."

It felt as if night was bleeding out from the shadows, rather than descending from the sky. It moved through the trees, setting Ellis's nerves on edge.

When they returned to the encampment, Ellis saw that the villagers had little fear of the night. The rich melody of a crwth rang out, and firelight spilled across the packed-dirt ground. A few couples whirled, arms clasped, far more graceful than he could have managed. In the flickering illumination, he could not make out many faces; they were shadowed and strange, but he thought he saw the older couple sitting together, sharing a cup. It made him smile; he could enjoy the camaraderie even if he did not share in it.

Aderyn skirted the glow of the fire, keeping to the shadows of the cabins. "If one of the ladies spots you, she may try to kidnap you for a dance," she said.

His shoulder gave a twinge, as if in response, and he rubbed his collarbone. "I'm not much of a dancer. But I am going to talk to the villagers before I turn in for the night," he said. "To ask about the mine's entrance—if it's barricaded or open, and whether any of them have ventured inside."

She hesitated, and he could see indecision playing out across her face.

"I'll see you inside," he added gently.

She nodded. But she remained in place, one hand resting on Catrin's door, her face half tilted toward him. The firelight burnished her red-brown hair to a blazing crimson, and something about the angle of her chin and jaw made his heart clench painfully.

For a moment, he considered telling her. Of every night he spent in wakefulness, of how he never quite dreamed of his family, of how his body felt more a battleground than a sanctuary, and of how he did not know who he was—but only that he wanted to be someone.

He said none of that.

Rather, he turned and walked toward the fire.

CHAPTER 17

DA HAD COME through here.

That thought beat within her again and again, until it seemed to drown out everything else. Ryn looked at the encampment with new awareness, her gaze tracking over the buildings, wondering if her father had seen them, too. Wondering what he had thought of them. Wondering if he had stood beside the communal stone oven or eaten with these people.

Something hot and bitter burned in her throat and she tried to swallow it down.

Her thoughts still raced with memories of her father, and part of her yearned to go outside and speak with everyone she could. Perhaps she could draw memories of him from these people like water from a well.

But that was not her journey's purpose.

As Ryn walked into the house, her eyes adjusted to the darkness.

A woman sat before the still-burning cook fire. Her back was to Ryn, and soft white hair cascaded down her shoulders. She wore an old nightgown, and her thin fingers rested gently on the arm of her crudely carved chair. Catrin's mother must have finally risen from her bed, only to take refuge by the fire's warmth. Ryn stepped toward her. "Good evening," she said.

The woman's fingers twitched on the armchair, but she did not respond.

"Sorry to bother you," said Ryn. "I'll just be going up to the loft—"

The old woman turned her head; the illumination from the fire struck her across the face.

She was indeed wearing a nightgown. It was clean and white, with flowers embroidered along the sleeves.

But she had no eyes, and her skin was stretched tight over her cheekbones. Her mouth was too large, peeled back over exposed teeth.

The woman reached out a hand. As if she were beckoning or entreating.

Ryn stumbled, tripped over her own feet. A wordless sound burst from her lips and she found herself crawling away.

The woman was—dead.

She'd been dead long enough for her skin to stretch tight, for desiccation to set in to the flesh, yet not so long that her hair had lost its shine. It had been recently brushed, and it was that detail that stuck in Ryn's mind.

Her hair had been brushed smooth, every strand lovingly cared for. Her nightgown was pristine. She was taken care of.

And she was dead.

The door swung open and Catrin walked inside. She carried a cup of something hot, tendrils of steam trailing behind her. When she saw Ryn, she smiled.

She *smiled.*

"I see you've met Mother," she said warmly.

Mad. Catrin had to be mad. And reckless, if she were keeping a bone house here, in her home. "She—she—" Ryn began to say, her voice shaking hard.

"Mother," said Catrin, laying a hand on the dead woman's shoulder, "don't be afraid—she's a guest."

The dead woman tilted her head, her sightless eyes fixed on Ryn. That gaze seemed to freeze the blood in Ryn's veins, and she felt sick with it.

"What are you—" Ryn began to say, but she faltered again. "She—she's one of them—"

Catrin's smile wavered. "Of course she is."

As if Ryn should have known. As if it were not some terrible secret.

"You knew," said Catrin slowly. "Isn't that why you came? That's why everyone comes here." She met Ryn's eyes, and there was a terrible kind of joy in her face. "Death cannot touch this place," she whispered. "If you are dying, if you have a father or a sister or a spouse who is dying... you can come here."

Or a mother, Ryn thought, but did not say.

"Your husband," said Catrin. "He—he is the one who is

dying, isn't he? I saw how he moves, as if his whole back pains him. I saw the willow bark he chews. You came here so as not to be parted from him."

Ryn opened her mouth to say all sorts of things: that Ellis was not her husband, and he was *certainly* not dying—

Was he?

Well, it would explain why he did not fear dying in the mountains. Death was cheap in a place where the dead rose every evening. He could simply come back and—

That was when she understood the encampment.

People did not come here to live.

They came here to die.

They came here so loved ones would continue on, silent, rotting versions of themselves that would rise every night. So they could cling to the remnants of loved ones. So that they would never have to put a body in the ground, and flowers on that grave. It was foolish and dangerous and—

So very *tempting*.

"We didn't come here for that." The words spilled out of Ryn. She could barely hear herself; her attention was wholly on the dead woman sitting in the chair. She looked so calm, so peaceful.

Ryn remembered the dead woman she'd encountered in the fields. She had been dead, but she had made no move to attack. She had merely wandered, her gait unsteady with her broken ankle. Wandered, as if searching for something.

Family?

Home?

"People *only* come here to live with their loved ones," said

Catrin gently. "And they stay because the magic won't work from afar."

Ryn had thought the cauldron's curse twisted the dead into something they were not. It made them attack, made them into monsters. But what if it had done no such thing? Her uncle had always been vicious, and it was not difficult to imagine he would try to drag Ceridwen out of their home to hurt her. The dead man who had attacked Ellis might have been a robber or a murderer. As for the soldiers of Castell Sidi—perhaps they had attacked merely because they were soldiers.

If death did not change a person...

A shudder ran through her.

She thought of the dead she had dismembered. She had placed bodies in the forge, thinking they were little more than unthinking monsters. If they were not, did that make her a murderer?

She could not think of that. Not now, not with a dead woman watching her and a living one waiting for her to explain.

"Neither of us is dying," said Ryn, and hoped that wasn't a lie.

Catrin's face was drawn with confusion. "Then why are you here?"

Her answer came haltingly. "We—we're...the mine. We're going through the mine."

Catrin's confusion flickered into the sharpness of realization. "You're going to Annwvyn. But that's—no one goes into the mountains. There's no reason."

"That's where the cauldron is," said Ryn.

Catrin's face drained of all color. For one moment, Ryn

thought it was concern for her. She was so used to people believing she would die in those mountains, it was the first conclusion that came to her. But then she saw the way Catrin's hand tightened on her mother's shoulder. That pristine gown draped over the dead woman's bony frame. Such care was due to the dead—and Ryn respected that. But there was something sickening about the image of Catrin washing and dressing her mother, helping the dead woman with fastenings that her rotted hands could not manage.

"You're—going to take the magic from this place," said Catrin, very quietly.

Ryn did not answer. She could not, because in that stretch of silence, she understood her mistake.

Catrin remained frozen for a heartbeat.

And then she threw herself at Ryn.

CHAPTER 18

MUSIC RANG THROUGH the encampment.

The song began slowly, the first few notes drawn out, before the rhythm took shape and dancers began to swing around and around, hands clasped and hair shining in the light of the fire. Ellis watched from a distance, his arms at his sides, listening to the pleasant music. The man playing the crwth was half shadowed by the awning of a cabin. He sat in a wooden chair, the instrument cradled to his chest as the bow moved lovingly across the horsehair strings.

"Not one for dancing, are you?" asked a young woman, stepping toward Ellis. Her golden hair was bound in a knot, and her smile was a bit too knowing.

Ellis gave her a polite little bow of his head and shoulders. "I fear I'd do your feet an injury, my lady."

“Well, you’re a sweet-tongued lordling,” she said, her smile widening. “None of that ‘my lady.’ We’ve all left our titles behind.”

That was interesting. Some of them had once had titles. Ellis would have thought that the squatters had been poor farmers or those who’d escaped servitude—those with nowhere else to go.

“Where’s your companion?” asked the young woman. “Gone to bed?”

“Yes.” He considered saying that he’d wanted a moment of solitude, but that would sound rude. “The music is lovely. I wished to hear more of it.”

“Caradoc.” The girl nodded to the man whose thin-fingered hands were a blur over the crwth. “Some say he played for princes before his horse bolted. A cart ran over his foot—the wound sickened, and he had barely enough time to make it here.”

Ellis blinked. He wouldn’t have thought the encampment’s healers would have the skill or the supplies to treat an inflamed wound—but again, he remained silent for fear of offending this woman.

“Now he plays only at night,” she continued, “but it’s better than never at all, right?”

Ellis nodded.

One song bled into another. This one was slower, a tune that seemed to tug at something in Ellis’s chest. “Come now,” said the woman. “Surely this tune would not cause too much injury.”

Before he could truly understand her meaning, the woman slipped her hand into his, and led him among the dancing couples.

He had learned to dance, of course. The prince saw to it that all noble children in Caer Aberhen knew the traditional steps. Even Ellis, who did not enjoy the scrutiny of his instructor, nor the effort it took to raise his left hand above his partner, had been saddled with lesson after lesson. Now he found himself whirling amid the other dancers, one hand twined with the young woman's, and the other rested lightly on her waist. She was smiling, as if overjoyed to have a new partner, and the other dancers made room for them.

At first he stumbled a bit. He could not recall how to move, where his feet should go. But as the song shifted again, memory slid into place. They spun—if not wholly gracefully, then at least enthusiastically. The light of the fire cast shadows and flickers all about them, throwing the other dancers into strange contrasts. One gaunt man with deep-set eyes moved past them, and something about his face made Ellis pause. But the man was gone before he could study him more closely. None of the dancers were truly skilled, but their enjoyment was infectious.

The music sped up, and Ellis's heartbeat kept pace. Something about the wild dance made him want to smile—and suddenly he was caught up in the rhythm of it. Thought fell away, and he realized this was why people enjoyed dancing: Because when it was done right, there was very little thinking to it. His mind retreated, and all that was left was movement. It was as heady as drink, as a stolen kiss, as all the things he'd been too afraid to try.

The shadowed figures moved through the firelight, spinning round and round, until he was smiling in earnest. The young woman was grinning, even when his shoe caught the hem of her dress. They stumbled together beside the fire pit. The heat flushed his bare forearms and neck. "Not bad," said the young woman with a careless little laugh. "And here you said you'd injure me."

He rubbed the back of his neck. The skin was damp, and sweat rolled between his shoulder blades. In the brightness of the fire, he could finally see the man playing the crwth. He was bent over the instrument, fingers darting as he finished the song. "I was sure I—"

His words strangled out.

Because at that moment, the man lifted his head. His fingers slowed, the bow gliding across the strings, and the tune ended. Cheers and cries for more rang out, but Ellis did not hear them.

The musician did not have thin fingers.

He had fingers of raw bone.

They were polished smooth and brown, like driftwood on a shore. His face had deep hollows—because there was no flesh beneath the cheekbones. The mouth grinned a skull's smile, and the man's high collar nearly hid the ridges of his spine. Only his hair remained glossy, well cared for and trimmed.

Shock rooted Ellis to the hard-packed ground. It was not fear—not yet. There was no room for fear. His mind was clawing for an explanation. Surely these people had not noticed. They must not have noticed, because otherwise they would have run. They would have reacted like those in Colbren, who took up arms to defend their homes and families. They would not have continued to dance.

But now he truly looked at them.

There was a child wearing a red gown and whose hair hung in ringlets around her shoulders. Her face was tight, as if the flesh had begun to pull away from sinew. Her mouth was a rictus of a smile. Then there was another man—an old man with a bald pate and eyes gone milky. And that man he'd seen before—not with deep-set eyes, but with no eyes at all.

Three, no four of them. Bone houses were dancing all around him. The hands of the dead clasped with those of the living, whirling in glorious abandonment.

"You all right?" asked the young woman. But her voice was light, unconcerned. A mere formality now that her partner had gone unnaturally still.

He had been dancing among the dead and never even realized.

The dead man put bow to crwth, every movement sinuous and practiced, and the music began again. The young woman tugged at him, but Ellis slipped from her grip, shaking his head in silent refusal.

What is this? he wanted to say. *What is this?*

The words remained behind his teeth; his jaw ached, and he realized every muscle of his body was drawn tight. His shoulder clenched in pain, but even that seemed distant.

For the first time, he was glad he had not found his parents among these people.

He strode away from the circle of firelight, from the movement and the song, toward Catrin's home. The shock was draining away, and fear rapidly swelled to take its place. A tremble began in his legs, but he forced himself to keep moving. He did not run—not out of any bravery, but because he wasn't sure his legs would not simply collapse.

He had to find Aderyn. He let that thought center him. He would find Aderyn and tell her that something was wrong, that they needed to leave, and—

His fumbling fingers found the latch, and he shoved the door open.

The interior was lit only by the embers of the dying fire. There were no candles, no torches, only a dim orange glow.

Even so, he saw the fight at once.

Aderyn was on her back, legs kicking wildly as Catrin pressed her to the floor. The woman's hands were on Aderyn's shoulders, gripping with bruising force, and she was saying "—can't, you can't—" as if this were a conversation. Aderyn snarled and threw an elbow, cracking into Catrin's chest. A pang of phantom pain went through Ellis as Catrin clutched her collarbone, staggering up onto her heels. Aderyn began to scramble upright, but Catrin seized her ankle and yanked.

Ellis started forward, and the movement must have caught Catrin's attention, for her gaze jerked up to meet his. He expected anger—but what he saw was terror. "We can't let them leave," she gasped. "Mother—"

At first, Ellis thought she must have gone mad, to refer to him in such a way.

Then pain flared across the base of his skull. The world went red at the edges, and he heard himself cry out, the floor driving up to meet him. He landed hard, jostling his shoulder. It was like kicking a hornet's nest to the ground—agony burst within him, burning and stinging through his collarbone, extending down his back.

The pain might have been debilitating—if he had not had a lifetime of it.

If Ellis knew anything about himself, it was pain. He knew how to sense it, how to avoid it, how to soothe his aches with heat compresses and herbs. He let the pain roar through him now, breathing in short bursts, and then he used his good hand to push himself upright. He glanced up to see his attacker.

It was an old woman in a nightgown, a wooden rolling pin in hand.

No, that was not right.

It was an old, *dead* woman in a nightgown, wielding a rolling pin.

That was slightly less embarrassing.

Ellis had little experience with fighting. But even he knew that when it came to reach, he had the advantage. He lashed out with one long leg, catching the old woman in the knee. He hooked his foot around, jerking her weight out from under her. The woman crashed to the floor, mouth open in a wordless snarl. Behind him, he heard the sickening sound of fist on flesh, but he could not help Aderyn. Not like this—unarmed and unprepared. He shoved himself to his feet and dashed for the ladder to the loft. Gritting his teeth against the pain, he hauled himself up and over, fingers scrabbling for his pack. He threw Aderyn's pack over the edge, heard it hit someone, and then heard a cry of surprise. His own pack went over his shoulder.

He hit the floor with both feet, settling into a crouch, his crossbow cradled between both hands. "Stop," he snapped, and aimed the weapon at Catrin.

She and Aderyn were in a tangle on the floor—Aderyn gripped Catrin's hair and had one leg hooked around the woman's arm, grappling for the upper hand. Catrin had scratches down her face but did not seem to notice. Blood spattered the floor beneath them, black in the dim light.

And the dead woman was struggling to rise.

"Let go of her," he said to Catrin. She went still, her eyes fixed on the crossbow. Her chest rose and fell in uncontrollable spasms, then her fingers unclenched. Aderyn crawled away on hands and knees, reaching for her fallen pack. Her hair was mussed and there was a red welt beneath her left eye. Her axe rested on the floor, and she scooped it up.

"I would have thought that'd be your first response," Ellis said, with a tight little smile. Aderyn glanced down at her weapon, then back at him.

"I'm not a murderer, for all my faults," she replied. Her voice was ragged but firm. "And I think—I think I've had enough hospitality."

"Let us walk out of here," said Ellis, turning his gaze on Catrin. "We walk out, and no one is harmed."

Catrin took half a step toward them. "No—you can't."

Ellis's finger touched the trigger, and she flinched.

"The magic," she said haltingly. "You can't take it. It's all that's keeping these people alive. Mother—Caradoc. They're—"

"Rotting," said Aderyn.

Catrin closed her eyes for a moment, then reopened them. "They're aware. They can't talk, but they know who they were. What they want. They're not a danger to anyone. I've heard—we've heard rumors of other risen attacking other people, but none of them do that here. They came here for a second chance."

Aderyn threw her arm out, pointing at the dead woman. She had managed to right herself, and her sightless gaze drifted between Catrin and Ellis, as if she could sense what was going on. "You call this a second chance?"

"Yes!" snarled Catrin. "You wouldn't understand. You've never lost someone. You've never had to see the end coming and know there are no other options. We came here because I couldn't lose her."

Her words rang with a terrible certainty.

Aderyn trembled; it was slight, but Ellis saw the way her axe shook. "The bone houses—"

"Don't call them that," snarled Catrin.

"The dead," said Aderyn roughly, "are *dead*."

Catrin took another step forward. "But they don't have to be!"

A flicker of emotion passed over Aderyn's face.

Ellis gazed at her—and a certainty struck him. He had seen her in the shadow of the forest—how her body canted toward the mountains, her face peaceful. For someone with little fear of death or magic, this place must seem a haven to her. A place where she would not have to lose her loved ones, where they could rise with the moon, silent and constant. She must have thought of her buried mother. It would be a temptation. It *was* a temptation.

"Aderyn," he said.

She did not look at him.

He might lose her to this place. It would be so easy for her to put aside her quest, to dig up her mother's bones and bring them here. Perhaps she could even find her father in the mine or the mountains beyond and bring him here, too.

As for what would become of himself—he could continue on alone. Try to find his own family, skirting the edges of the forest, always searching, always half-lost.

Or he could retreat home. Return to Caer Aberhen, sleep in a soft bed, smile at the nobles, and when the master mapmaker's hands became too stiff, Ellis might take his place.

All he had to do was run. All he had to do was turn his back on Colbren, on those travelers who might be caught unawares on the road, on the deaths that would follow if the bone houses were allowed to exist.

No. He'd come here to find his parents. He'd found peril and magic instead, but he would not run. He had no surname, no family, no ties at all—but he had his pride.

Ryn was trying to make this land safer.

He could do no less.

"Aderyn," he said again.

Her eyes came up to meet his—and he saw the war raging in her. Grief and need and fear seemed to freeze her in place. But he could not do this without her.

So he did the only thing he could think of.

"Ceridwen," he said.

It was like submerging her in frigid water: She shuddered and seemed to come awake, eyes wide. She shook herself, taking a step back, away from Catrin.

It had been a gamble, but he'd seen how she regarded her little sister. And perhaps there was a bit of himself in that gamble, too—he imagined, if he'd had a little sister, he would have done anything to keep her safe.

"N-no," Aderyn said. "This—this isn't right."

Catrin edged forward, but Ellis raised the crossbow a little higher. She went still.

"We're leaving," said Ellis. "I'm sorry." He wasn't sure to whom or for what he was apologizing, but it felt necessary. He reached behind himself, fumbling for the door handle. Part of him knew that to turn his back would be to invite another blow to his head. The latch came undone with a heavy clack, and the coolness of the night air touched his neck. He took a step back, and then another, until the glow of the fire faded and he found himself standing outdoors. Aderyn followed a moment after, her pack bouncing on her hip. She moved as if she were halfway between waking and dreaming, and her mouth kept forming words he could not catch.

"We need to leave now," said Ellis. A terrible fear had descended upon him—and before he could voice it aloud, Catrin began to scream.

It was a terrible sound. The kind an animal made when it

was pierced through, when there was no hope of survival. The music fell away, and the sound of dancing went with it. Ellis could almost feel the eyes straining through the dark, trying to find the source of the noise.

Ellis took off at a run. He heard Aderyn behind him, fumbling for a moment, and then she fell into step. His strides were longer, but she knew how to run in the dark. They kept pace.

Together, they sprinted around one of the half-collapsed cabins. If these villagers caught them, he had little doubt of what they'd do to protect their loved ones. Even their dead loved ones. If breaking the curse threatened them—

Something flew through the air, slamming into the underbrush. Ellis felt its passage as a whisper of movement and sound, but it was gone before he understood. Arrows. Someone had a bow—likely for hunting rabbits or deer. Biting back a curse, Ellis ducked low and tried to keep moving, darting from one side to the other, trying to elude the hunter.

"The bone goat," said Aderyn suddenly, and she veered to her right. How she remembered the goat in this mess, he did not know. He yearned to keep running, but if he rushed headlong into the dark forest, he might end up even worse off than he was now. Forcing his breathing to slow, he followed Aderyn, more by sound than by sight. The thick foliage drowned out the starlight, leaving them in suffocating darkness. He heard her murmur something, and then the snick of a knife cutting through rope. A rustling as a four-legged beast rose to its feet.

There was a shout somewhere in the distance.

Ellis felt Aderyn's hand seize his arm. "Do you know where we need to go?" he gasped. In the dark, and full of fear, he had lost all sense of direction.

"Yes." The word was curt but sure. "This way." She pulled, and he followed—or at least he would have, if the bone goat had not chosen that moment to step in front of him. He staggered, half tripping and half falling around the animal. He heard Aderyn snarl beside him.

It was terribly painstaking to run from the others. Ellis and Aderyn could not sprint, not without breaking their necks on tree roots or sharp rocks. Rather, they ran in short bursts, keeping low to the ground, trying to put as many trees behind them as they could. Aderyn seemed to have a good sense for when to move and when to go still. A hound bayed, and Aderyn hissed through her teeth.

He did not know for how long they ran. But as they moved, the undergrowth thinned out; the texture of the ground shifted, from soft moss to hard-packed dirt and rocks. Even the scents changed: from bright greenery to a heavy metallic tang. It was only when his foot slipped in a puddle, when he touched hard rock and felt the coolness of it, that he understood.

They were in the mouth of the mine.

Aderyn paused, and Ellis leaned on his knees, panting hard. Every part of him ached, but he knew there wouldn't be any rest. Not tonight, when they could be followed into the mine. He heard her fumbling in her pack, and then the familiar sound of tinder catching. Brilliant light made him blink tears from his eyes; a lantern burned merrily in her hand. She looked haggard, the hollows beneath her eyes deep and her lips pressed tight.

He remembered the silent words her mouth had formed as she'd stared at Catrin. He had not heard them, not then, but looking at her now, he saw the shape of them.

I'm sorry. I have to.

CHAPTER 19

THE MOUNTAIN WAS called Carregdu—the black rock. There were tales that said the mountain had been named for the fire it had once spat into the sky, covering the stars with black clouds. Even after the Otherking left the isles, very few would venture through the forests to the mountains. The trees in those forests had thick roots, and bark that seemed to repel axes; there was no great game to be hunted; even the herbs and berries could be more safely picked elsewhere.

It had only been the copper mine that had drawn humanity through the tangled trees. The promise of wealth within the mountain was a lure, and Ryn wondered if it had been enough for those who had built homes and paths, fought back the creeping undergrowth and the sense of otherness that still lingered in the air.

Ryn walked through puddles of water; rusty sediment had settled in them, and even in the darkness she could see the way the copper had stained the land. This had once been a place where hundreds of men and women had come to eke out a living bringing copper to the surface, the pay keeping food on their tables.

The ground was rocky and sloped upward, the trees thinning out. Abandoned carts were strewn about; they'd been scavenged for metal pieces and useful tools. Remnants of a better time, left to rot where they stood.

She tried not to find any deeper meaning in that.

Her emotions still ran too high; her fingers were numb at the tips and her forehead fevered. She could not close her eyes without seeing Catrin's mother—those sightless eyes boring into Ryn, as if the dead woman could see through her. And worse, the pleading on Catrin's face. The woman had begged, and Ryn had understood. If someone had tried to take her own mother away again, Ryn knew she might have done more than tackle a person to the ground and try to talk them out of it.

When she'd decided to end the curse, it had been to save lives. Not to end them a second time.

She closed her eyes and reopened them.

"You don't have to come with me," she said. Her voice shook.

She gripped her axe more tightly.

She was a gravedigger. She would bury her fear.

"I believe," said Ellis mildly, "we are well beyond that decision." He smiled with the corners of his mouth. "And just because I did not find evidence of my parents at the encampment doesn't mean I won't find something in the mine. Or perhaps beyond." His gaze sharpened, and she felt the full weight of his attention. It made the hairs on the back of her neck stand. "Besides, I have a job to do. Mapmakers have a responsibility to the world to portray it as accurately and carefully as they can. Wars are won with maps. Trade routes are created. And lives can be saved or not—all depending on the stroke of pen across paper. I would be a sorry excuse for a mapmaker," he said, "if I were to walk away now."

That got a laugh out of her. "You speak of mapmaking as if there's nobility in it."

"There is," he agreed. A moment, and then he added, "Just as there is in gravedigging. Neither occupation is particularly romantic, but I suspect the world would be a sorrier place without us."

"I hope so," she replied. She squared her shoulders, taking a deep breath. "If we wait for daylight, those at the encampment might find us."

The mine smelled of old metal; the ceiling was low, and Ryn had to duck her head to step inside. At once, she felt the presence of stone all around her. The weight of the mountains seemed to press down, and the air was thick and damp. The lantern light made the shadows quiver, and she hoped her hands were not visibly shaking. She heard Ellis walking behind her, and then the sound of hooves as the bone goat trailed after. Their footsteps echoed from the mine shaft, wobbling back to her.

"You feel that?" Ellis murmured.

Ryn looked at him sharply. "Feel what?"

He gave a little shake, as if trying to rid himself of something. "Like—I don't know. Something's waking up."

His face was lifted to the darkness, prey scenting a predator. It unnerved her, even as she said, "Don't let the mine rattle you. We can't linger here."

Ellis nodded, and unrolled the sheet of parchment. "It's a rough map," he said. "The one I used to get to Colbren."

"The one that got you lost," she answered again. "That's reassuring."

"Well, it's all we have."

To Ryn's eyes, it was a mess of crisscrossing lines and shapes, of crudely scribbled words, many of which she'd never learned. She did know how to read, thanks to her mother's teachings, but the map seemed to use a kind of shorthand. As Ellis studied the paper, something about it changed him. It sharpened him, brightened his eyes, and made every movement a little faster, a little more certain. "I see," he murmured, fingers whispering over the paper. He slipped a compass from his pocket, laid it upon the ground, and watched the iron needle. It was all very practiced, very precise, and Ryn found herself watching. It was always fascinating to see people do what they did best—Gareth's hands steadied when he tallied the graveyard's account books, and it was the only time he ever appeared truly relaxed; Ceri was smiling and friendly until she went to war against a dough that would not rise, and then she was all narrowed eyes and thin-lipped determination.

Ryn didn't know what she looked like when she worked. Smudged with dirt, most likely.

"We need to go this way." Ellis tapped the parchment.

The walls of the mine were stained golden with copper. Stalactites clustered along the ceiling, reaching down like the fingers of some clawed beast. Every so often, she heard the sound of moving water. The air smelled—wrong. Perhaps it was the stillness of the air, the stagnation of the world around them.

The miners had driven spikes into the walls to hold narrow planks of wood placed like the rungs of a ladder. The planks were about an arm's length apart, and they ascended into the darkness.

"Ladders," said Ryn. "To the other levels of the mine. Some'll go up—and some down. They would've dug in both directions."

"Are these safe?" asked Ellis. He touched one plank, as if testing its strength.

"Hardwood," replied Ryn. "They won't have rotted yet." She hauled herself up and onto the first plank, and extended a hand to Ellis. He took it without hesitation, cool dry fingers sliding against hers. The climb upward would have been grueling, if not impossible, had these crude ladders not been left behind.

Ellis glanced down. The bone goat remained there, head slightly cocked.

"Right," said Ryn. "I forgot about her." She flapped her hands at the goat. "All right, girl. You can't—"

Before she could finish the sentence, the goat tensed. Her haunches bunched with muscle, and then she leapt into the air. Hooves found invisible grooves along the stone wall and—and the bone goat stood on a small ledge. The movement had been so sudden, Ryn flinched and Ellis caught one of her arms, holding her steady. For a moment, they both gazed at the dead animal.

The bone goat looked back.

"I don't think we have to worry about leaving her behind, then," said Ellis drily.

Ryn let out a breath—half laugh and half sigh. "Looks like."

It was slow going, and Ryn listened all the while. She almost expected to hear the shouts of those coming after or the grinding of bone against metal. But she only heard the drip of water and the rustle of wind through the tunnel.

One of the wooden planks had fallen away, leaving only metal spikes. Ryn went first, testing the handholds as she climbed. A childhood of tree climbing had left her with no fear of heights. Ellis waited a moment longer, judging the ascent, before grasping the first of the handholds.

The mine had several floors. Most were artificial—made of bracken mixed with stone and mud, with wooden planks to hold everything together. Some of the shafts were so narrow they had to crawl on hands and knees, Ryn using one arm to hold the lantern as she shuffled along, her hip dragging on the stone floor. Water soaked into her clothing and a chill settled into her bones.

They reached another floor, and Ellis had to study the map again. Ryn held the lantern while he studied the paper, both their heads bent low over the whorls of ink. His lips moved silently as he read, and one of his fingers traced the lines.

A sharp sound echoed down the mine shaft. They both jumped.

"Rocks," said Ryn. "It sounded like rocks falling."

"What disturbed them?" Ellis replied. His gaze jerked every which way, trying to take in everything at once.

"I'd rather not think about it."

The shaft narrowed until she could have touched both sides if she stretched out her fingers. There was that sense of heaviness all around, the weight of something unseen pressing down on them. She heard Ellis's raspy breath behind her.

They came upon the first collapsed section perhaps an hour into their journey. A large swell of gravel stood before them, forcing them to crawl up and over. Ryn went first, handing the lantern to Ellis so she could use both hands to get over. Her fingers slipped on the debris, and some of it scattered down, bouncing along the floor.

The bone goat was the only one to remain completely unfazed. But then again, this was a creature who hadn't let death stop it.

"Right," Ellis said, when they came to a fork in the path. There was an old cart there, one of its wheels shattered. A single bone rested beside the cart—and the sight made Ryn's body clench.

She felt a hand on her shoulder.

She looked up. Ellis stood beside her; his face was cast into harsh lines by the lantern light, but she read concern in his eyes. "He was here," she said. "He must have been. Seen this—and—" She shook her head, and a tendril of hair pulled free of its braid, slipping down her shoulder.

When she thought of her father, she remembered fingers creased with calluses and how, no matter what he was carrying, he would shift the burden so as to settle his hand on Ryn's shoulder. Smile lines were etched into the corners of his mouth, and he liked feeding the chickens, giving them names and telling stories about how the birds probably had adventures when no one was looking. He had been solid and smiling and always there—

Until he hadn't been.

He was dead. Of that Ryn had no doubt. Only death would have kept him from returning home.

"When did you—" Ellis began to say.

His head jerked around, the question dying on his lips.

A moment later, Ryn heard it, too. A scraping sound emanated from near their ankles.

A spidery-thin form crept out from under the cart. A hand, she realized. It was a hand, pulling itself along. Gristle dragged in its wake. Ellis made a startled sound and took a step back.

Ryn brought her boot down on it. The bones shattered and skittered across the floor. One finger bone twitched and went still.

No one spoke for a moment.

"If you make a jest about hands or 'handling' that," said Ryn, "I will shove you down a mine shaft."

Ellis wrinkled his nose. "Furthest thing from my mind. That's possibly the most disgusting thing I've seen yet."

The bone goat nudged one of the bones with its nose. "Don't you dare eat that," said Ryn sharply.

"Never mind," said Ellis. "*That* is the most disgusting thing I've seen yet."

The goat's gaze flicked up, but it nuzzled the bone again. Ryn grabbed it by one horn and dragged it away.

The journey took them up another floor, and this time, Ryn

found a ladder. It was in good condition, but she still tested her weight on the lowest rung.

The ladder was sturdy but she took her time, glancing down every so often to check on Ellis. Lines of pain gathered around his mouth and eyes, and she frowned.

At the top of the ladder, a rung was missing. Ryn reached up and shoved the lantern onto the stone ledge. She placed her hands on the smooth stone and heaved herself up, using all the strength in her arms.

Something cold grasped her arm and hauled her over. She went with a cry, kicking out even as the bone house pinned her to the ground.

It was a miner; it wore rough-spun clothing and most of its teeth were missing. Ryn could not tell if it had been a man or a woman. Its flesh had long since rotted away, leaving only bone and cracked sinew. Like the water, it was stained by copper. Red flecked its skull, and its empty eye sockets were focused wholly on Ryn. She felt its hands on her, and she struck out with her fists. Her axe was strapped to her back, pinned beneath her, and she could not reach it. Pain flared in her arm as it was twisted and pressed to cold stone.

Ellis shouted something, his voice echoing off the cavern walls. The words blurred in her ears, and she did not care. Her attention was on the bone house—its weight and smell, its closeness and threat. She did not know if the bone house meant to hurt her, or if it wanted to speak with her, or even if it felt like a dance—it didn't matter. Not when she could fall to her death so easily.

"Sorry about this," she panted, before she bucked like a startled horse. Her legs wrapped around the bone house's waist, and she rolled hard. With all her strength, she flung the creature off her and over the ledge.

There was a startled cry, and then the sound of a shattering impact. Ryn rose to her hands and knees and scurried to the edge. "You all right?"

"Missed us by a hairsbreadth, but you missed us," called Ellis. He heaved himself up and onto the ledge, and a moment later, the goat clambered after.

"I see why this place was never reopened," said Ellis. His voice was even more hoarse than usual.

Ryn willed her hand to be steady as she picked up the lantern. "Why do some of them attack us?" she said, still breathing hard. "Those soldiers—that man. But others . . . don't." Her gaze flicked to the bone goat, who was scratching her rump with one horn.

"I don't know." Ellis leaned against the wall. "Do you think . . . death has a way of changing people?"

In the daylight, she could push away most memories or drown them out with work. But night was when remembrances returned, like chickens to roost, and she could not be rid of them. She glimpsed the bone goat trotting closer, and for the first time, she was not glad for her presence. She'd always felt as if she had death nipping at her family, taking them one by one—she didn't want to see her sister's pet goat slowly rot away.

Her foot slipped on a rock. She fell, knee hitting hard, and a grunt of pain escaped her. She knelt there for a moment, until she felt Ellis's hand on her shoulder.

"Are you all right?" he asked quietly.

"Yes," she said. The lie came to her lips of its own accord. But it rang false, even to her own ears.

She set the lantern down on the rocks. The flame guttered but did not go out.

Revulsion churned within her, and she wasn't sure what made her say it. Perhaps because the truth had been burning a hole in her gut for months now, and someone needed to know.

"I knew," she said.

"What?" He sat beside her, but she kept her gaze averted.

"I knew about Uncle." Her fingers tangled together, and she held on tight.

There was a moment of quiet, broken only by Ellis's sharp intake of breath. It echoed off the cavern walls.

"I knew he was dead," she said.

His voice was soft now, and it made her want to turn away. She did not deserve his gentleness, not for this. "You knew already?"

She wasn't sure what made her say it—perhaps it was the night pressing down on her, the intimate closeness of the dark, or the memory of the dead at the encampment. They all had their dead—she just had more than most.

"I buried him," she said hollowly.

His hand touched hers. "Tell me?" he asked.

She didn't want to—the words threatened to unravel her. But perhaps to speak them would be to release the heavy burden.

"We were happy," she said, because wasn't that how every story began? "My family—my father, my mother, my brother, and my sister. We had a good life, for a while. Our uncle moved in with us after Da vanished into the mine—and he helped Mam around the house.

"We weren't overly fond of him," she continued. "I mean, he was our mother's brother and she loved him. But then she fell ill. It was the lung rot—it got into her chest and never left. When she died, we were given into the care of our uncle.

"He looked at us as if we were a burden. We all tried not to be." Ryn had done so by leaving the house often: She tarried in the forest, picking berries and acorns, and digging graves when the need arose. Gareth had put away his childish notions of play and took up his mother's accounts ledger. He ran the business of burying the dead and learned how to speak so that adults would treat him accordingly. As for Ceri, she learned how to put food on the table. Even as a young child, she crafted meals from the smallest scraps, churned goats' milk into butter and cheese, and baked lovely sweets that could be sold on market day.

Ryn said, "We managed as best we could. But... a few months ago, Uncle came home from one of his nights at the Red Mare. He was soused, angry that he'd lost yet another game of cards. He'd been borrowing coin from Eynon, which we only discovered afterward. He blamed us for his debts, saying that if he hadn't been forced to live in Colbren, he would have gone on to do better things. He was drunk and angry—and he slipped on the stairs." Ryn could still hear the crack of skull against wood. "His head hit the door frame, and he tumbled into the yard. We all stood there for a few moments, waiting for him to rise and continue yelling at us—but he didn't."

She looked at Ellis's face for the first time since she'd begun the story. His expression was steady and he gave a small nod, as if encouraging her to go on.

"Gareth wanted to tell someone," said Ryn. "But if we'd told... I'd have been sent to a workhouse—and perhaps Gareth with me. We didn't know what would happen to Ceri. And when faced with that... I knew what I was supposed to do with the body, but I didn't care."

Respect due to the dead was one of the many things her father had impressed upon her. That was why he took such care of the graveyard, why the little rituals were always observed, and why he entrusted the care of it to his eldest. Because he knew she would understand.

Until it became inconvenient.

"We buried him in the woods," said Ryn. "An unmarked grave in the forest, because I wouldn't risk my family. And I knew—I knew that he *could* become a bone house. But even if he did, I thought he couldn't leave the forest."

And while she had never liked her uncle, Ryn felt the shame of the deed. It was the most monstrous thing she had ever done, but she had done it. For her family, and for herself.

Once the hole had been filled in, she and Gareth had returned home. They washed the dirt from beneath their nails, covered the blood in the yard with hay, and told the villagers their uncle had gone to the city on business.

They did not speak again of what transpired that night.

"For a while, we didn't have to think about it," said Ryn. "We just went on, pretending Uncle was away. But two weeks ago, a bone house appeared outside the forest. It stumbled into Hywel's farm and we destroyed it. I helped him carry the pieces to the forge."

Fear had taken hold of her—after all, if one bone house could leave the forest...what would stop another? What if the magic found her uncle and forced him to rise? What if he returned, only to be recognized? Everyone would know that he'd died, only to be buried unmarked in a forest grave. That was when Ryn took her axe and began spending nights in the graveyard.

Waiting for a monster to appear.

CHAPTER 20

THE LANTERN FLICKERED. She barely seemed to notice. Her gaze was faraway, her voice deceptively even. Ellis listened as the confession spilled forth.

When she finished speaking, her gaze remained on the damp stone. "I'm not going to apologize for what I did," she said. "It was terrible, and I know it makes me a terrible person, but I won't be sorry for it."

Perhaps he should have been disgusted. Or horrified. But rather, Ellis wanted to find a way into that story—to step between the uncle and those children. He had never known an adult who had berated him—not like that. He knew what it was to be ignored or treated like a burden, but not what it was to be hated by family. "It wasn't your fault."

A bitter half smile tugged at her mouth. "Oh. So I should blame my uncle, then?"

Ellis said, "His death was an accident. Terrible things happen. Your parents—I'm sorry for your loss. As for your uncle, he sounds like—"

"Not quite a loss?"

"I was going to say, 'an ass,'" Ellis replied. A startled little laugh burst free of Aderyn. "You did the best you could. And if I were in your place, I might have done the same."

"You would have told the truth." Ellis opened his mouth to protest, but she continued. "You're a good person. But I've never pretended to be." She bowed her head, and a strand of hair fell before her eyes. "I buried the last of my family in a forest, in an unmarked grave. To be forgotten and unmourned."

Ellis shook his head. "Not the last of your family," he said. "You still have your brother and your sister."

At that, she smiled—but only with her mouth. She patted his arm. "Thanks."

Something inside him lurched. It felt like the times he slipped on a patch of ice or a slick rock—weightlessness in his belly and anticipation of the fall.

Her hand withdrew, and he felt the loss of it keenly.

"Thank you for listening," she said. "For... understanding."

"Of course," he said.

His shoulder ached fiercely. When Aderyn had her back turned, he dug into his pack for fresh willow bark. His supply was dwindling, and his stomach sank when he saw how little was left.

He'd have to be more careful—but after. For now, he needed it. The familiar bitterness coated his tongue and he swallowed hard.

As they walked, the mine suddenly swelled open. They'd come into a cavern. Aderyn made a soft sound, and a moment after, Ellis realized why. Water sloshed across his boots. The cavern was a natural one; its walls were bulging and misshapen, and there was none of the careful smoothness that accompanied the places were human hands had dug out tunnels. This cavern had been carved by time and water.

He held his compass in one hand. And with the other, he reached for Aderyn. His fingers found hers, and he gave a squeeze. He expected her to pull away, to feel her cold hand slip from his. To be pierced with one of her looks.

Rather, she held on. She squeezed back, as if she, too, needed something to grasp. Something alive. The bone goat moved with the placid ease of an animal who didn't mind its surroundings, only stopping occasionally to sniff at an interesting rock.

Ellis wasn't sure how deep the water was; he hoped it would remain shallow. Even so, they kept to the edges of the cavern, tripping over stalagmites and holding on to each other for balance. The light bobbed as Ellis tripped, nearly dragging Aderyn down, and he barely caught himself on a rock. The chill numbed Ellis's feet, the pain of it creeping up his knees and into his thighs. The water was utterly opaque, and he found himself looking at it again and again to reassure himself that nothing was there.

That was how he saw the ripples.

A glimmer of movement caught his eye—as if someone had skipped a rock.

Ellis's whole body drew tight. "There's something—"

He never finished the sentence.

A hand emerged from the water. It was slick; the smell that wafted up was sour, and it made bile climb Ellis's throat. The hand had only four fingers, one of the bones cracked through at the knuckle. Light glinted off its finger bones.

There was no time to scream. One second, Ellis was upright. And the next, he fell.

He plunged into darkness and icy water.

It was blackness of a sort he had never known. In the city, there wasn't true darkness. There were candles, fires, and oil lanterns. In the country, there were torches and moonlight and even the gleaming of stars.

Deep beneath the mountain, there was nothing.

Utterly empty, cold nothing.

Terror tightened around his throat like a noose.

Something gripped his ankle, and he kicked out. His head broke the surface and sound returned to him.

There was shouting, and it was far worse than the silence.

Aderyn's voice was the first sound he heard. He croaked out her name, reaching about the air, trying to find something—anything.

He hit something but it slipped away before he could grasp it. There was splashing and he stumbled, a knee slamming into a rock. Ellis found himself on his knees in the water, his fingers combing through the muck. He found his pack and dragged it onto his shoulder.

Something knocked into him. Suns burst behind his eyes as

his shoulder slammed into the ground and he choked out a cry, and then water closed over his nose.

It wasn't deep. But water did not have to be deep for a person to drown in it.

He tried to push himself upright, but something hung on to him tightly. He struck out at the thing, bubbles emerging from his lips. He blinked and the water stung his eyes, but there was nothing to see, nothing to hear. His elbow connected with something hard and he felt it give, snapping beneath the blow.

He surged above the water, dragging air into his lungs. It hurt, his chest burning, and someone was yelling his name.

He fumbled, and his fingers found soft fur, skimming up until he realized he was touching the bone goat's horn. His fingers tightened, and he found himself being dragged away, as if the goat were determined to keep him moving.

Light flared.

It was a mere handful of flame—Ryn had used her flint and firesteel to set her scarf alight. He pulled himself upright, the bone goat beside him, and he saw another bone house. Its flesh was gone, clothes hanging in ragged strips from its arms, and its jaw clicked and clicked as if it were trying to speak. It reached for him, its posture almost beseeching, but he kicked its hand away.

One handed, Aderyn swung her axe at another bone house. The creature jerked and fell, slipping and vanishing into the churning water.

The water was churning, he saw. Alive—no, not alive. Dead things were crawling free, some moving with one leg or none at all, pulling themselves along with their bony fingers. Others had no head, and some were broken in other terrible ways.

All of them were coming closer. "Move!" Aderyn shouted, and Ellis did not have to be told twice. Water splashed before them as they tried to run—the ground was too slick for a true sprint. When another bone house drew near, the bone goat lowered its horned head and charged into the water. Ellis felt a pang of fear for the animal.

"Keep moving," Aderyn snarled. The firelight was flickering, the scarf dangling from her fingertips.

If it went out, they'd be lost again.

They rushed through the cavern, the sound of their footsteps bouncing off the walls, magnified with every echo. It sounded as if a hundred people were running for their lives. When Ellis glanced over his shoulder, he saw the forms of those following behind.

The miners were ragged and decayed, having spent years in these waters. Their flesh must have long since floated to the surface, carried away on some tide or eaten by animals. And while they had none of the training or weapons of the knights of Castell Sidi, the creatures were still terrifying.

Ellis and Aderyn broke free of the water, of the cavern, and suddenly they were slipping on stone, their steps stumbling as the ground rose to a sharp incline. The light guttered, and for a moment the world vanished around them. Then Ellis heard Aderyn blowing on the flames, and the light kindled again, weaker this time, sparks vanishing into the blackness. The cloth swung in her hand, making the cave seem oddly unreal—there one moment and gone the next. Every step was a guess, a silent prayer, and Ellis could only hope that he would not fall again… or that nothing would grab him.

Another look back. The fastest bone house was only a few paces away, unhindered by darkness.

He didn't know what had become of his crossbow. The weight of it was gone from his back. For a moment, he considered reaching down to scoop up rocks or something to throw at the bone house, but—

Hooves clattered on the rock. He chanced another look back, and he saw the bone goat, horns lowered and back legs churning the water as it charged the dead. Perhaps it was trying to avenge its own death.

Or perhaps it was trying to save its people.

Sound clashed behind them. He could not tell if it was a bone house or the goat. Aderyn cupped the flame between her hands, heedless of how it was likely burning her.

"Come on." Ellis barely managed to say the words. He took the second tunnel, and sent up a quiet hope that this one would take them outside.

The tunnel rose up at an impossible angle, and a half-rotted ladder glinted in the firelight. Most of the wood was gone, but the iron remained.

Without a word, Ellis went first. He grasped the metal stakes where they had been pounded into rock, using them as handholds to drag himself upward. He grunted softly when his foot slipped, but he held on.

Aderyn released the burning cloth. For a moment, the flame

was visible, and then it hit the damp stone and everything went dark.

His left shoulder burned as if it had been branded; heat rushed through him and for one dizzying moment, Ellis wondered if he would simply faint, if he'd fall and be left here. If his bones would join those in the water. He bit down on his lower lip, forcing his gaze to steady. He tried to take more weight on his right arm, to use that one to pull himself along. But his right arm began to tremble.

Fallen kings. He couldn't do this. He went still, unable to pull himself higher or to climb back down. His chest was ablaze with pain, and it felt as if his heart were trying to climb his rib cage and crawl out of his throat. "I—can't," he rasped. His body simply could bear no more of this—no matter how much he tried to force it to cooperate. His shoulder screamed at him and he wanted to scream in reply, but he caged every painful sound behind his teeth.

For a few terrible moments, they were frozen on the wall. He could feel Aderyn's hand on his ankle, her grip tight as she tried to tell him to move, to keep fleeing, but he remained still. Then her hand fell away.

He felt her begin to climb past him—and he understood. She was getting around him, escaping before the bone houses could drag her down.

Good. Relief crashed into him—not for himself, but for her. He would fall, but she did not have to. She could go on, continue their task, and perhaps save everyone else. Her journey did not have to end in the damp and the dark, to rough fingers and snapping jaws.

And then he felt her hand on his arm. She wrenched his grip from the wall, and she hauled him upward to the next rung.

It hurt. Like molten fire being poured into the shoulder joint. He may have screamed, but the noise was lost in the caverns. Gritting his teeth, he forced himself to continue.

The climb was a blur—feet and arms, cold metal and slick rock. Ellis heard Aderyn give a sound of surprise, and then fresh air caught in Ellis's shirt. He felt the chill of it, the cold sweep through his collar and down his chest, and it was welcome.

He scrambled out of the mine. One moment he was surrounded on all sides by rock, and then he stood beneath splashes of crimson and gold, light spilling through the trees.

He sank to his knees, one hand on the soft moss of a forest floor.

CHAPTER 21

RYN HAD HEARD many tales of Annwvyn. How it was the Otherworld, the Not-Place, where Arawn had ruled over his court at Castell Sidi, where red-eyed hounds caught game for their master, where men vanished for a decade only to reappear not a day older, where maidens heard songs so beautiful they wept, where Gwydion fought a great battle and called the very trees to fight on his behalf, where Arawn finally turned away from the isles and sailed far beyond the reach of humanity.

But for all the stories, Ryn was unprepared for the beauty of the mountains.

These trees had leaves of gold. Not autumn-brown or rust-red, but gold as the dawn. White lichen crept up the trunks, catching the light. The ground was thick with moss, and delicate flowers studded patches of sunlight. It was the kind of beauty that could not be created by human hands.

And for the first time, Ryn understood why a human might have coveted this place.

She crouched on the mossy ground and watched as the first rays of dawn crept through the trees. She wanted to wrap herself up in that daylight.

"We need..." she said, and her voice faltered. She tried a second time. "We need to dry out our clothes. Eat something, rest."

Ellis did not reply, but he gave a small nod.

He was bent over, chest heaving and clothes soaked through. He trembled hard, and he made no move to rise or speak.

"Are you all right?" she asked.

He kept his eyes averted. "My pack is wet, but I'm fine." The pleasant rasp of his voice roughened. He offered nothing more, and she did not press.

"I can hear running water," she said. "I'm going to refill our flasks and take a look around."

She was almost glad of the solitude when she walked deeper into the woods. There was a profound silence in this forest, a stillness that she dared not break. The trees themselves were broad with age, their trunks whorled and knotted, untouched by axes. Their thick canopy kept the sunlight at bay, and the undergrowth was not overly thick; it wasn't difficult to walk among the trees, her steps muffled by soft ferns and mosses. She followed the sound of water, descending a small ridge.

The creek was small, likely fed by a mountain spring. She knelt beside the water. It was the kind of cold that made every muscle seize. But it was also clear and clean, and she used it to scrub the mud from her face and arms. She pulled off her tunic, rinsed the garment as best she could. It still smelled of the mine—copper and rust. Her hair was a tangled mess, and she tried to re-braid it, with some success. Once her fingers were clean, she drank handfuls of the water. A small fish darted by and she twitched, wishing she had brought a net with her.

"Oh—I'm sorry."

She looked up. Ellis stood a few paces away, his gaze averted. She frowned. "What are you on about?"

Still he would not look at her. "You're—ah—" He waved about, the gesture meant to encompass all of her.

"Oh, come on," she said. "I'm not naked. There's cloth covering all the relevant bits."

"I wouldn't want to embarrass you."

She rose to her feet. Ryn knew how she looked: freckled arms corded with wiry muscle. A pale stomach, and a chest that was easy to bind with a strip of cloth. Her body was like her axe—perhaps not the most beautiful, but it was useful and familiar and comfortable. "I'm not embarrassed," she said. "Seems you're the one out of sorts."

His mouth made a funny expression, as if he were trying to laugh and grimace at the same time. When his gaze finally met hers, it was with the hesitance of someone trying to look at the sun. A glance and then away, then another. "What," she said. "I'm not terrible to look at. Not one of your fine ladies, perhaps."

He made a noise. As if that laugh snagged in his throat. "I wouldn't know."

"Not one for the ladies?" she asked. "If you prefer the lads, that's fine. Though you're not Gareth's usual type. He likes blonds."

"I have not been eyeing your brother, either." Ellis finally managed to hold her eyes. He exhaled a sharp laugh. "The reason I could not climb—why I froze back there."

"Are you dying?" The words came out in a rush. Ryn's doubts rose up to meet the memory of Catrin's words.

Ellis looked taken aback. "Well. I know I don't look so dashing after being doused in coppery water and climbing through a mine, but—"

"Ellis," she said.

He laughed, but it was small and short-lived. "You're one of the few people who never make my name sound as if it's lacking something—a surname or a title."

"Probably because I'm irritated," she replied drily. "Ellis the Elusive."

"Fair enough." He inclined his head. "I'm not dying. It's my shoulder—it pains me. It always has."

Ah. Suddenly things made more sense. "Old injury?" she asked.

He touched his chest gingerly, fingers sliding along his collarbone. As if testing it. "The prince's physician thought so. She thought the bone had broken and never been set right." For a moment, a vein of bitterness slid into his voice. "Sometimes sliding my arm into a shirt is more than I can stand, and other days, it's merely a throb that I can ignore. I always have willow bark with me, so I can dull the pain if needed. I chose mapmaking not only because I love it, but also because I needed a trade that wouldn't injure me. I'll never be a soldier, or a smith, or anything that requires full use of both arms." He shook his head. "And if you think of pitying me—do not. For the most part, I truly enjoy my life. But there are limitations.

"Sometimes I wonder if this is the reason my parents abandoned me," he said in a low voice. "If perhaps they could not afford to keep a son who would never be able to help on a farm." And she knew, by how he said the words, that this was the secret he took with him to bed. This was the most raw, most painful thing he could have entrusted her with.

Fallen kings. It made her heart ache for him—and suddenly she hoped they would find his parents so she could yell at them. Perhaps she could help find them. She could ask the village elders, see if anyone had lost a child around Ellis's age.

If they survived this, of course.

"Can I help?" she asked.

He blinked. "Pardon me?"

She gestured at his muddy clothes. "You said it hurts to put your arm in a sleeve. And you need to wash out your clothes, unless you want that muck to dry and harden. Can I help?"

Silence fell between them, and Ryn was sure she had overstepped. Gareth would have known not to push, and Ceridwen would have been too polite to ask in the first place. She felt the beginnings of an apology on her lips, but then Ellis said, "I—if it's not too much trouble."

She stepped closer, placing her fingers on the hem of his mud-spattered shirt.

Getting it off took a few minutes—it was a matter of not straining his arm too badly while not ripping the garment. In the end, he gave a small grunt of pain, but the shirt slid away. Ryn tossed it into the shallows, where it snagged on a fallen branch. Mud began to sluice away on small currents of water.

As they stood beside that creek, clad in little more than their smalls, she chanced a look at him. True enough, his left arm had less muscle than his right, and there was a thin scar just beneath his collarbone, as if the bone had pierced through the skin. And yet, there was a strength to him, a stillness that bespoke quiet confidence.

"You could have told me before," she said.

His gaze was on the creek and the small fish. They had come to investigate the dirty shirt, touching it, then darting away and back again.

"To tell people is to invite pity," he said, a bit wearily, "or worse, advice."

"Advice?"

"Herbs to try," he said. "Stretches. Leeches, one time. People cannot simply let me be. They have to find a way to fix me."

"You're not broken," she said.

"I know," he said. "But it's difficult to convince the world of that most of the time. That's why I've enjoyed solitude. People think pain makes me weak—or worse, strong. If I have to endure one more person telling me that I'm 'so strong' simply for living…" He shook his head.

Ryn knew something of pain; she had seen enough of it.

Death and pain were close companions, often twined around each other.

"Pain doesn't make a person weak or strong," she said. "Pain just—is. It's not a purifier, it's part of living."

That made him laugh. It was a good laugh—the kind that scrunched up the corners of his eyes. "Ah. Well, I suppose I should be glad of it, then. I quite enjoy being alive." When he looked at her, it was through the fringe of his hair. "And thank you."

"For what?"

"Not leaving me to die in that mine," he said.

She snorted. "As if I would."

"You could have." He tilted his head, and his dark hair slid out of his eyes. It was a steady look he gave her, and it felt as if it went deeper than skin. As if he had peeled away flesh and bone and was looking at the heart of her. "Most people would have. When faced with darkness and terror, most people will run—and forget those around them."

"Death doesn't frighten me," she said. "It never has." She closed her eyes, feeling the bitterness of the lie on her tongue. "Losing people is what I fear. The uncertainty and the... not knowing." She pressed a hand to her forehead as if she might push back the memories.

"I understand," he said simply. There was no *I'm sorry*, no awkward silence.

Because he did understand. He'd lived with his own uncertainty for most of his life.

She smiled, just a little. "Come on, you. We need to eat."

She reached into the creek, retrieving their clothes: soaked but clean. They would dry in the sunlight.

He walked after her. "And what are we to eat?"

She gestured about the forest. "Look around us. There's plenty."

That earned her a skeptical noise. "Truly?"

She flashed him a grin. "Watch me."

She had the provisions in her pack—the flour and the pickled seeds, the berry preserves, and even a small iron pot. She could eat out here for weeks, if she had to. She made for the trees, bending to pick handfuls of sorrel. She used the edge of her cloak to take some nettles—which would taste just fine after they'd been cooked. Mushrooms were riskier fare, but Mam had taught her which sorts were dangerous. She found a clump of hedgehog mushrooms clustered about the base of a tree. She pulled a small knife from her belt and went to work harvesting them.

"Hold these," she said, giving Ellis the mushrooms.

He cradled them gently in both hands, as if afraid to crush them.

She built a fire as best she could with green wood. It took a few locks of her own hair and several tries before a trickle of smoke trailed between her fingers.

They dined on a soup of sorrel, nettle, and mushrooms. The pickled seeds were sprinkled atop, and they sharpened the flavor with mustard and pepper. It was a good meal, but Ryn saved the last mouthful, scraping it into a thick leaf. She carried it several steps away, and then she set the food on one of the mossy rocks.

"For later?" asked Ellis.

Ryn shook her head. "You would probably call it superstition. After all, this forest is supposed to be abandoned."

He nodded, understanding. "Pwca."

Her brows shot skyward.

"We have the old tales in Caer Aberhen," he said mildly. "I heard them, too. I just never believed them—until a dead man tried to strangle me."

"That does tend to change one's worldview." Ryn threw him a smile, then went back to their small camp. Well, to call it a camp seemed overly optimistic—it consisted of their packs, her axe, and their cloaks strewn across branches. She'd scrub out the iron pot later, refill their flasks with water, and clean the mine muck from their boots. But for now the food was settled comfortably in her belly, the sunlight felt warm on her back, and it was a simple matter to curl up on the mossy ground.

"Aren't we supposed to move?" said Ellis, but he sounded as exhausted as she felt. "Keep going?"

"We won't do ourselves any good if we're too tired to think," she replied. "We'll rest a few hours, then find our way."

He grunted a soft acquiescence. She felt him curl up beside her—his back to hers, and the warmth of him was a comfort.

She closed her eyes and fell asleep swiftly.

They began the true journey that afternoon.

Rather than try to forge their own path, Ryn decided they should keep to the banks of a small creek. It had cut a swath through the rock, so deep in some places that naked cliffs surrounded them on both sides. Rays of sunlight pierced the canopy overhead, illuminating the mists and mosses. The water was shallow, coming up to just below her knees. With the autumn foliage all around them, Ryn could only hope they would find Castell Sidi before snowfall. Winter would fall upon this place like a wolf on a fresh carcass. Its jaws would close and it wouldn't let go.

By keeping to the river, they wouldn't run out of fresh water. Ryn kept her axe in hand at all times, striding through the mud and the rocks.

Ellis followed a few paces behind. The rest seemed to have done him well; he moved more easily, and he appeared raptly interested in the trees and in the slope of the mountain. When they stopped to get their bearings, he withdrew a small, damp book from his pack and wrote down numbers. "Distances," he said, when he caught her looking. "If I can make a map to Castell Sidi..." He seemed at a loss for words. "Well. I don't know what the equivalent would be to a gravedigger."

"Burying princes?" she said with a wry little smile. "We still don't get much recognition for that."

The forest was clotted with moss and ivy, and the trees themselves were so wide she could have stretched her arms around some of the trunks and not touched her own fingers. Their thick roots shaped the very ground, jutting into the air before descending into the earth. The golden-leafed trees were some variant of oak, she decided, with perhaps a touch of magic.

The afternoon passed quickly, as Ryn fell into the rhythm of walking. Her calves burned pleasantly, and the heat of her body kept the river's chill at bay.

"There's no sign of people," said Ellis, when they stopped to refill their flasks. The water was bright and sharp against Ryn's dry throat, and she gulped it down.

"We're in Annwvyn," said Ryn. "Of course no one is here. Only we're fool enough to try."

His gaze swept across the forest. "Exactly. We got in—I thought it would be more difficult."

"Nearly dying in the mine wasn't enough for you?"

He frowned, but the expression was directed at the forest, not at Ryn. "This place is . . . well, the lumber here could be worth a fortune. If the cantref could bring in workers, we might manage to enrich the villages nearby. Bring in trade. Make this place a center of commerce, rather than a nowhere. Surely if people could come this far, they would have."

"You think we've had too easy a time of it?"

"Yes," he said simply. "Which means there'll probably be more monsters ahead."

"Cheerful thought."

She remembered the tales of red-eyed hounds chasing lone travelers, of the monstrous boar that took ten knights to bring down, of lake-dwelling maidens who would drown those who came too near, and of keen-eyed dragons. If the otherfolk had left the cauldron behind, there could be other magical artifacts, as well.

"We'll be careful," she replied.

That evening, they dined on dried meat, both too tired to seek out fresher fare. She brewed a tea of pine needles and laughed when Ellis grimaced. "I suppose it's an acquired taste, Aderyn," he said.

"Ryn," she said.

He looked at her sharply.

"None of that Aderyn nonsense," she said. "When you've seen me covered in mud and without a tunic, I think you've earned a bit of familiarity. Besides, every time you call me that, I twitch. Usually when I hear my full name, it's someone scolding me."

"Ryn." Ellis threw a look over his shoulder, searching the forest. "You think bone goat will catch up?"

"Of course she will. She didn't let death keep her from us. She'll find us."

If they lived through this, Ellis thought, perhaps bards would sing the tale. *The gravedigger and the mapmaker, and their dead goat.*

"Boat," he mumured. "Float. Moat."

He felt Ryn's gaze on him. "All right. What are you on about?" she said.

He glanced up at her. "Oh. Um. Just wondering if we'll be well known if we end this curse. And if the bone goat might merit a verse of her own, should the bards decide to retell our tale."

A startled laugh made her cough, then press a hand to her mouth. "You," she said, "never say quite what I expect you to."

Ellis shrugged.

"It's not a bad thing," she said. She flashed him a grin that made his stomach turn over. Then she added, "Along with our heroes was the bone goat. A great creature of note." She grinned. "To the eldest daughter, she was devote."

Ellis added, "Who, hopefully, will help end the curse before she begins to bloat."

Ryn tried to hold back her laugh, which transformed it into a choking snort. Which only made *him* laugh in turn. It was the kind of laughter that took hold of a person and wouldn't let go—not until the stomach ached and the lungs burned. His shoulder gave a painful twinge, and he pressed a hand to his collarbone. The sharp pain drained the last of the mirth from him.

He had no willow bark left; the thought felt like a splash of icy water. He had no way to stave off the pain. His fingers dug into a knotted muscle, and he forced his lips into a smile. "As much as I dislike lying on the cold, hard ground, we should try to get some sleep."

Ryn raised a brow. "Yet you're still sitting upright."

He forced himself to lie on his right side. His cloak rumpled, digging into his ribs, and he gave it a sharp yank. "I've never been a very good sleeper," he admitted. "The cook—the older woman who helped raise me, she knew as much. When I first came to Caer Aberhen, she used to tell me stories. Unfortunately for her, all that did was keep her awake, as well."

"Where I come from," said Ryn, "people cannot afford to stay awake at night. Candles are too costly, and so is oil for lanterns. When it's dark, you sleep."

"Well," he said, "you'll have to excuse my odd habits, then."

She curled onto her side, using a rolled-up shirt as a pillow. "All right, then. Tell me a story."

He raised a brow.

"I told you one," she pointed out. "The bone houses and all. Seems only fair you should tell me one, too."

He considered. "All right." He settled more comfortably, eyes a little unfocused. "Have you heard the tale of the prince's hound?"

"No."

"There was once a prince. He enjoyed hunting, and kept several hounds for such a purpose. His best hound was a faithful creature, so gentle and sweet that one day the prince entrusted the hound to guard his newborn babe while the prince was away.

"When the prince returned, he found the cradle had been overturned. He called out for the hound, and it trotted dutifully to his side. The prince saw its muzzle was stained with blood—and fury kindled in his heart. He struck the dog a mighty blow, and the creature perished. A moment after, the prince heard the cry of a babe—and he found his child on the other side of the fallen cradle. Beside it was the still-warm body of a dead wolf.

"The prince wept with mingled joy and sadness, and he buried his hound at the center of a village. He left a message carved in stone, so that any who saw would know the bravery of his hound."

His voice faded away, leaving only the crackle of burning wood and the drip of rain on leaves.

Then Ryn said, "That's a terrible story."

"It is," Ellis agreed.

"Appalling. The cook told that to you as a child?"

"She did." He sounded fond. "What stories did your parents tell you?"

"Monsters," she said at once. "Dragons. Pwca. Dramatic battles."

"And that is any better?"

"Yes," she answered. "I grew up thinking monsters could be slain."

"Ah," he said. "And I grew up thinking people were the monsters."

CHAPTER 22

SHE DREAMED OF damp earth.

She dreamed she was drowning in it.

Dirt filled her nose and mouth, and when her fingers dug into the ground, she could not find purchase enough to sit up. She may as well have been buried in bedrock; she could not claw herself free. Panic swelled within her, threatened to burst from her lips in a scream, but she knew it would do her little good. They'd buried her far from the village, away from the graveyard. She was alone—and—

Ryn sat up, her breath coming in heaves.

She was wrapped in a wool cloak, not in soil. For a few moments, all she could do was breathe. The rain fell in patters, and the forest smelled of sharp pine and damp greenery. Her eyes went to the place where she'd last seen Ellis, but he was no longer there. It was fine, she told herself. He had probably left their camp to relieve himself. He'd be back in a moment.

She touched the woolen cloak and realized it wasn't hers. The finely stitched edges and embroidery—this belonged to Ellis. He must have put it over her at some point during the night. Perhaps she'd looked cold or he hadn't needed it. Her fingers played across the soft material.

Then she realized what had woken her.

It wasn't the solitude—but the smell.

The scent of rotting flesh was one a person never got used to. If it had to be compared to meat, she would have likened it to pork. The thick meatiness of it, the way it became sweet and heavy, coating her throat and clinging to her hair.

Ryn rose to her feet.

She moved with care, so as not to disturb the ground. Every step was based on memory rather than sight, and when she felt the thick roots of the trees around her, she lifted her feet high. Tripping now would be to invite her own death.

The smell intensified.

She had to breathe through her mouth. Even then, the taste washed over her tongue and made bile rise in her throat. Her chest gave a juddering heave and she forced the retch down.

The clouds slid by, and sudden moonlight spilled across the forest floor, illuminating spruce needles and pale white mushrooms and—

A deer. A dead deer. The carcass was strewn across the forest floor, ribs pulled open by some carrion-eater. The sight made her shudder—not with revulsion, but relief. It was so commonplace.

She took a step back, shaking her head. This journey had rubbed her nerves raw.

She turned to walk back to their camp—

And saw the soldier before her.

In the dark, few details were visible. Its outlines were traced by moonlight: the sharp edges of armor, the slight build, the hollows of its skeletal face.

Ryn's fingers skimmed to her belt—and found nothing.

Her axe wasn't there. Of course it wasn't. She always took it off to sleep so she wouldn't roll over and gouge herself accidentally. All she had was a borrowed cloak and in her pocket a small knife. It was the kind meant for skinning rabbits, not for defending herself—but it would have to do.

She bent her knees, angling her fingers toward the knife.

The bone house took one heavy step toward her.

Ryn froze. The dead creature moved like liquid shadow, and suddenly it stood before her. So close that Ryn could see the cracks through its teeth, the small flecks in its cheekbone. It was shorter than her, and Ryn wondered if this soldier had been a woman.

The bone house drew a rattling breath across its teeth—and it felt as if it were drawing the very air from Ryn's lungs. She would jab the blade into its spine. Or the knee—if she could just go for the knee—

The dead soldier moved like a striking serpent. Bony fingers seized Ryn's cloak and yanked hard. The clasp bit into her throat and the next thing she knew, she was gazing up at the trees, the breath knocked out of her. She could not even cry out, not when the bone house took hold of her hair and cloak and began dragging her deeper into the mountains.

Ryn snarled. Her fingers clawed at the soft earth, seeking any handhold. She got snagged on an old fern—its roots must have gone deep, because she stopped moving. The bone house pulled harder, and pain flared in Ryn's scalp. There was a terrible yank, and she felt some of her hair come free.

The knife slipped from its leather sheath, and Ryn felt the blade bite into her thumb. Her hand twisted, finding the hilt, and then she shoved the iron blade into the bone house's wrist.

Iron. The mortal's best defense against magic and all of its perils. She twisted the blade, expecting the creature to recoil.

It did no such thing. Rather, the bone house shook its arm like a dog trying to dislodge an irritating flea.

Ryn gritted her teeth and thrashed, trying to break free.

It hadn't worked—why hadn't it—

Fallen kings. Some of the bone houses wore armor. Crafted of *iron.*

It had never repelled them. Her axe had hurt them, dismantled them, but its metal blade hadn't been enough to frighten them away.

Foolish. She had been foolish, and now she growled and fought like a mad animal, trying to break free of a snare.

If the tale was true, these creatures had been born of an iron cauldron. Of course cold metal wouldn't affect them. Which meant—if the iron fence hadn't kept them at bay...what had? The distance from the forest and the cauldron? Something else?

There was no more time to think, because the bone house

shook her so hard, her teeth rattled. Pain flared in her neck and her fingers loosened on the fern, slipped free, and then she was being dragged along the forest floor.

It had been his bladder that awoke him.

Ellis blinked his eyes open, then grimaced. Sleeping on the cold forest floor left him stiff and he took a few moments to stretch his arms.

When he glanced across the dying embers of their fire, he saw Aderyn yet asleep. No, not Aderyn—Ryn. She was curled tightly on her left side, eyes closed and hair slipping across one cheek. A small shiver ran through her.

Ellis rose, moving quietly so as not to wake her. He slipped his cloak from his shoulders, easing it across her and fastening the clasp so it wouldn't fall.

A moment of sentimentality that he could ill afford. The cold would seep into his bones, stiffen every sinew. But he would allow himself this foolishness, if only because no one else would see it.

He did reach down and pick up Ryn's axe, his fingers across the wooden handle, nails catching in the worn grooves. It was a heavy, old thing, but he could see why she liked to carry it. The heft was a sort of comfort.

The fire burned low, and he added a fresh branch to it. The green leaves sputtered and smoked, and he winced, hoping he hadn't accidentally put it out.

He strode from their small camp, looking for a place to relieve himself with some amount of privacy. He chose the shadow of a Scots pine. When he was finished, he turned back toward camp.

The clatter of falling stones made him whirl. He kept the axe in both hands and strained his gaze at the darkness, trying to see any movement.

A creature stepped into the moonlight. Ellis raised the axe for a swing, and then he froze in midair.

Moonlight shone from the creature's white fur. Long horns angled from its head, and there was a pickaxe protruding from its flank.

"Bone goat?" he said, aghast.

The goat blinked at him, then shook the mist from her fur. The pickaxe wobbled, but remained in place.

"Fallen kings." Ellis put down his own weapon and hastened to the animal's side. "I can't believe you found us."

She must have followed once the sun fell, picking her way up the mountainside with more ease than her human companions. He didn't know if all goats were this stubborn, if death had somehow made her more implacable. Even so, her state had... deteriorated. The smell of rot had begun to cling to her, and the pickaxe didn't improve things.

The goat looked at him.

He looked back.

"Do not make me regret this," he told her, and then he reached for the pickaxe.

He didn't like hurting things. He couldn't look when Cook

broke the necks of chickens, and he'd done badly in any attempts to learn combat. It simply wasn't in his nature. He hoped the bone goat wouldn't feel it when he took hold of the handle and pulled the weapon from her flank. It came free and he tossed it to the ground, wiping his hands on his trousers and shuddering violently.

"Those miners weren't pleased when you fought back, I assume?" he said.

The goat opened her mouth in a silent answer.

He shook his head. "You are the strangest animal I have ever met."

At this, the goat flicked her tail and began nuzzling his hand. Hesitantly, he scratched between her horns, the way he had seen Ryn do.

She leaned against him, eyes half lidded with pleasure.

"But sort of nice," he said.

The goat's ears flicked. Ellis heard it a moment after: a shout. It tore through the forest, setting fire to his chest.

He picked up Ryn's axe and sprinted back toward camp. His every sense sharpened: In every breath he tasted the spice of juniper and fresh rainfall; the shadows seemed to part as he gazed into them; he heard the sounds of a scuffle.

He bolted into the clearing, found it empty. But then he spun around—and saw movement. Ryn was on the ground just out of the circle of firelight, throwing her weight against an armored figure. Ryn sank a small knife into the dead soldier's arm again and again, but the blows did little.

Fury burned bright at the edges of his vision. He raised the axe and charged—

But the bone goat was faster.

The goat hit the bone house in the thigh. Horns met armor, and the soldier's leg crumpled beneath it. Ryn rolled out from under the bone house, slamming her elbow into the creature's exposed face. A crack resounded through the woods, and the bone house twisted back. It staggered upright, seemingly dazed but functional. Its skeletal fingers reached for Ellis's cloak, which was tangled about Ryn's legs.

Ellis swung the axe with all his strength. Even as he pulled back, he felt the muscles in his shoulder blades sear with fresh pain. But anger pushed the sensation away, made it manageable.

The axe bit into the bone house's exposed spine, lodging between shoulder and skull, and it fell, twitching. It looked like a half-squashed bug—more pathetic than terrifying. Ryn stumbled upright, then brought her heel down on the bone house's skull. Once, twice, a third time, and then the struggles slowed. The creature's arms and legs moved dreamily, reaching for something it could not find.

At least until Ellis wrenched the axe down and swung again and again.

Once the dead soldier was little more than shattered bits of iron and bone, Ellis looked at Ryn. In the dim light, he could just see the blood trickling through her hair. Her chest heaved with labored breaths, and she bent, resting her weight on her knees. For a few moments, neither said a word.

The bone goat nuzzled one of the pieces of armor, as if trying to see whether or not it could be eaten. Dissatisfied, the animal trotted away.

Ryn turned to watch it go. Hoarsely, she said, "They wear armor."

Ellis felt his brows draw tight. "The—the goat?"

Ryn coughed, then straightened. She threw him an exasperated look. "Not the goat. The soldier."

Ellis returned her look. "Soldiers generally do, yes."

Ryn threw her arm out, gesturing vaguely at the forest. "We're in Annwvyn. Magic. Iron is supposed to repel magic—that's why Colbren built that iron fence back when things like the pwca and afanc were threats. I thought that must have been the reason the bone houses came into Colbren—because Eynon took down the fence."

Finally, Ellis understood. "But the iron doesn't affect them," he said. "They wear it."

"The cauldron of rebirth is *made* of iron, if the stories are right," she said, nodding. "I mean—it makes sense. It just never occurred to me before. That iron might not bother them."

Ellis's gaze flicked down to the dead soldier. "You—you thought all this out while being dragged into the woods by a dead man?"

"Pretty sure this one was a woman," said Ryn.

"Not my point."

"Yes." The corners of her mouth twitched. "Yes, I did. Like I said before—something has changed. The bone houses are leaving the forest, attacking people, and ignoring how magic is supposed to work. And if we're going to end this, we need to know what changed."

She turned to face him fully—her hair was a mess and the borrowed cloak askew. Without thinking, he reached out and touched the blood at her temple. "You're bleeding."

"I think it tore out some hair. It'll grow back."

"Come here," said Ellis, and before he could stop himself, he stepped closer. One hand rested gently on her jaw, angling her face to one side, while he used his sleeve to wipe the blood away. She winced, and he kept his touch light. "There," he said quietly. "Now you won't bleed into your eyes."

An amused breath escaped her. "Well, thanks for that." Her eyes met his and it felt as if the ground had been yanked out from under him.

She looked a frightful mess, but her skin was warm beneath his fingers and her mouth was crooked at one corner. *Fallen kings.*

He wanted to kiss her.

He felt half sick with yearning. Even now, dirty and exhausted, she remained undaunted. She would see this quest through. It was her surety, her fierce sense of purpose; he wanted to draw it into himself. Her eyes were steady on his, and she did not pull away.

A wave of pain racked him; his hands dropped and he stepped back. He drew in an unsteady breath—already, he could feel the overextended muscles in his back screaming at him. He should have taken more care with swinging that axe—but he couldn't bring himself to regret it.

"Here," he said, holding the axe out. Ryn's face flickered

through several emotions, each gone so quickly he couldn't put a name to them. She took the axe, then reached up and unclasped the gray cloak.

"Trade you," she said, handing it back. "You're shivering."

He was. He hadn't noticed—some aftereffect of the battle, perhaps.

They returned to their camp, and Ryn stoked the fire with dried pine needles. Sparks flew into the air, glittering and bright, and Ellis tried to focus on them rather than on the burning discomfort settling into his shoulder.

"Hey," said Ryn, and he looked up.

She sat crosslegged and the bone goat leaned against her. She was absentmindedly scratching the goat's rump. "Thanks," said Ryn.

Ellis considered several replies, discarding all but one: "Glad to be of use."

She twitched one shoulder in silent agreement.

Ellis settled on the ground beside the fire. He hoped the warmth would unknot some of the muscles in his back. His eyes slipped shut and he tried to rest.

But sleep was a long time in coming.

CHAPTER 23

RYN ROUSED WITH the dawn.

She glanced over at Ellis. He was still asleep, curled into a ball on his right side. A smile stole over her, and then she gave herself a little shake.

She hadn't slept well after the attack. Even with the bone goat watching over them, Ryn knew she would find very little rest in this forest.

"All right," she said, standing. "It's time to pack up."

Ellis did not move.

"We can't remain here too much longer," she said, reaching down.

He did not move—rather, he remained curled on his side.

A noise escaped him. It was a thin sound, an animal noise of pain.

Ryn's blood iced over.

His eyes, when they opened, blinked several times. A rattling hiss, and he placed a hand on his chest.

"Are you—what's wrong?" she asked. She hated that her voice was unsteady.

His eyes closed, then opened again. His fingers knotted in his own shirt, as if he needed something to hold on to. He rolled onto his back, a cough shaking him.

"Fallen kings," he rasped. He cursed, the words coming out as a sharp groan.

"What's wrong?" she repeated.

"It hurts," he said, teeth gritted. His fingers clawed at his shoulder and his eyes squeezed shut. "Damn it."

She reached for his pack. "Where's your willow bark?"

A muscle in his neck spasmed. "No more."

Her fingers went still. "It's gone?"

"No apothecaries in the wilds," he said, mouth twitching into a painful smile. It was the kind of smile that was all muscle and no true emotion—hollow reassurance. Ryn's nails dug into the leather. For one moment, frustrated anger welled within her.

"You should have said something," she said. "I could have—"

"Fixed this?" This time he made no effort to smile. "Pretty sure that's beyond even you." He seemed to make an effort to steady his breathing. "It'll pass," he said raggedly. "It always does. I just—rest. And heat, if we can manage."

She rocked back on her heels. "I should have realized something was wrong."

Again, that flickering little smile—more self-deprecation

than amusement. "Considering how much effort I put into concealing any discomfort, that would be quite the achievement."

She closed her eyes. Her own supplies consisted of food, some clothing, her axe and a knife, firesteel, and a few sprigs of dried yarrow. Which would help with wounds—but not this.

She stoked the fire until it was dancing on green wood, flames merrily sending sparks high into the air. She helped Ellis move a little closer to it, hating every flash of pain that crossed his face.

It wasn't just that he'd likely injured himself to help her—it was that Ellis was supposed to be calm, his face mildly amused, a journal in one hand and a quill in the other.

The smoke from the fire stung her eyes, making them dry and achy. She blinked several times and the world blurred at the edges.

She should have paid better attention to him. He would have done the same if she'd been the one hurt. He was good and kind and she—she was a girl who carried an axe and dismembered the dead.

The day passed with excruciating slowness. The sun moved overhead, and morning drifted into afternoon. Ryn did go to the creek, stripping out of her dirtiest clothing and rinsing her skin with the clean water. It was so cold she gritted her teeth to choke back a scream, but when she was finished, her skin was pink and she no longer smelled of dead goat.

She returned to Ellis and brought him a cup of water. He nodded his thanks, but did not say much more. She could see the pain behind his eyes, despite the way he tried to hide it even now. And he did this every day? She could not imagine it.

"It's not always this bad," he said, as if he could hear her thoughts. She gave a start, then glimpsed his faint crease of a smile.

"I saw your face," he said. "And no—it's not always like this. Some days it's just in the background. I don't even notice. Other times it's nagging. And once in a while if I strain myself or sometimes out of nowhere it just... flares up."

"Like now," she said.

"Like now."

She watched as his fingers dug into the muscle of his shoulder, as if trying to release some of the tension. "You can't stay here forever," he said.

Ryn's gaze fell to the fire. "You're right; we need more wood."

"No, I mean." He drew in a long breath. "You can't stay here on my account."

She blinked at him. "You think I'm just going to leave you?"

"I think," he said, "you have to. With your family, with your home, with everything at risk. You came here to end the bone houses—and I came for my own reasons. You shouldn't put everything at risk for my sake."

She thought of it. Of how it would feel to walk from this forest, to follow the river to its source. To cross Llyn Mawr on her own, throw open the doors of Castell Sidi, and find the cauldron of rebirth.

One thing was certain: If she left Ellis on his own, he would die. He couldn't navigate the wilds, forage for food, or defend himself should the bone houses attack again. He would perish—of cold, of starvation, of being torn apart by dead creatures.

"I'll be fine," said Ellis.

She threw him a disgruntled look.

"Your face is rather expressive," he said. "And I believe I'm beginning to tell the differences in your scowls."

Her frown deepened.

"Like now, you're wishing I would stop being so lighthearted about this," he said.

"That wasn't hard to guess."

CHAPTER 24

EVENING CAME ON. Ryn snared a rabbit and cooked it over the small fire; gristle bubbled into the coals and the smell of roasted meat seemed to rouse Ellis a little. She gave him the larger portion before settling down to watch the sunset. There was no more talk of her leaving him, but even she could feel the urgency beginning to tug at her.

Clouds filled the sky, blotting out stars and the moon, and the only illumination came from the fire. It crackled and spat, the green of the wood too damp for easy burning. Ellis slept—or rather, he remained quiet and still, his fingers knotted in his shirt. She watched his chest rise and fall, rise and fall, until she was sure he was resting.

Ryn rested in fitful moments. She woke when the fire began

to sputter out, she woke when Ellis stirred, and she woke when she heard the sound of footsteps.

Her axe was in her hand at once. She rose to her feet, knees slightly bent, her every nerve at the ready. The forest was still and quiet, and even the sound of the creek seemed to have faded away. Ryn ventured a few more steps.

Something approached. Grasses rustled and the undergrowth stirred. Ryn pulled her axe back, jaw clenched and arms shaking with readiness.

A goat emerged.

Ryn's shoulders slumped.

"You," she said in an undertone, "need to announce yourself before scaring people."

The bone goat blinked slowly. Then it walked forward and nudged her, as if asking for food.

By all the fallen kings, the creature was beginning to smell. Ryn grimaced and gave it a quick scratch behind the ears before sidestepping it.

"Are you going to keep following us all the way to Castell Sidi?" she asked, sitting down on a large rock. Its surface was rough with lichen, and she found herself absentmindedly using her thumbnail to pick at it.

The goat sniffed Ellis.

"He doesn't have food, either," said Ryn.

The goat lay down beside Ellis. Ryn wrinkled her nose; she considered grabbing the goat by the horns and trying to coax it away from Ellis, if only so he wouldn't smell like death tomorrow.

A branch snapped behind her. She whirled so swiftly she was on her knees, one palm pressed to the mossy earth, the other trying to grip her axe.

Someone stood over her.

Another bone house.

He wore a tattered gray cloak—the garb of a traveler, not a soldier. There was no flesh to him, and his bones had the brown quality of someone who had spent time in the mine. He must have followed the goat here.

The bone house stood there, the firelight flickering across the hollows of his face. He took a step closer.

"No," said Ryn softly.

As if sensing her anger, the bone house retreated a few steps. The empty eye sockets remained fixed on her, and she felt the weight of his gaze.

Ryn lowered her axe, letting the heavy iron blade rest on the ground beside her. So long as he did not attack, nor would she.

"You out for a stroll?" she asked, as if they were merely strangers who had met on the road. "You don't look like a miner. Did you follow us from the encampment? Is there a dead grandmother on my trail, seeking to end our quest?"

The bone house raised one shoulder in a half shrug. Even without features, she could sense something like amusement in the gesture.

"Well, if you're not going to attack, I'd appreciate it if you left us alone," she said. "My friend isn't doing so well, and I can't stare at you the whole night."

She'd wondered sometimes if the bone houses could understand her. But this one seemed to—his gaze fell to Ellis. He took a step back, and then another, and Ryn watched as the bone house slipped soundlessly into the undergrowth.

Ryn leaned her elbows on her knees, eyes slipping shut. Exhaustion pressed down on her and she fought it, but she knew it would be a losing battle. Time slipped by—minutes or hours, she couldn't be sure.

A root snapped.

Ryn's head came up. The world swam into focus: the moonlit clouds, the forest, and the gray-cloaked figure before her.

Panic ripped through her. Her fingers scrambled for her axe, but before she could take a swing, the bone house dropped something into her lap.

Her shaking fingertips brushed over delicate white flowers. A few petals fell, and the sweet scent of cut greenery reached her nose.

She remained there, crouched over Ellis—flowers in one hand and axe in the other. Neither one moved. And then the dead man silently pointed a finger to Ellis.

She finally recognized the flower. Feverfew.

It was meant for treating headaches and fevers, of course. But she knew several elders who used it for their joints, who sipped it in tea and said it helped with their aches.

"Did you want me to have this?" she asked.

The bone house nodded.

A well of confusion opened up within her. She thought she'd known the dead, known them better than anyone else. She'd met one when she was a child and lived to tell about it; she had made it her life's work to keep the peaceful dead in the ground and the risen dead in the fires. But they still managed to surprise her.

Ryn emptied a canteen of water into her small iron pot, placing it over the fire. Once the water was boiling, she sprinkled the water with the feverfew leaves and set it aside to steep.

When she looked up again, the bone house was still there. He stood with his arms at his sides, unthreatening and unmoving.

"Thank you," she said. She hesitated. "Is there—I don't know. A message you wish to give me? Do you have relatives nearby that I could contact? Let them know that you're dead?" It was the least she could do.

The bone house did not reply for a moment. Then it raised a hand and beckoned to her.

In the old stories, heroes always went with the monsters. Ryn remembered thinking it was such a foolish decision to make; surely those heroes of old knew better than to accompany the monster into its lair.

But, standing here, she understood.

She rose to her feet.

The bone goat lifted her head, gazing at Ryn. Death had crept into the creature's body with sickly sweet rot; it was becoming less goat and more monster. Even so, Ryn laid her hand on its forehead. "Keep an eye on him, all right?" she asked.

The bone goat nuzzled her fingers, then rested her head gently on Ellis's stomach.

It would have to be good enough. Slowly, ever so carefully, she followed the bone house.

He moved as shadows did—grace without weight, shape

without form. Those who did not know how to move in a forest could not have kept up. And Ryn felt glad she was half-wild, raised on the edges of Annwvyn—her feet found footholds and her fingers slipped through brambles without snagging.

She followed for the same reason she had begged her mother for tales of monsters. Monsters were unrestrained, unbound, and beautiful in their destruction. They could be slain but they would never be truly defeated. And perhaps, even back then, Ryn thought that if she could love the monsters—then she could love those monstrous parts of herself.

They walked through the forest, dead man and living girl. The air smelled of the late harvest, of sun-ripened berries laced with frost. They went up into the mountains, around boulders and over mounds of stone that must have once been homes. The trees thinned and then vanished all together, until Ryn found herself in a field of dead grasses.

They walked in silence—that was the one thing Ryn had always liked about the dead. There was no need to talk.

The path wound farther upward, until Ryn found herself reaching for rocks and weeds to stay upright. Her palm came down on a dusty ledge and she hauled herself up and over. When she rose, she saw how far they had come.

They stood on the edge of a mountain.

When the clouds parted, she saw the forest sprawled below, a dark smudge against the earth. And beyond that, she glimpsed the shape of rolling hills and fields, and the place where Colbren resided. It felt as if all the isles were laid at her feet.

Perhaps this was why Arawn had chosen to make his home

here; the Otherking could look down upon the human lands at a glance.

A tremor ran up her legs, and the bone house seized her arm. It was a tight grip, but not restraining. It was as if the dead man feared she would fall.

"I'm all right," she said, rolling her shoulder. He pulled back, jaw working silently. She could only imagine his reply—and somehow she thought there might be a quip and a laugh tangled up in it. "Why did you bring me up here?" She gestured at the ledge. "It's pretty, but a bit of a climb."

The dead man merely looked at her. And then he ducked low, and she saw the gap in the rock.

It was small—barely the width of a man's shoulders. The bone house slipped into the space and crawled into the dark.

There was an old tale of a man who'd crawled into a rabbit hole and found himself in the land of the tylwyth teg. The immortals had welcomed him, asked him to join their revel, and he pleased them with his fine manners. They said he was welcome to return. He'd used the hole to come and go, until his pride got the better of him. He bragged to a lady that he could show her the otherlands. But the next time he tried to get inside, he found only a rabbit's warren.

Ryn knelt beside the hole.

Someone had cut into the rock; it was crude, as if a blade had been jabbed repeatedly into the stone. It looked a bit like a star. Her thumb slid across the etching.

She thought of a man seeking treasure in the mountains using a hunting knife to mark his way. Her hands found the smooth rock, and she began to crawl. The air tasted of dirt, and roots brushed across her back. Pebbles scattered, heard but unseen, and she hoped no rats or other creatures had made their home here.

Something dripped onto her shoulder and she flinched, a curse snagging between her teeth. She scuttled forward, and nearly tumbled headlong when the path angled down. She scooted on hands and knees, rocks biting into her palms, her axe banging against her hip, and when she left the tunnel behind, it was with a gasp and a thud.

She half scurried, half crawled from the hole. Her fingers clawed at damp earth, and she dragged herself into a sitting position.

The bone house stood a few strides away, arms still at his sides. She looked past him.

Everything seemed to slow.

She saw a shore of broken shale. The dark gray rocks overlapped one another, shattered to pieces by time and wind. And against those rocks lapped water.

Her gaze was drawn past the water, to the smudge of dark against the sky. She could not see it, not truly. But she knew it was there, across the lake.

Castell Sidi.

Elation propelled her forward, and she walked until she stood at the edge of the shore, eyes straining into the dark. As the bone house led her a little farther, the scents changed, became crisper and damper, and she heard the flap of wings and a splash as a bird descended into the water.

The heart of Annwvyn—she'd *found* it.

No, no. A bone house had led her to it.

She might never have found it without his help. After all, what kind of person would have crawled into a deep, dark hole, unknowing if it would lead anywhere at all?

Rocks clattered behind her and Ryn whirled. The bone house stood a mere arm's length away.

"Were you a knight?" she asked. "Did you come here seeking the cauldron, too?"

A shake of his head.

It was true—he bore no armor. He wouldn't be a soldier, then. But perhaps—

She shivered.

The story of the cauldron never said what had happened to the thief. Perhaps—perhaps. She looked at him and wished for the first time that he could speak, if only to utter his name.

"I have to be getting back," she said. "But thank you for this."

The bone house nodded. He held out a hand, and she recoiled. The dead man's hand dropped, and he retreated a few steps as if apologetic.

He had not harmed her. She had no reason to draw away, not when he had done all he could to aid her. "Sorry," she said. "I just—I'm not used to..."

Her voice drifted.

Silently, the bone house took a step toward her. His brown-edged fingers were raised, catching in the moonlight. He moved slowly, as if trying not to startle a wild animal.

Ryn's heart slammed against her ribs, but this time she did not pull away.

The bone house touched a lock of her hair. He was gentle, so soft she barely felt the contact. His hand shook and then she felt the whisper of bone against her cheek, down her chin. The touch was cold and dry, but she held still.

The dead man simply looked at her. For a few moments, all she could hear was the lapping of the lake against the shale shore and her own breathing.

The bone house's hand fell back to his side. He retreated, watching her all the while, and before she could utter another word, he had vanished into the hole.

She stood there, waiting to see if he would reappear.

He didn't.

She waited another minute, then returned to the other side herself. Giddiness made her steps light; she had done it. She had done it when no one else could—she'd found Castell Sidi.

They were going to do this. For the first time, she truly believed it. She and Ellis were going to finish this, end the bone houses, and return home as heroes.

When she reemerged from the small tunnel, she glanced about to see if the bone house would be waiting. "Hello?" she called.

There was no answer, of course. And no sign of the dead man.

Even so, she knew what was owed. "Thank you," she said, into the empty night.

Returning took less time; she was more certain of her footing, and when she crawled onto the ledge, she found herself alone. She hastened back to their small camp.

The fire was all but out; she rekindled it with a few dry roots, blowing over the embers until sparks flew into the air. Ellis was still, his chest rising and falling evenly. The bone goat rested beside him, but her eyes were open. She lifted her head in silent greeting.

The feverfew tea had a vaguely greenish color. She wasn't sure if it would help, but anything would be better than leaving him like this. She reached down, resting her hand on his arm. "Ellis?"

It took him a moment to wake up. He blinked several times, firelight in his eyes, before his gaze settled on her.

"Why," he said, "do you look as though you've rolled in a mud puddle?"

Oh. She touched her cheek and her fingers came away brown.

She handed him the warm tea. "Drink this."

As he drank, she turned back to her pack. She could store what was left of the feverfew, and if it worked, perhaps Ellis would be well enough to leave in the morning.

That was when she saw the thing resting on her pack. It was perhaps the length of her middle finger, dark and smooth.

It had been placed there, like an offering.

She frowned, her fingers scrabbling for the object.

Half of a wooden love spoon.

Hands trembling, she traced the edge of the carving. Whorls of familiar wood slid against her thumb.

She reached into her pocket.

The broken handle was carved in an intricate woven pattern; flowers were etched into the wood.

With shaking hands, she pressed the two wooden halves together.

They fit perfectly.

Ryn lurched to her feet. She spun around, glancing every which way. Her heart thundered in her ears and she felt as if she might fly apart.

Fallen kings. Fallen kings.

She wanted to scream, to rend the forest with the sound of her voice, to hear her own grief howled to the sky.

"What is it?" Ellis sounded croaky, but he made an effort to sit up. "What did you find?"

But her lips only formed two words. She gave them voice, even when she knew they would go unanswered.

"My father," she said.

CHAPTER 25

SHE DID NOT mean to fall asleep, but she did. She awoke with something soft against her temple. A shoulder. She opened her eyes and blinked into the dawn light. One hand rested on her axe, the other on Ellis's arm. The fire was little more than smoking ash. The night seemed unreal, something that must have happened in a dream. But the stems of feverfew were sprinkled across the ground.

Ellis sat up, scrubbing a hand across his face. He drew in a breath—at first tentatively, then a little deeper.

"How is it?" she asked.

He probed at his collarbone, fingertips skimming along bare skin, pushing his shirt collar aside. There was the faint scar—white and dimpled. "Better," he finally said. "The feverfew—it helped. I've always used other herbs for the pain, but I'll have to remember that one."

"It probably grows nearby," she said. "That bone house didn't go far—I'll see if I can find more."

His lips moved in a slight smile. "Planning to keep me in a state of slightly drugged good cheer?"

"Planning to keep you," she said, "regardless of what state you're in."

The words slipped out—and she didn't know if it was relief or exhaustion that gave her tongue such freedom.

She wasn't sure when she'd begun to regard him as *hers*. Her friend, her ally, and one of those few people she wanted to keep safe. And if she liked the way his dark hair fell across his eyes or how his voice rasped when he said her name—well. That was beside the point.

He cleared his throat. "All right," he said. "We should go."

They packed up their small camp; dried meat and a handful of berries made for a quick if not wholly satisfying breakfast. And when they were finished, Ryn led them deeper into the mountains. They left the bone goat resting in a patch of sunlight.

The foliage around them shifted from lush to rugged. Lichen clung to bare rocks; the river thinned into a narrow creek; the trees were bare, stripped by wind and some of them only clinging to the mountainside with their thick roots. The grasses were yellow, and the wind had a sharp chill. Winter was closing its teeth around the mountains.

They did not speak. Ryn was lost in her own thoughts and Ellis would not disturb her. The tale she had told sounded like something from a legend—a dead man appearing to her in the moonlight, a climb up a mountain to a forgotten passage, and the lake beyond. But he could not doubt her; for one thing, she'd never lied to him. For another, she showed him the twin halves of the wooden spoon. "Do you think he'll come back?" was his one question.

Ryn had glanced away and not replied.

She kept her pace slow, but Ellis still breathed hard. The path wound upward, the slope steep. In some places, he found himself reaching for rocks as handholds, using them to pull himself along. The journey took the better part of an hour—which was his fault, Ellis knew.

"I would apologize for slowing us down," he rasped, "but I fear you'd push me off this cliff."

"Your fears are not unfounded." She flashed her teeth in a wolf's smile. "You apologize too much."

He gave a rueful shake of his head, hair falling into his eyes. He pushed it back. "I hope the waters of the Llyn Mawr are good for bathing. I think I need one."

"You do."

"Flatterer."

"You look like a corpse," she told him. "And you smell like a dead goat."

He laughed. "Ryn," he said, shaking his head. He said her name for the sheer joy of it—because he could. "Ryn."

The passage through the mountain was small. He had to angle himself so his shoulders wouldn't get stuck, one after the other. He moved with little grace, shuffling along on forearms and knees, teeth gritted against the discomfort. Ryn had gone ahead, calling out encouragements. Even so, it was slow going. By the time he emerged from the tunnel, he was covered in dirt and sweat. His head swam and he leaned on his knees for a few heartbeats to catch his breath.

When he lifted his head, he blinked several times.

Daylight glittered on the surface of a lake. It was nestled in the heart of the mountains, surrounded by jagged rocks on either side.

They stood on the edges of Llyn Mawr.

And beyond: Castell Sidi.

Waves lapped gently at the broken shale shore and weak autumn sunlight touched Ryn's face. The remnants of old docks still clung to the shore. The shattered prow of a boat rested among the rocks, its surface soft with moss. A black bird sat upon it, gazing at the humans.

It was only when she saw the ruin of the docks that a sense of loss struck Ryn. This had once been a place of trade and travel. Otherfolk—and perhaps even humans—had crossed Llyn Mawr to reach the castell. In their absence, time had waged its war on the place, leaving only the scattered remains.

"It's beautiful," said Ellis quietly.

Ryn nodded. "It is."

"Are you getting in first, or shall I?" This time his voice was laden with good humor.

She snorted. "Yes, of course. Once I've drowned, you can float my bloated body across."

Ellis grimaced. "For once in this trip, I'd like a plan that doesn't involve bodies."

"You shouldn't have befriended a gravedigger, then," said Ryn. "Should've taken up with a baker or a blacksmith."

"I shudder to think what a baker might have done with the bone houses."

Ryn walked toward the dock. "Come on. Let's see if any of these boats are usable."

There were several small vessels strewn alongside the lake. Slate clattered beneath her feet as Ryn strode around them, trying to find a boat that wouldn't sink the moment she pushed it into the water. The first two were rotted through, wood so soft it crumbled beneath her fingers. The third had a long crack through its underbelly. The fourth had some promise.

It was a smaller boat, the kind likely used by couples to take a leisurely row around the lake. Ryn grasped the prow and yanked, dragging it up and out of the earth. It took a fair amount of pebbles and dirt with it, scattering detritus along the shore as she hauled it into the water.

It did not sink. She pressed down, waiting to see if water would seep into the belly. A little swirled around the bottom, but nothing overly worrying.

Ellis dragged two oars from a different boat. They were beautifully carved: etched with a leaf-and-dragon pattern, the wood lacquered against rot.

"I wonder how long it's been since anyone used these," said Ryn, slotting the oars into place.

"Since the thief came here to steal the cauldron, I assume," said Ellis. He gave the boat a dubious look, but he stepped into it. A little water sloshed over the edge, but the boat didn't sink.

Ryn sat on one of the smooth planks and began to row. It took a few strokes, but she soon fell into a steady rhythm, and they were gliding away from the bank.

With her back to Castell Sidi, it was almost easy to pretend they were out on a lake for fun. The water lapped at the boat in a way that she found soothing, and the autumn sunlight warmed her bare forearms. With no current to drag at them, the boat churned a path through the water with ease.

Ellis skimmed his fingers across the water, dragging gentle furrows—and then his arm jerked up. His gaze sharpened and his mouth pressed tight.

"What is it?" she asked.

Water dripped from Ellis's hand; he cradled it against his chest. "I—I don't know. I touched something. A fish, perhaps."

Ryn lifted the oars out of the water and stilled. The boat bobbed in place. In the swirling water, Ryn saw something move.

"If there are fish," she said, "perhaps we can think of sup—"

The words fragmented.

At first, she thought it must be a shadow or a cloud reflected in the water. Something too dark and too large to be truly in the water. Sunlight caught on its form. Its body was segmented, and scales glittered down its sides. It had the flat form of a lizard—but it was far too large, and its feet were webbed. Its long tail propelled it seamlessly through the lake, so smoothly that barely a ripple followed in its wake.

In all the stories of the bone houses, there was always mention of soldiers dying in Llyn Mawr. But the stories never mentioned *how* they'd died.

Now she understood.

"Do not move." Ryn spoke out of the corner of her mouth.

Her axe sat at the bottom of the boat because what use was there for an axe on water? Now she cursed herself for sliding into complacency. She'd thought they were safe in the daylight, but there were magical creatures not bound to the night.

One of the many stories her mother had told her was of a creature who lived in a lake. When the creature raged, the lake flooded nearby farms and villages. For many years, the villagers lived in terror of the creature—until a blacksmith proposed a plan. He would forge chains strong enough to hold the monster, and they could drag it away. Oxen were brought to the village, and the blacksmith spent days laboring in his smithy. The villagers decided they would lure the creature from the lake with a maiden. She sang so sweetly that even the birds would fall silent.

On one fateful morning, the blacksmith brought his chains to the shore of the lake. The oxen shifted uneasily beneath their yoke, and the maiden walked into the water. The hem of her gown grew damp, but she did not shy away. She opened her mouth and began to sing a joyful song.

Nothing happened.

The villagers began to fret, fearing their plan would not work, when the maiden decided to try something else. She sang a mournful melody, and all those who listened wept.

Something emerged from the water, and the villagers cringed. All but the maiden. She sang and sang until the lake creature heaved itself to the lakeshore and fell asleep beside her.

The villagers lashed the creature with the chains, and the oxen strained. The creature awoke, thrashing and furious, and in its struggles, it nearly dragged the oxen into the lake. But the animals were too strong, and the creature was dragged free of its home.

The blacksmith and a few other men accompanied the oxen, keeping a watchful eye as they bore the monster away. Once they were well away from the village, the men released the creature.

It vanished into the wilds, to find a new home.

When she was young, Ryn had wondered why the blacksmith had not forged a blade rather than chains. To kill, rather than confine.

But as she looked into the depths of the Llyn Mawr, she understood.

"Afanc," breathed Ryn.

This creature was untouched by time and blades. It was a remnant of another age, and she could not kill it. Not even if she'd wanted to.

The creature drifted beneath them, so large it might as well have been a shadow of a cloud. Even so, Ryn considered leaping from the boat like one of those heroes of legend. But for one thing—she was only a passable swimmer. And for another—she was sure that if knights and soldiers hadn't managed to kill this afanc, she had no chance at all. But maybe she could delay it long enough for Ellis to row to shore.

Her gaze met Ellis's, and one of those moments passed between them: that silent language that she'd only ever shared with her family. Ellis's eyes narrowed and he gave a sharp shake of his head.

Ellis reached into Ryn's pack. Ryn twitched—an aborted little movement as she held in the desire to grab at him. What was he doing?

He withdrew a jar of rowanberry preserves.

Then he pulled his arm back, drew his brows together, and flung the jar as hard as he could. It flew high, tumbling end over end, sunlight shimmering along the glass. It fell into the water with a soft plop.

The afanc lunged. With one powerful sweep of its tail, it propelled itself through the water toward the fallen jar and away from the boat. The monster vanished into the depths, in pursuit of the unknown thing that had dropped into its territory.

"Row," said Ellis. His jaw was tight. "Fallen kings, *row*."

There was little point in conserving movement now—all that mattered was getting to the shore before that thing realized its prey was escaping. Lake water churned beneath the oars, and her arms burned. An ache made itself known in her lower back, but she ignored it. She didn't look; she didn't dare. She kept her eyes on her own knees, focusing on the motion of her shoulders. Her arms were strong from years of digging, hands worn with calluses, and the boat lurched forward with every stroke.

"Keep going," said Ellis quietly, the way one might chant a prayer. "Keep going, keep—"

"What," said Ryn through gritted teeth, "do"—downward stroke—"you think"—the oars lifted from the water—"I am"—and then another stroke—"doing."

The talk was almost a comfort—familiarity in a situation that felt so very other. Ryn rowed and rowed, felt the water moving beneath her, and as their speed picked up, her heart did as well. Perhaps they'd make it. They'd have to make it. They would make it—

Her left oar plunged into the water and hit something solid. For a moment, Ryn thought they'd hit land. But the prow of the boat should have struck the shore first, not an oar. And certainly not only one oar. She pulled upward, but the oar would not move. It was as if it'd become stuck in something.

Or been grabbed by something.

Ryn's gaze yanked to her side, and she saw the *something*.

This close to the surface, she could appreciate the creature's beauty. It had small scales that glittered in the sunlight like small opals. Its teeth were as sharp as daggers, angled inward. Meant for ripping and tearing. And its eyes—its eyes were the palest gold, with the sharp pupil of a cat.

The left oar was yanked from Ryn's hand. She heard Ellis cry out, and then a claw settled on the side of the boat, tipping it precariously. Ryn brought the axe down, but it was too late.

The world flipped sideways and they plunged into the lake.

The cold of it drove the breath from her lungs. Every muscle seized painfully and she sank for several moments before she began to struggle against the water. Her cloak was a noose around her throat and she fumbled with it, fingers clumsy, until the clasp gave and the fabric drifted away, caught on some invisible current.

It was quiet; the chaos replaced with the heavy silence of water. Ryn kicked, felt her foot make impact with something alive, and she pushed herself upward, arms churning through the water.

Her head broke the surface and she gasped for air. Her hair was in her eyes and she hastily tried to shove it away.

The boat was overturned, and the last remaining oar floated uselessly beside it. Ellis clung to the boat, his long legs kicking at the water. His dark hair was plastered to his forehead and his lips were bloodless, but he was alive.

Ryn swam for him. With every kick, she was sure she'd feel claws or teeth sink into her flesh and drag her under. Fear seemed to slow the world around her, dragging moments into minutes, and several eternities passed in the time it took to get to Ellis. He had seized the oar and thrust it at her. She took one end and he the other—and together, they swam for the shore.

Something shifted in the water. Ryn wasn't sure what made her want to look down, but she did.

The water beneath them was dark—too dark. As if a creature swam beneath them, just out of kicking distance. Scales glittered, and she caught a glimpse of ridges along its joints. The afanc moved below them as easily as an eel.

This was its home, after all. And they were intruders.

If this were land, they might have been able to run. There was no such opportunity with the cold water tugging at their clothes, with every kick taking them only a short distance. She could not even cry out; she did not have the breath. And even if she had, fear had stolen her words. Her fingers slipped on the oar and she had to grab for it a second time, and then a third. The chill of the lake was slowing her, and she knew that it would kill her just as easily as the afanc could—it would just be a slower sort of death. And she would join all those corpses at the bottom of Llyn Mawr. Her body would rise, with the rest of them, never allowed to rest in the quiet of a grave.

She wondered if this were the afanc's plan: to let the cold and exertion sap their strength. Perhaps the lake was not only its home, but its trap.

"Keep going," Ellis was saying—or rather, wheezing. He sounded terrible, and Ryn wondered if they were even going to make it. If the afanc didn't strike, they still might not be strong enough to reach dry land.

Something caught her around the ankle.

Then she was dragged under.

She thrashed. Arms and free leg cut through the water, stirring up bubbles. The creature's grip on her was like a band of iron and she could not break it.

She looked down, eyes stinging as she forced them wide, to look upon the afanc.

It must have been a guardian, once. A creature of magic and the depths, trusted to keep Castell Sidi safe from intruders. It was doing so even now, even after the fortress's residents were gone.

The afanc drew her down, down, into the heart of the lake,

and Ryn let it. There was no fighting such a creature with raw strength. The light dimmed, and then something hard rolled along Ryn's back. A rock.

The bottom of the lake. It had taken her to the bottom. The afanc's claws pressed her down, but gently so as not to slice her open.

They did not cut and they did not devour. They *drowned*.

Ryn blinked; the sun was a distant, wobbly thing. Bubbles rose from her lips and nose, and an ache was building behind her ribs. That pain would soon turn to burning agony, and eventually she would try to breathe. Her body would force her—and she would draw in only water, and she would choke on it.

The afanc watched her, impassive, its tail in constant motion. Back and forth, swaying, keeping itself steady amidst the currents. It was waiting, just waiting, because this creature had an eternity while Ryn had only moments.

Her fingers scrabbled along the rocky ground. The soil was soft with silt, crumbling at her touch. Her lungs were beginning to catch fire, and if she was going to act, it had to be now.

She touched a stone that seemed larger than the rest. Her fingers curled around its rough exterior, and before she could hesitate, she drove the rock into one of the afanc's golden eyes.

The pain startled the creature into a fury. It writhed, tail lashing through the water, and for a moment the claws squeezed Ryn so tightly that her ribs creaked. Its mouth worked, and she thought that if the creature had been human, it would have been screaming.

It pawed at its face, seemingly forgetting its prey. Ryn found herself on the lakebed, freed, her chest hurting so badly that for a moment she wondered if she could even swim. She flipped over, pressing her boots to the ground. A glance, and she saw what she'd used to hit the afanc.

There was a half-shattered skull in her hand. It was a muddy brown, and her fingers had been wrapped through one eye socket.

Ryn realized what she'd been resting upon. Not river rocks—but bones. These shattered fragments must have been too broken for the curse to touch them—or perhaps they simply lacked the pieces to claw their way to shore.

Ryn pushed upward with her legs, using the ground to propel her toward the surface. Her boots felt too heavy, but she dared not pause to pull them free. Her fingers cupped the water, and she pulled herself upward. Her vision was flecked with gray, and she hurt so badly, she thought she might cry out.

Something behind her ribs seemed to snap; she inhaled—a reflex, and it felt as if someone had poured mud into her chest. It burned and was heavy and she was going to die here. Alone, in a lake, so close to Castell Sidi. Like so many others. She'd been arrogant to think she could survive when so many others had perished.

She broke the surface. At first she didn't realize it, and her arms kept moving, trying to swim. The air was warm and sweet as summer sunshine, and she dragged it into her. It still hurt; her lungs were on fire, even as the rest of her was freezing.

She swam. She wasn't sure she had anything left to give to the swim, but she threw herself into the motions, heading for the dark smudge that was Castell Sidi.

With every stroke, she was sure she would feel the touch of

the afanc again. That it would recover and come for her, driven by pain and fury.

Her fingers struck something hard. She'd never been more exhausted or scared, and all she wanted was—

Shore.

She was touching the shore.

With what little strength was left to her, Ryn dragged herself out of the lake. The ground was pebbled and damp, and as comfortable as any bed. She lay there, cheek pressed to the ground, breathing. Just breathing.

And then there were hands on her. Warm hands, pushing the sopping hair away from her eyes and touching her throat. She was distantly aware of someone saying her name, helping her onto her side.

Ellis. It was Ellis.

She wanted to sob with relief. She wanted to throw her arms around him, hold on until she was sure they were both all right, until she'd worked up the nerve to press her face into the hollow of his shoulder.

Ryn didn't do any of those things. What she did was roll onto her side and vomit lake water.

CHAPTER 26

IT WAS NOT her most dignified moment.

There was a lot of gagging and gasping, throat burning and eyes streaming. And then there was Ellis, helping drag her farther up the shore, away from the lapping waters of the lake. She was glad to get away from it; she didn't think she'd ever swim in a lake for the rest of her days.

Once she'd stopped sputtering, she lay on her back, focusing on one breath and the next.

Finally, Ryn pushed herself to her elbows. Ellis sat beside her, legs crossed. He'd pushed his waterlogged hair out of his eyes, making his forehead seem even higher than usual. A red welt was raised along his cheek, and she could see the places where it would deepen into a bruise. "I saved my pack," he said, sounding both exhausted and triumphant. "Only a little water got in."

"Good," she rasped. "At least we'll have plenty of parchment."

He inhaled deeply, and then released the breath. "What about you?"

The loss of an axe shouldn't have sent a pang through her, but it did. She closed her eyes, then reopened them. There was little to be gained by wallowing. "I didn't manage to keep anything. Too busy trying not to die."

"I appreciate that," he said, smiling a little.

He held out a hand and she took it, allowing him to haul her upright.

Her gaze swept past him, and she felt her breathing quicken.

Castell Sidi stood before them.

There was no drawbridge—there would be no need, with the lake guarded by a monster. But she could see the battlements, the chipped stone where arrows must have struck. There were at least eight distinct towers, taller than any trees, and they cast long shadows across the ground. She tried to conjure up the old tales of the battle of Gwydion of Dôn and his family against Arawn and his court.

In the end, Gwydion had won. Not with magic or swords—but with a name. He'd called out the true name of Arawn's champion, thus reducing the champion's power and ending the battle.

Her hand rose and touched the heavy fortress wall. Wind had worn it smooth.

"Come on," she said. "Let's find a way inside."

As they circled the castell, Ryn could see how the place had once been a community: Inside the fortress walls, the main structure was accompanied by several smaller buildings. Cottages were set alongside the stone walls, and the shape of a barn was farther west. The grass was overgrown with late-harvest wildflowers. Beads of white blossoms gleamed amidst the grasses. Birds circled overhead, chittering at one another. Nests had been tucked into the broken stones, high above the reach of any predator.

They entered through the granary tower. All that remained of the outdoor oven was a pile of rocks, making it appear more like a burial mound than a stove. There was a small door, and using one of those rocks, Ryn managed to bash the hinges until it gave. With a push, the door fell half in. It was enough space to slip through.

The air was still. Almost too still, untouched by breezes or the movement of animals. It had a stale dampness to it, and she shivered as she walked into the large room. There were tables of all sorts, barrels stacked high, and gleaming glass jars sealed with dusty wax. Her hand came up unbidden, but Ellis touched her arm, drawing her back. "I wouldn't touch anything," he said quietly. "What if there are other enchantments?"

Ryn understood his trepidation; she felt it, too. The ceilings were too high, the rooms too large, and the shadows too thick. This fortress was not meant for humans, not unless they were invited to join the wild hunt or were guests of the tylwyth teg.

They walked through a hallway that led into one of the inner wards. It must have been some sort of meeting room, with a long slab of wood serving as a table. It looked as though it had been cut from the heart of a thousand-year-old tree.

There was no one living there; of that she was sure. The dust was settled, the stillness absolute. There were no signs of occupation, of anything breathing or—

Something whooshed overhead and Ryn found herself ducking, falling to her knees. Ellis made a sharp, startled noise.

A bird sat on a chandelier overhead, gazing down at them.

The chandelier was not made of metal or glass—but of antlers. The bird bobbed its head, examining the intruders. Ryn raised her hand in silent greeting, as if the bird might understand. Perhaps it would.

She stepped through another doorway, and the room opened up. She felt almost as if she'd stepped outside again—the ceiling was so high.

And at the center of the room was a statue.

It looked to be made of wood, but that could not be right—wood would have lost some of its luster. It was only when she saw the dried and scattered leaves that she realized the sculpture was a living tree, dormant for the winter. Its branches, trunk, even the roots were shaped to give the appearance of a man. He stood in still repose, one hand raised as if in greeting and the other clasping a sword. His helmet curved into the lines of a buck's horns, giving him an otherworldly beauty.

"King Arawn," she said. She half expected the statue to answer, but it remained still. She bowed her head, if only for a moment.

This must have been a great hall once, a place where visitors might see the wonders of Castell Sidi. Its beauty yet remained—like a flower pressed between the pages of a book. The colors had faded, but the lines and form were still lovely. The revels of the Otherking must have been held here, and for a moment, she let herself imagine it. Gowns of seafoam and lace, brows adorned with leaves and glittering gems, chalices brimming with spring wines, and above all, the Otherking with his antler crown. She found herself moving slowly, fearing to disturb even the leaves with her footsteps. This was the hall of a king, and she felt grubby and gawky, still shivering from the chill of the lake.

"I can't believe he would have abandoned this place," said Ellis softly.

"He must have despaired of humans," said Ryn. "After Gwydion stole from him, then waged war upon him, Arawn must have thought humans weren't worth staying for. He took his court and all his magic and sailed away."

Seeing the great hall was bittersweet, a taste of a world long past, and she longed for more. Part of her yearned to sweep away the fallen leaves and cobwebs, light the candles, and bring warmth back to Castell Sidi. It had the sense of a slumbering beast, one that might awaken if the right hands tended to it.

But even as she marveled, she knew this place could never be hers. It was not meant for the likes of humans. The mother and her infant son had dared to live here, and the mother's actions had awoken the bone houses. It would be folly to remain, to dwell here—but Ryn could see why a person would want to.

"We need to find the cauldron," she said, keeping her voice low.

Ellis's eyes roamed over the great hall, taking in the high windows and birds nesting overhead. His lips moved silently for a moment. Then he shook himself. "Ah—right." He pursed his lips. "We could search more quickly if we split up."

"Do you think that's safe?"

Ellis twitched his good shoulder in a shrug. "Nothing about this place is safe. Which is why I wouldn't tarry here. Your legend said that the cauldron needed to boil the water within it—we should check those rooms with fireplaces first."

"All right." Part of her yearned for solitude; the chaos of the last few days pressed down on her, and she might buckle under the weight. "But we should meet back in a few hours. Say... two?"

"I'll take the eastern towers," he replied. "You take the west." He hesitated, sliding a look toward the living-tree statue before turning away. He seemed distant, distracted. He strode through a doorway and vanished into the corridor beyond.

Ryn did not move. Her chest shuddered, and the noise she made sounded like a hiccup. Her legs trembled and she found herself sitting in one of the dusty chairs. She was not sure why this place affected her so, but it did. It was every old tale, every bedtime story, every glimpse of wicked wildness she'd seen at the edges of the forest, every monster and every hero. And she wished so badly she might have shared it with her father.

She thought of the dead man wandering the wilds, in a gray cloak, carrying half of a wooden spoon.

Another sharp rasp pinched her lungs; she was not quite crying, but close. She squeezed her eyes shut against the burn of tears.

Her father had led her here—as if he'd known what she intended. And perhaps he had. Perhaps he'd always known she would come here, chasing the old stories to their source, because she was the kind of person who did not know how to let go.

She thought of her hand in his, of gripping his worn fingers with her small ones.

She thought of an old dead woman in a rocking chair, because her daughter couldn't bear for her to leave.

She thought of the Otherking, leaving his home because he could not stay.

And she thought of a mother, holding her dead child and the broken cauldron of rebirth.

Her hand tightened around the broken spoon and she let the jagged waves of grief wash over her.

Ellis had not been sure what to expect of Castell Sidi.

He knew some of the stories. Bards had sung them in the hall at Caer Aberhen, trading songs for a bowl of warm rabbit cawl and a straw mattress. He had heard tales of the immortal tylwyth teg, of great bloody battles, and of feasts. He had expected the castell to be something risen from a myth: unknowable and unwelcoming.

He had never expected to feel so comfortable here.

As he walked the halls of the old fortress, his heartbeat eased into a steady rhythm and his breathing evened out. Perhaps it was because he had grown up in a place much like this: Caer Aberhen was less grand, but it was still a fortress. It had towers and walls, a great hall, high windows, and servants trying to keep birds from the rafters.

To him, home was—it was letters slipped between the pages of a leather-bound book and the small white wildflowers that grew beneath his bedroom window. It was honey over warm porridge, the scent of wet stone in the spring rains, and the humming of the cooks in the kitchen.

Home was taste and smell and sensation. It was not a place.

But this place felt like it could be *someone's* home.

He walked through one corridor after another until he found himself in the deepest rooms. These had to be the king's sitting rooms; with several walls of stone between these quarters and the outside, it would be the safest place in the fortress. A large fireplace stretched out along one wall; there were still ashes dusting the floor, and the tapestries were heavy with cobwebs. But it did not detract from the majesty of this place.

He reached out to skim the long oaken table with his fingers. He could almost hear the clatter of tureens and cups, imagine the scent of braised meats and old wines. He closed his eyes; Castell Sidi might have been built of memories, rather than rocks.

"Where did you go?" he murmured.

A gray culver perched on a high-backed chair. Of course—the messenger birds would have been left behind to fend for themselves. It eyed him warily, unused to humans in its home.

The door to the king's bedchambers did not open easily. Ellis frowned, and then on the second try he gave the latch a hard twist, lifting so that the hinges would not stick. It swung open slowly.

The rooms smelled of mildew. For all that they had once been Arawn's chambers, now they served as a home to some animal that had made a nest of the bed. Dust lay heavy on the floor, and every step kicked up a fresh cloud.

If the cauldron of rebirth were anywhere in this fortress, Ellis figured it would be here—tucked away behind fortress walls and heavy doors, inside a castell that no one had visited for nearly two decades.

He looked toward the sweeping expanse of woolen blankets and goose-feather-stuffed pillows. One of them had been pierced through and feathers were scattered about.

He did not think a cauldron could be hidden under the bed, but he checked regardless. In the pillows, beneath the bed frame, and then in the wardrobes, and the desk. On hands and knees, he swept his fingers into every nook and cranny of the room.

There was a small side door that led to the queen's bedchambers, and he slipped through it, angling himself sideways so as not to touch the cobwebs. The queen's chambers were smaller, with soft rugs and elaborate curtains draped over the windows. He could see a row of love spoons, their handles intricate and lovely, hanging just above the bed. He pushed one curtain aside. Sunlight cascaded into the room.

He gazed out across the expanse of grass below. There were cottages and sheds; fortresses often had outlying buildings for tanneries or blacksmithing—anything that would disturb the castell's occupants with smell or sound. Perhaps those small buildings once housed the legendary smiths who forged dragon-killing swords. And they'd be worth a search, as well.

When he ventured outside, he found Ryn. She sat beneath a twisted old tree, her gaze faraway.

"I see you're looking hard," he said drily, sitting down beside her.

Ryn gave him a look.

"I'm jesting," he said, holding up both hands in surrender. "You've earned a rest."

He settled beside her on the grass, moving a little stiffly. His shoulder ached and he wondered if tonight they would find a place to boil water for a bath. To soak in heated water sounded like bliss.

"I searched three towers," she said. "One must have been the dungeons, for I found chains and... other instruments. Another was full of bridles and tack. And the last..." She held out her hand. A short dagger rested in her palm. The scabbard's leather was buttery soft, and old runes were etched into the pommel. And while Ellis preferred pens to swords, even he could admit it was a lovely weapon.

"You found the armory?"

"I did," she said, and dropped the dagger in his lap. "That won't tax your shoulder. You should hold on to it, just in case."

It was then that he noticed the longsword tucked beside her hip. It was less ornate than the dagger, but no less deadly. "It's not my axe," she said. "But it's better than nothing."

Of course she would prefer her axe—old and straightforward and familiar—to every weapon in Castell Sidi. The thought tugged at his mouth, and he hid his smile behind one hand. He'd never thought stubbornness could be an attractive trait in someone, but it was so very much a part of her.

She stretched out her legs, her gaze fixed on the lake. It was deceptively peaceful in the afternoon light, the water still and opaque. As if no monsters lurked beneath the surface.

A thought had been nagging at him, and he finally gave voice to it.

"What if we never find it?" he asked.

Ryn did not ask what he meant. Her fingers knotted in her lap. When she spoke, her voice was level. "The dead will continue to rise. We won't run out of food here, not with the granary stores, but Colbren probably won't survive. My family will probably run—Gareth's a survivor. He'd take Ceri and go to one of the southern cities."

"Could it spread?"

"The curse?" She shook her head. "I believe what Catrin said. Magic must have its limits—distance being one of them. The bone houses were not deterred by iron or gorse. The nearness of the magic in the forest must have kept them caged. If they wander too far, perhaps they simply go back to being dead." She tipped her head, gazing at the lake. "Maybe this is what Arawn intended. Part of me wonders if he didn't leave the cauldron on purpose, so that humans would doom themselves with it."

There was quiet.

"That's a tad morbid," observed Ellis.

Her eyes moved, meeting his for the briefest of moments before returning to the lake. "Sorry, I've never been the chipper sort."

"I rather like it."

She turned the full force of her gaze upon him. He felt it like being pierced through: the sharpest, sweetest pain he could imagine. Her lips were slightly parted, reddened where she'd bitten them. The late-afternoon sunlight set fire to her hair, and in that moment, he thought her truly lovely. It did not matter that dirt stained the beds of her fingernails or that she smelled of lake and mud. She was *here*. In this impossible place with him. He wanted to touch the hollow of her throat, feel her heart beating beneath his fingertips. He wanted to push the hair behind her ears and kiss the freckles scattered across her shoulders. He wanted to tell her that he wouldn't leave—not like the others had. If she wanted him, he would stay. She would never have to lose him, not like she'd lost so many others.

But he did none of those things.

He merely smiled and said, "Shall we see what food stores the Otherking left behind?"

The moment of tension snapped and Ryn shook her head—not in disagreement, but amusement. "All right," she said. "We'll find food, and then see if we can look for a place to sleep for the night. Preferably in part of the castell that still has working doors that we can lock. We'll continue the search tomorrow, once we're rested."

He nodded and they rose together.

CHAPTER 27

HIS DREAMS TASTED of bitter smoke.

Ellis knew what smoke was supposed to smell like, knew the slight sweetness of cherrywood, the tang of oak, the heavy scent of ash. But this smoke, this was unnatural. It was heavy and damp and somehow Ellis knew, just *knew*, that he was smelling bodies as they burned.

And then he was on the lakeshore, the water lit up by the fire of evening sunlight. Someone rose from the water—not the afanc, but a man. He could not make out the stranger's features, but the sight sent a bolt of panic down his spine.

Look at me. Ellis could hear someone say the words, but he felt strangely disconnected. It was a woman's voice, and one he had only ever heard in the moments between waking and dreaming. *Ellis, look at me.*

Pain lanced through him. It centered beneath his collarbone, in his left shoulder. His fingers grasped uselessly about, trying to find a way to make it stop—

His fingers looked odd. He held them up to the sunlight, and the light poured between the finger bones.

He was dead. He was nothing but bone.

And then he realized that *he* was the one burning.

Ellis came to. He was sweating hard, his shirt soaked through. It was all too hot and close, and he found himself desperately trying to untangle himself, trying to escape the blankets and the memory of the dream. He tried to draw in a steady breath. It had been years since a nightmare had woken him.

They'd found barracks in a northern tower. The circular room was packed with cots that were little more than rope and blankets; it was a place for guards to catch a few hours' sleep. But after days of resting on roots and rocks, even the meager mattress felt wonderful. Soft moonlight gleamed through the slots in the stone and a gentle breeze tugged at his hair. Ellis sat up, rubbing at his face. As if he might push the dream away.

He stole a glance at Ryn. She was unmoving beneath her own blankets and her red-brown hair spilled across the mattress. Asleep and safe. Ellis released a shaky breath. It was a foolish fear, he knew no dream could touch him, but he was glad to see her resting.

There was a cup of cold feverfew tea beside his cot, and he

gulped the last of it down. For all that it tasted of bitter flowers, it did help with the pain.

Ellis slipped out of the bed. The stone floors were cold on his bare feet, but it grounded him, made him feel more awake. He strode to the door and pulled it open. Sleep felt like a distant hope. Perhaps he could walk for a bit—and in doing so, tire himself out.

The halls of Castell Sidi were made for nights. The palest sliver of moonlight came through the cut stone overhead, reflected by shining glass and mirrors. It was a place of starlight and old magics—not meant for people like him.

The softest footfall made him look up. Ryn stood in the hall, wearing only her long undershirt and leggings. Her face was drawn, and it took Ellis a moment to see the sword in her hand. "It's all right," said Ellis quietly. "It was . . . it was nothing."

Ryn stepped forward, her free hand reaching for him. She laid her palm on his chest, just beneath his left collarbone. Her touch was cool against his feverish skin, and it felt nice. "Are you in pain?"

He tried to smile for her. But she deserved more than the lies he was used to offering casual acquaintances. "Always," he said. "But that isn't what woke me."

Her hand didn't move, and Ellis found himself relaxing into the touch. "Tell me," said Ryn, quiet but somehow still commanding.

If Ellis weren't so exhausted, he might have felt embarrassment. Because what kind of person lost his nerve because of a dream? But Ryn didn't move, didn't speak, just waited. "It was a nightmare," admitted Ellis.

She appeared to consider him. Her hand dropped away, and he felt its loss at once. "Come with me."

"Where?"

"I have something to show you," she said.

He fell into step beside her. "Where are we going?"

"You'll see." They walked through the great hall, and Ellis found his gaze drawn to that statue of Arawn. Its features were cast in shadow, its eyes fixed on something far away.

Ryn took a side door he had not wandered into; this must have been part of the fortress that she had explored. A spiral stairway was cut into the stone, and he found himself descending, the walls close and ancient, and he felt as if they might be leaving the world behind entirely. The darkness swallowed them up, and then he heard the snap and hiss of flint catching on firesteel. One of the torches flared to life, the light dancing across Ryn's face. She was smiling, and in the firelight, she looked like she belonged here. One of the tylwyth teg, untouched by time and amused by some mischief.

They walked deeper still, and when the room opened up, Ellis realized they'd entered a cellar. The ceiling was just a little too low, and he had to hunch so as not to feel the touch of cobwebs. Barrels lined the walls, along with jars filled with unidentifiable liquids. Some were muddy and others clear, the glass kept clean by some magic. Ryn went to one of the shelves, blew the dust from it, and reached inside.

It was a bottle.

"When the Otherking took his court and his magic away from the isles, he did not bring his wine stores," she said, and he suddenly understood the edge to her smile.

"That is either going to be atrocious or delicious," he said. "Or perhaps drive us both mad." He'd heard stories of humans drinking and eating the food of the otherfolk—and it never ended well.

"It's doing no one any good collecting dust down here." Ryn grinned at him. "Come on. Want to climb to the tallest part of a tower?"

They found a circular stairway and Ryn took the lead—one hand on an old rope for balance and the other holding the bottle of wine. Ellis glanced downward once—only once—before he swept his gaze upward. The tower narrowed as they ascended, and he found himself a little dizzy when they came out onto a ledge.

The view during the day must have been wondrous; it would look out upon the mountains and beyond, stretching nearly to the sea. In the darkness, Ellis could barely make out the shapes of trees and hills. He thought he saw the silhouette of a building—perhaps a storehouse or a stable. They sat with their legs over the edge, and Ellis could feel the place where her leg touched his. Just a small brush of sensation, but it made his stomach jolt.

Ryn unsealed the bottle with a small knife, the wax coming away in small strips. She held the bottle under her nose, sniffed, and a wheeze caught in her throat.

"Not a good omen," said Ellis.

Ryn threw him a look. "I am going to taste this. Even if it does turn out to be only vinegar, I'm going to be able to say I have drunk the Otherking's wines in his fortress. This will be a story to tell my grandchildren."

"Far be it from me to deter you from a dream realized," said Ellis drily. "I'll try to catch you if you stagger about."

She put the bottle to her lips. A small shudder ran through her, and for a moment Ellis worried that the wine would indeed drive her mad. But then she threw her head back and laughed. "Oh, you have to try this."

The bottle was crusted with dust. He took it with a bit of trepidation.

The liquid was thick in his mouth. He swallowed hastily, but even in its absence, the wine lingered on his tongue. It tasted of burnt honey and orange rinds. Warmth bloomed in his chest.

"Seems to be all right," said Ryn. "I wouldn't drink too much of that, though, not if we want to find the cauldron tomorrow."

He gave the wine back. "Are you really so certain we'll find it?"

She kicked her dangling legs back and forth, as if she needed the movement. "We've made it this far, haven't we?"

"Yes, but—"

"No," she said, breaking into his words. "We have made it this far. We ventured into an encampment of the risen dead, through the mines, made it into the mountains, past an afanc, and now we're drinking wine in a fortress that no one has lived in for nearly a century. Well, if we're not counting the woman who caused the curse." Her fingers tightened on the bottle's neck. "We've done the impossible thrice over. We're going to manage it one more time."

Her certainty was more intoxicating than the wine.

"And then what comes after?" he said.

She gave a little shrug. "I go back. See if Eynon has managed to pry the house from my family—or if Gareth finally cracked and bashed him over the head with his accounts ledger." Some of her bravado slid away, leaving her voice softer. "I . . . I don't know. We'll bury our dead, I suppose. Or at least our memories of them." She took another swig from the bottle, then cleared her throat. "What about you, mapmaker? Going to continue your search for your parents? Or maybe map these mountains? Go back to Caer Aberhen?"

He hesitated.

She'd answered honestly. He would do the same. "I'm not sure. Still planning on charging me for this little journey?"

"Maybe," she replied. "Depends on what kind of valuables I find here. Maybe I could just take a few bottles of this wine and buy Eynon off with that."

Ellis took the bottle, drank deeply, and handed it back. He wasn't one for drink, but he hoped it would give him courage. "Can you miss something before it's gone?"

Ryn clinked her nail against the bottle. "I think I'm going to miss this, once it's gone."

He shook his head. "I mean—something else. A place, or a person."

The silence that followed was full of unsaid things. He wondered if he'd blundered into painful territory, if perhaps he shouldn't have said anything at all. But then she said, "I think so. The anticipation of the loss hurts nearly as much as the loss itself. You find yourself trying to hold on to every detail, because you'll never have them again."

"Aderyn," he began, then corrected himself. "Ryn. I must say, I won't miss this journey. The sleeping on the ground, the rain, the rotting corpses, the constant fear that something might leap out of the night and murder us both." Well, this was going well, part of him thought, but he forced himself on. "But even with the monsters and the dead bodies about, part of me wishes this wouldn't end. I mean, I want it to end. The bone houses and all. But when we go back—I will miss—well, what I'm trying to say is that—I will miss you."

Silence fell thickly between them, and for one terrible moment Ellis considered simply throwing himself off that ledge. It might prove a less painful end.

And then Ryn started laughing. It was just a snort, a stifled little sound that dissolved into giggles.

"This is wonderful," she said, once her mirth was under control. "I mean—it wasn't quite as spectacular as the time the peat cutter's son tried to court me by taking me on a tour of the bog and one of my boots got stuck and I had to leave it behind."

"Well," said Ellis, a little tartly, "I'm glad I rate above the bog and your lost boot."

"Do all your confessions begin with that bit about rotting corpses?"

"Well, I tried bringing the last girl flowers, but she preferred knights to mapmakers."

She laughed again, but this time it was quieter. "Ellis. Ellis." He liked how she said his name, the syllables soft in her mouth. "I'm a disaster. You know I am. I'm prickly. I prefer dead people to living ones. I'm only good at digging graves and surviving in a forest. My brother thinks I've abandoned the family, and my sister loves me, but then again she loves a dead goat, so her standards are a bit off. Oh, and the last family member that irritated me? I buried him in an unmarked grave."

"And I'm a mapmaker who gets lost quite often," said Ellis. "I have no family to speak of, I couldn't survive two days in the wilds, and I'll probably never be able to lift anything heavier than a tankard with my left arm."

"That isn't you," she said, and she took his hand. "You're—you're good, Ellis. You're kind and you're good and I'm—not."

"Well, I like you that way."

That seemed to startle her into silence.

"I like you prickly and disastrous, with grave dirt beneath your nails and forest leaves caught in your hair," he said. "You refuse to be anything other than what you are. And I only wish I could be so brave."

She looked down. "I'm not brave."

"Ryn—"

"If I were brave," she said, "I would have done this days ago."

And before he could finish whatever he'd wanted to say, her mouth met his. His words crumbled, and he found himself holding very still.

She kissed him like she did everything—with a determined ferocity. She took and he gave willingly, feeling the warmth of her body pressed against him. His hands swept over her, touching where he could. The corded muscle of her arms. The silken sweep of her hair. The breadth of her shoulders, and the ridges of her spine, flexing as she shifted, trying to find a more comfortable position. This wasn't the ideal place for kissing; he was dimly aware of the height, and the knowledge that one wrong move and they'd both tumble from the fortress. A soft noise escaped him—longing turned into sound.

In that moment, he did not care if they ever made it back to Colbren. They could live here, in this otherworldly fortress, with the wine cellar and their dead goat. If that dead goat managed to get across the lake without being eaten by an afanc.

His thoughts were fragmenting, running wild as he felt Ryn's hands skim down his chest. Fallen kings, all he wanted to do was lose himself in that touch. To want and be wanted in return was a heady knowledge, and he felt almost giddy with it. All the people in the world that she might have kissed, and she'd chosen him.

Even so, he broke away. His breath came in little gasps, and he could see a flush blooming high on her cheeks. "Was that... all right?" she asked.

"Yes." Part of him wanted to lean in again, to feel the softness of her mouth, but he forced himself to remain still. "But we're—on a ledge. And as much as I'm enjoying this, I'd prefer not to fall to my death."

"Understandable." Even so, he kissed her a second time—a brief flash of heat and sweetness—before he stood. "I'm going to return to the barracks before the wine reaches my blood." He gave a rueful shake of his head. "Perhaps now I'll get some true sleep."

Ryn nodded. "I'll be down soon." Her gaze drifted to the horizon, and her fingers tightened on the bottle's neck. "I just—need a moment."

He wondered if half the reason she'd come up there was for a good vantage point. Perhaps she hoped to catch a glimpse of her father. "I understand."

She gave him a short, honest smile that made his stomach turn over. Then he turned and began walking down the circular stairs. His head was spinning, and with every beat of his heart, elation surged through him. She had *kissed* him. She had kissed *him.* He touched his mouth with one hand. He could scarcely believe his own memories. It felt like some kind of fever dream, and he half expected to wake up.

It was a scant distance to the barracks, but he was so caught up, he did not realize that he'd walked a little too far. Too many corridors, too many doors. He pressed a hand to his face, trying to rub away his rueful little smile. He was acting like some lovestruck fool, which he'd never thought—

He did not see the hands that seized him. They were cold and slick with lake water, nails raking across his shoulder. A startled shout burst from him, and he whirled, trying to wrench himself free.

The moonlight cast this bone house in shades of palest gray, even the etched emblems on its armor and the hollow places where teeth had fallen out. The remaining teeth were stubby, worn smooth by a lifetime of chewing hard food.

A soldier. Likely in the lake, dragged to the depths by the afanc. They drowned—and they hadn't even been allowed the dignity of death. Rather, they'd found themselves forced to rise, again and again, to carry out the bidding of some curse.

For the first time, Ellis felt a swell of sympathy for the bone houses.

He thought of the old woman in the nightgown, those dancing by the fire, the musician—and all those forgotten dead who could not rest. Ryn told him she'd been able to speak to one. Perhaps he could, as well.

"I'm—I'm trying to end the curse!"

The bone house straightened. It regarded him with its hollow eye sockets, head tilted as if in question.

What might you say, if you could speak?

The bone house that held Ellis did not move. It merely held him in place. Every instinct screamed at him to struggle, to thrash his way to safety, but perhaps if he could make it understand—

The bone house's hand moved.

Ellis forced himself to stay still. The thin fingers touched his chest, moved to his shoulder the way a spider might ascend a web. His heartbeat thundered.

The bone house leaned close. Lake water slipped down its jaw, dampening Ellis's shirt.

The creature drew in a breath. He wasn't sure how; it had neither nose nor lips. But he could hear the inhalation as it snagged on the broken teeth.

It was *smelling* him. The way a hound might follow a scent through the forest.

Then it drew back, and its mouth opened in a silent howl.

CHAPTER 28

RYN SAT ON the ledge, legs still dangling, until the clouds blotted out the moon.

She'd wanted a few moments to herself, to gather her own thoughts before she faced Ellis again. Her mind was a tangle, and a strange sort of calm had descended upon her. She did not know what would happen when they found the cauldron or returned to Colbren, but she knew one thing: She wouldn't face it alone.

It was a thought that both warmed her—and made fear squirm in her gut. To love someone was to face the possibility of losing them, and she feared another loss could shatter her.

There was another reason she had remained here; in the bright moonlight, she had been able to see the grounds. To watch for any moving creature—living or not. Part of her yearned to see a dead man in a gray traveler's cloak, to catch a glimpse of him again.

She saw nothing.

And when the clouds crossed the moon, Ryn rose to her feet. There was little point in keeping watch, not when she couldn't see a thing. Her hand found the smooth stone wall, and she made her way by touch and memory. The stairs were simple to traverse—the rope led her spiraling downward into the castell, and she remembered the way back to the barracks.

The air was cool against her skin and she shivered. It would be a pleasure to sink beneath the woolen blankets of her cot, even if they did smell of damp lanolin and dust.

She crossed the threshold to the barracks and blinked.

It was not Ellis that awaited her. It was a goat.

None other than the bone goat was nuzzling her pack, searching for something to eat.

For a heartbeat, Ryn simply gaped at the creature. She looked terrible—she'd begun to bloat and she smelled of fresh rot. But she stood there, as lively as any dead creature could be.

"You made it," said Ryn. "You swam across the lake, you daft creature. And the afanc didn't eat you?" She wrinkled her nose. "Then again, I can't blame it. You're not exactly appetizing."

The goat gazed at her.

"I can't believe you," she said. She reached out to touch the creature, then thought better of it. "You followed us all this way. You're the most loyal, the most foolish, the—"

Her voice trailed into silence.

The goat had followed them here. She had slipped into the

castell unseen and unheard, and found her humans. And if she could do it, then—

"Ellis?"

There was no answer, and fear twisted at her stomach. She held her borrowed sword a little tighter. At once, the fortress seemed too quiet and too still. It brought to mind how cats froze just before they pounced on prey. She did not know precisely what she feared—whether it was magic or bone houses or something monstrous—but she knew something was wrong.

She moved quickly but with care, keeping her footfalls soft. She did not call out again but listened instead. She heard the quiet click as the bone goat followed, hooves against the stones; she heard the rustle of wind overhead and a flutter of wings; and—there.

She heard the distant clatter of metal on metal, and a muffled voice.

Ryn adjusted her grip on her sheathed sword and quickened her steps to a jog. She wished she had taken more from the armory than just blades; she wore little more than her nightclothes. She thought longingly of chain mail and breastplates, but there was no time to armor herself. She would have to fight in her loose shirt with a borrowed sword.

She heard another sound—the scuffle of feet and a door on old hinges. Ryn's lips drew back in a silent challenge and she rushed ahead. She gathered her anger around herself, stoked it to a burning fire in her chest, used it as fuel for each stride. If she could be angry, perhaps she could burn all the fear from herself.

She rounded a corner and saw them.

They were armored like those who had attacked Colbren. At least five of them.

And two had Ellis caught between them.

He struggled, snarling as one of the bone houses kept its skeletal fingers pressed across his mouth. Biting did him no good.

The thought of losing him to those dead creatures gave Ryn's anger a keener edge—and something to attack. A wordless cry burst from her lips and she threw herself at the bone houses. Without hesitating, she spun around. Her sword was raised high, and she brought it down with all the strength in her body. It was a shattering blow; she had felled small trees with her axe.

The first bone house fell to one knee, and its arm came up. Her sword struck an iron shield and sparks flickered.

She caught a glimpse of the bone house's face—it wore a helmet and its face was frozen in the rictus of a skull's grin. The bone house shoved forward, forcing Ryn to retreat several steps. Now she was on the defensive, trying to parry a blow with her own sword. She had no shield—and far less experience with a sword than any of these dead soldiers.

The cantref princes sent their best knights into the mountains.

And now they had no flesh she could cut, no arteries to sever. Death had only served to make them more dangerous.

Ryn heard Ellis call her name, but she did not reply. All her focus was on the bone house. It pushed again, harder, and she felt her feet sliding back, giving ground. Jaw clenched, muscles straining, she placed her palm on the flat of the blade, taking the weight on both her arms. A droplet of sweat rolled down her neck, catching in her shirt. Her muscles shook with the exertion.

The bone houses dragged Ellis through the door and into the courtyard. One of his hands seized the frame, fingers straining, but then he was jerked free. He vanished into the darkness.

With a curse, Ryn kicked out. Her heel caught the side of the bone house's knee and it bent the wrong way. Something cracked and the creature's mouth yawned wide in a silent scream. With only one functioning leg, the bone house fell to its knees. Ryn took its head off with a single blow. She moved on to the next one, sword slicing through the air as another bone house crowded forward.

She counted time not by moments but by how many blows were exchanged. She felt recklessly invincible. She caught a sword pommel on her shoulder, and a throbbing pain began in her back. She ignored it, parrying blow after blow, striking back, fighting with such ferocity that it did not matter that she was outnumbered and outclassed. These knights and soldiers had been trained to survive, to take weapons on shields and armor, to duck out of the way of attacks. Ryn had no such qualms; she threw herself into the battle, snarling and spitting like a wild animal.

Some instinct had taken over, and all she knew was that she had to get to Ellis.

Death had taken too much from her—she wouldn't let it take him.

She slammed her sword through another bone house, cutting a path through ribs and armor, until the blade's tip skittered along the stone wall. Sparks lit the darkness. The bone house was pinned—but so was her weapon. The dead man's hand lifted, grasping the sword's blade, and it pulled itself forward. Iron dragged along its rib cage as the bone house struggled closer, one hand reaching for Ryn's throat.

Ryn twisted the sword and threw her weight against the hilt. The sword became a lever, and iron crunched against bone. Vertebrae broke, fell to the floor—and the bone house went with them. Its legs were still, even as its arms grasped for her.

Ryn kicked it aside and rushed into the night.

Her fear drew her body tight and sharpened every sense to the point that it felt as if the world had slowed around her—the weight of the sword in her hand, the sight of moonlight on grass, and the tang of winter in the air. Every part of her strained forward. The courtyard was empty, but she heard the sounds of a struggle. She turned one corner so swiftly that she had to throw up a hand to keep from hitting a wall, palm slapping against stone.

The castell seemed larger in the dark, towering over her—around her. She tried to remember what was before her, which direction the lake lay in. If the bone houses were trying to give Ellis to the afanc, she'd need to reach them first. Or perhaps they would merely try to drown him, to make him into one of them. There had to be a reason; the dead were dead, but they weren't mindless.

Another bone house lurched out of the dark; she slammed the pommel of her sword into its jaw. The bone came away, and the dead man staggered in surprise. Ryn took its head off with a single swing, barely losing her stride.

She rounded another corner and saw them. The bone houses bore Ellis not toward the lake—but to the rows of cottages. Confusion pierced her anger and fear, but it was only a moment's pause. She threw herself into a sprint.

Something crashed into her with bone-jostling force. She hit the ground and all the breath left her in a rush. She lay there, gasping, fingers groping uselessly for her fallen weapon.

A bone house straddled her; it wore no armor, only rags, and it moved with the languid grace of a snake. *A scout,* she thought. *Or one of the spies the cantref princes sent.* It had long silver hair and bones the color of lake silt. It pinned her arm, holding her in place as it leaned down. Bone whispered along her cheek as it smelled her, drawing a long breath over her skin.

Revulsion made her kick out, but her legs were useless—flailing against the air. This bone house seemed far more adept with weaponless combat, and Ryn didn't have the element of surprise.

The bone house drew back, seemingly satisfied with its examination. Metal glinted at its belt, and it drew a short hunting knife.

Ryn thrashed like a rabbit caught in a snare; there was no strategy to it, only fear-given strength and desperation. She could not die here. Not like this, not with the cauldron unfound and Ellis being dragged away. She had not come this far only for a dead scout to cut her throat. She imagined the warmth leaving her, imagined lying on the ground until the next night.

Perhaps she would rise again. Perhaps she would be herself,

or perhaps she would become a monster: one of those legendary creatures she had loved as a child. She might wander the night, silent and restless, until a proper hero arrived to end the curse. Perhaps she would even find her father in the forest.

For the briefest moment, her struggles slowed.

And then she thought of Ellis, *his mouth against hers*, of Gareth, *that last embrace before he told her to return*, and Ceridwen, *her hair shining in the sunlight*. She thought of her father's hand in hers, and how he'd told her not to let go.

She hadn't let go.

It was time to let go.

And to *live*.

Her knee came up, catching the bone house in the curve of its spine. The creature lurched, but its tight grip did not loosen. The skull grinned down at her, and it placed that hunter's blade against the soft flesh of her throat.

Panic burned within her. *No.* It couldn't—not like this. *No*—

And that was when the goat slammed into the bone house.

Horns caught on bone and the dead scout released Ryn. She gasped, dragging air into her lungs with jagged relief. She lay there for a few moments, just trying to breathe, before she pushed herself to her elbows.

The bone goat was attacking. Long, curved horns lowered, hooves pawing at the ground in a silent warning. It barreled toward the bone house a second time, hitting it with such force that Ryn heard something snap. The scout twitched like a half-squashed bug, fingers moving spasmodically.

The goat huffed, then trotted back to Ryn's side. If a goat could look pleased with herself, she did.

"You daft, beautiful, rotting thing," said Ryn, a giddy laugh rising out of her. "Come on."

Her wrist ached but she picked up her sword and took off across the grass. The bone houses were nearly out of sight.

They were taking Ellis to the farthest cottage. One of the bone houses was dragging him along by his leg. Ryn lengthened her stride, but the bone goat got there first.

The goat caught the dead soldier head-on, and its leg buckled beneath it. Ellis cried out, kicking wildly as another bone house tried to take hold of him. He slipped free, scrambling to his feet. His eyes alighted on Ryn, and she saw relief spread across his face. Not for himself, but for her. Of course the fool would be more worried about her when he was the one being captured, she thought.

She thrust her sword into another bone house, breaking its ribs and wrenching it to the ground. She brought the flat of the blade down on its face, cracking the skull wide. Its helmet fell away, and the creature twitched on the ground, grasping at its own broken head.

Ellis grappled with a third bone house, his fingers catching on the skull. With a mighty wrench, he twisted the head to one side. A crack resounded through the night, and the bone house fell limply to the ground. Ryn brought her sword down and felt the creature's back break beneath the blow.

And then all was quiet—but for the sounds of the living. Ryn breathed so hard there was a gasp on every inhale; Ellis leaned against his knees, shaking so hard she heard his teeth click. "Are—are you all right?" she managed.

He nodded. His own voice had yet to return to him. His hands sought hers, and then they were clutching each other. A smile touched her lips even as she panted for breath. "Alive," she said, and it seemed the only thing she could say. He pulled her close, only for a brief moment, and then he whirled, one arm catching her around the middle and dragging her back.

She saw them a few moments after he did.

Moonlight danced across the surface of Llyn Mawr. The water lapped against the broken-shale shore, and it would have been beautiful.

If not for the creatures emerging from the water.

Dead things. All sorts of dead things. Men and women. Hundreds of them—some broken and some whole. Ryn remembered the piles upon piles of bones stacked upon the lake's bottom and she went cold.

"Fallen kings," she heard Ellis whisper.

So many. Too many.

They could not fight them all.

Ryn's hand went to the cottage door. She shook the knob but it was locked. It wasn't much, but four walls would be *something*. A place they could fortify and hold out in until sunrise. All they needed was sunrise. Ryn took a step back, eyes darting over the door. It was heavy oak, and the emblem of the Otherking was etched into the frame. A beautiful piece of work—and she yearned for her axe so she might cut it down.

She struck at it with the heel of her booted foot. A jolt ran up her leg, but nothing happened. Cursing, she hefted her sword and brought the pommel down upon the door latch. Sparks glittered in the night and fell to the damp ground. Ryn hit the latch a second time, then a third. Her sweaty fingers slid along the hilt and she gripped it tighter. If she slipped, she might flay her own hand open on the blade, but there was no time.

On the fourth blow, the latch cracked free of the wood. She saw splinters, and then she threw her weight against the door.

The door opened by a fraction; the wood had swollen, making it scrape across the hard-packed ground. Ellis seized it and they pushed together, until the gap was wide enough for Ellis to slip through. Ryn angled herself, then glanced back.

The bone goat stood there, watching them.

"Come on," said Ryn, beckoning. "Bone goat, come here!"

The animal blinked at her.

"Damn it," Ryn snapped, and began to step outside.

Ellis caught her by the arm, and she jerked to a halt. "No," he rasped. "We can't."

"But she—"

"We can't," he said again, and she saw how near the bone houses were. So close she could see the web of cracks in one's skull and the gleam of silt on another's fingers. The bone goat lowered her head in challenge and turned to face the attackers.

"No," said Ryn again. A denial, when she knew there was nothing more she could do.

Ellis pulled her inside, and then he threw his weight against the door. She heard the creak of wood as it jammed into the door frame, and then he was moving, dragging something. A chair, she saw. He shoved it against the door, then dropped to his knees.

Ryn rested her forehead against the wood, her own breathing harsh in her ears.

Even so, she heard the sounds of the dead things outside.

CHAPTER 29

IT WAS DARK in the cottage. Ellis sat with his back to one wall; his legs had given out and he had little desire to stand again. Every part of him ached. He hadn't noticed the small cuts and bruises when he was fighting with the bone houses, but now they all came rushing back to him.

He waited. For the sound of people throwing themselves against the cottage, for the noises of battle, for . . . for anything.

Everything had gone silent.

When he met Ryn's gaze, he saw her eyes were wide. "Why does the quiet not reassure me?"

"Because you're not a fool," she replied. "Come on. Let's see what frightens bone houses away."

There was a lantern hanging by a hook near the door—likely so that whomever lived here could venture outside at night.

Firesteel rested on a small nook by the door, and Ryn handed Ellis her sword, then struck a flame alight on the first try.

This small room was meant for sitting; there were carved chairs and a table. Without thinking, Ellis picked up an embroidery hoop from that table. He trailed his fingers along the smooth surface, felt the grooves, and the memory of stitches. There was no fabric, but his mind supplied the sensation.

"What is it?" Ryn peered over his shoulder. "I didn't know magical beings did embroidery."

He did not answer, but gently set the hoop down. Another step, and he was through a doorway, into what must have been the kitchen. A stove rested in the corner. The chimney was crooked, and he thought he heard a rustle, as if there were something nesting inside. Several bottles and jars remained on shelves, the glass smudged with dust.

"Blackberries?" Ryn murmured.

"Currants." The answer sprang to his lips without thought—and he knew he was right, even as he didn't know why.

He felt very far away. As if he were watching another young man wander through this cottage, as if it were a wholly different person exploring this place.

He watched this other person—because it wasn't him, it couldn't truly be him—explore the small kitchen and then walk into another room.

There was a cot in the corner. The blankets smelled of moths, but they were still intact. A quilt, with blue embroidery. A leaf pattern, and he knew without touching that the stitching would be soft as butter beneath his fingers. He knew it would smell of dried grasses, because the blankets were hung on a line outside. And part of him wanted to curl up on that cot, to be small enough to fit there, and perhaps if he closed his eyes, the world would vanish.

He dared not look around that room any longer. He could not.

So instead, he walked through the opposite door. This bedroom was larger, with a window that looked out upon the lake. Lace curtains were hung around it, and the bed was neatly made. There was a desk—and parchments. A leather-bound book, with a quill still stuck between the pages. He remembered the softness of the feather, tickling someone with it, then feeling a gentle kiss against his hair before it was taken away.

He heard Ryn's intake of breath. A sharp hiss against her teeth, and he sensed more than saw, her reach for a weapon.

He didn't want to turn around. He didn't want to see. Seeing would make it all too real, would draw him back into the present moment, into the cottage with the bone houses waiting outside, and he desperately wanted not to be here.

"Ellis."

His name had been many things—a rebuke, a question, a warning—but no one had ever spoken it like Ryn did. As if it might be an endearment.

Ellis forced himself to look.

In the corner was a chair. And on that chair rested a figure.

It was a woman. Or rather, it had been a woman. She still had hair, straight and fine, falling around her shoulder bones. She was draped in silvery fabrics and a fur-edged cloak. And beyond that, Ellis could see very little. She had no skin, no lips, no eyes.

She was all bone—blanched by time, untouched by the silt of the lake. Her hair was a dark brown, and there was something familiar in the lock that slanted across her eyes.

And in the woman's lap rested a cauldron.

It was smaller than he expected. The edges were rusted and a crack ran through its side.

Ellis made a sound of surprise. Ryn's fingers squeezed his wrist, a silent acknowledgment that she'd seen what he had.

It was the woman from the tale—the woman who'd tried to save her child, the boy who'd been murdered by a thief.

He took a step forward. He felt like his body wasn't under his control; he had been compelled to come here, just as the dead were compelled to rise. He had no say.

"What is this?" he said, his voice shaking.

Ryn's gaze never left the woman. "I think…this is what we've both been looking for."

Of all the ways Ryn thought she might find the cauldron, she'd never expected this. Ellis's hand came up, as if he wanted to touch the bone house. Ryn seized his shoulder, trying to pull him back. He made a sound of pain, and she realized she'd seized his left shoulder. She let go at once, but it was too late.

The bone house's head snapped up. Its eye sockets were hollow, but somehow Ryn knew it was staring at her. The jaw moved, silent but for the click of teeth, and then it surged to its feet. The gown was in tatters, a bit of borrowed finery that had survived decades—

The sound of Ellis's pain seemed to rouse the bone house. It cradled the cauldron in its left arm, pressing it close. In its other hand, it held a knife.

The blade belonged in the hand of a butcher; it was meant for slicing meat. The bone house threw itself forward, the blade's edge a hiss through the air, and Ryn felt the whisper of it pass by her ear. She ducked beneath the blade, kicking out.

Her leg caught the bone house in the side. It staggered, one elbow slamming into the bed. Its refusal to drop the cauldron and the knife meant it had to fumble to stay upright, and its jaw clacked again and again, as if it were shouting. Its arm came up, knife flashing, and Ryn slammed her forearm into the bone house's elbow, knocking the blow aside. The blade hit the wall, sank into the wood.

Ryn saw Ellis in the middle of the room. His left arm hung limply by his side—and his right hand held her sword. His face was frozen in an expression that she never wanted to see again. It was how a child looked when they scraped their knee or burned themselves on a fire. Startled that such pain could exist. She took a step toward him to seize the sword. If either of them was going to bring this bone house down, it should be her.

Agony cleaved her skull in two.

The room spun around, and then her cheek was pressed to the wooden floor. She was breathing dust and there was a leaf stuck to her arm, and she was on the ground and wasn't sure why. She blinked, and—and reopening her eyes was a struggle.

Something warm seeped down her neck, and she tried to lift her hand, to see what was wrong. Her fingers came away bloody.

The cauldron. The bone house must have struck her with the cauldron.

It hurt so badly she wondered if the bone house hadn't managed to break something vital. She tried to sit up and nausea swept through her so strongly that she didn't dare try again. She closed her eyes, hoping her stomach would remain where it was, and tried to breathe.

It happened too quickly.

Ellis knew that sound would follow him into his nightmares—the resounding crack of the cauldron striking Ryn, and then the thud of her body hitting the floor. She was so still that she might have been dead. And for one terrible heartbeat, he thought she was. Then her fingers twitched and she made this noise. A whimper at the back of her throat.

He'd grown used to the idea that Ryn was invincible. That she could shake off any threat with a quip and a glare, her axe hefted on her shoulder and a smirk on her lips. The sight of her, still and bloodied, snapped something inside him.

He brought the sword down on the bone house. The creature lifted an arm, and the blade snagged on bone. The creature opened its mouth, as if wishing it could scream, but it did not have the voice.

Its fingers wrapped around the bare blade and it pulled.

Ellis stumbled, caught off balance. His left arm came up, and he grasped the pommel with both hands, trying to hold on.

Pain burst behind his collarbone. He caught a cry between his teeth and ground it into silence.

He would not lose his weapon.

He couldn't lose his weapon. Not with Ryn on the floor, not with this thing staring at him with its hollow eyes.

His feet shifted as he widened his stance before he threw himself forward. The blade surged through the bone house's fingers, and the creature sprang aside. The sword whispered through the creature's hair, and several strands fluttered to the ground.

His step brought them together, and this close, he could smell the death upon it. He swung the sword, trying to bring it down upon the creature's neck. If he could just take its head off, he might be able to end this.

He thought of Ryn and her axe, swinging again and again, that night they first met. She'd apologized to the creature as she'd dismantled it, and right now he couldn't imagine why. The dead should stay dead. They had no place here.

The bone house tried to pull the sword from him. He crashed into the bed, the sword skittering from his hands toward Ryn. He rolled over and over, until he fell to the floor. Grimacing, he pushed himself to his elbows—and his left arm crumpled beneath him.

The cauldron rolled to the floor.

Ellis saw it—the red-rimmed edges, the crack down the side. It was dark, so dark that light did not seem to reflect off its surface. It gaped wide, like a hungry mouth, and Ellis did not want to touch it.

Even so, he had to. He grasped one of the handles and threw it.

The cauldron clattered along the floor until it rolled within Ryn's reach.

The bone house seized him. He half expected to feel the whisper of bone across his throat, to feel a stranglehold and the crushing weight of its hands.

But the bone house did no such thing. Its hands settled on his shoulders, skimmed up his throat, then gently rested on his jaw. The dead woman tilted his face toward her—and then tucked the stray lock of hair away from his eyes.

He went utterly still.

That small gesture was a single point of familiarity in this strangeness. Hair brushed from his eyes.

No one moved. Not the bone house, nor Ellis, nor Ryn. It felt as if they were frozen in this moment.

And then Ryn spoke.

"Your shoulder," she said haltingly. "The left one—the one that hurts you. It was a broken collarbone, right?"

His answer came slowly. He dared not move too much, for fear of disturbing the bone house. Its skeletal hands rested on his shoulders. "I—yes. The healers said that the bone had been broken and was not set right." He sounded baffled. "I must have broken it when I was a child—"

"Or perhaps an arrow broke the bone."

He imagined a fallen child, his mother pouring water from the cauldron of rebirth into his mouth. Pouring cupful after cupful, until the magic took.

"It was you." Ryn said the words first. "The child who died. It had to have been you. The stories got it wrong—the child was brought back before the cauldron broke."

"No." The word burst forth, and he whirled on her. He wore the face of a child who didn't want the monsters to be real, and the face of an adult who'd fought them. "That can't be right. I'm not—I'm not—"

His voice failed him, and when he spoke again, it was in a whisper. "I'm just a mapmaker."

Her voice took on an urgent edge. "How long did it take you to get to Colbren? How long were you traveling?"

It took a few tries to answer. "I—a week and a half from the southern ports? I went slowly, so as to chart my progress."

She nodded, as if his answer were unsurprising. "The first bone house left the forest about the time you began to approach—and then more after that. Don't you see?" A shaky breath rattled through her. "I kept asking what had changed—and it wasn't the iron fence. It was *you*."

He laughed and the sound was terrible—a jagged rasp. "You think they were looking for me?"

"I think *she* was," said Ryn, with a glance toward the bone house.

He thought of that first night on the fringes of Colbren—of that bone house that had tried to drag him into the forest. Toward Annwvyn. Of how the bone goat had followed them without ever wavering. No, the goat hadn't been following *them*, it had been following *him*. He thought of the bone house in the woods, trying to bring Ryn deeper into the mountains—because he'd given her his cloak, of how he'd danced among the dead and they'd never noticed he was different—

Because he was one of them.

No, no, he thought. He was *alive*.

He was shaking all over. "No, I can't be—"

But he could be.

And more than that—he *was*.

His gaze slid up, resting on the dead woman. She knelt before him, fingers still resting on his shoulders. Like any mother would with her son. She'd never been attacking him; and she'd only attacked Ryn after she'd grabbed his bad shoulder.

Ellis turned to look at Ryn.

"Break it," he said. "Before she stops you."

"Why would she—"

It took a moment for her to understand.

The cracked cauldron was what kept the dead rooted here—bound in a mockery of life. To end the curse, she needed to break it. But if it had brought Ellis back, if he had truly died—

He saw when she understood. All the blood had left her face. "No," she said. "No."

He could not hesitate. To hesitate would be to undo everything. All their efforts to come here, all the spent blood and those left dead in their trail—it would have been for naught. He couldn't let that happen.

"Do it," he said.

He grasped the dead woman's wrists. She flinched. He held on.

Ryn's eyes were too bright and too full. She looked at Ellis as if she could not bear to look away.

"Break it!"

The words ripped from his mouth, hoarse and full of fear. He held the creature that had been his mother, and he was panting, his face creased with pain.

Because he did not know if it was true—if magic had brought him back to life, if he'd grown up here, if his mother was the woman who'd dared use a magical cauldron from Castell Sidi.

But he did know this: It had to end.

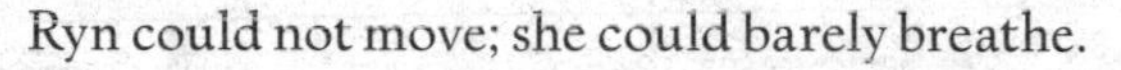

Ryn could not move; she could barely breathe.

The cauldron rested beside her. It was so small. So much smaller than she'd imagined. She had to break it.

To end the curse. To save Colbren. To be a hero.

Ryn looked up. Ellis's gaze met hers, and she saw his chest rise and fall. Rise and fall.

"Do it," he repeated. But quietly this time—a plea rather than a command. "Do it to protect your siblings. For every dead person that hasn't been allowed their rest. For your father, Ryn."

Fallen kings. She wanted to. She didn't want to.

In the end, there was no choice. "I'm sorry."

With a cry, she gathered all the strength in her arms—and then she brought the hilt of her sword down.

And the cauldron of rebirth shattered.

CHAPTER 30

RYN DID NOT look up. She couldn't.

Her gaze was locked on the cauldron.

It lay in pieces on the floor. Ryn stared at them. If she looked up, it would be real. Everything would crystalize. She would no longer be Aderyn the gravedigger—she would be the girl who'd killed Ellis.

And then she heard the noises. Bone scraping over stone—the rasp of breath against teeth.

Ryn looked up.

Ellis was alive. He leaned heavily on the bed, breathing raggedly as he watched the bone house.

They were both alive. At least, mostly.

It had not worked.

It—*it hadn't worked.*

Ryn could not move. The cauldron was in pieces, yet the curse remained.

Defeat made her whole body slump. Everything hurt. The back of her head felt as if a hot poker had been pressed to it, and her neck ached. Ryn swallowed again and again, measuring out her breath so that perhaps she might regain some control of herself.

"Why didn't it work?" she croaked. The words were a child's plea. She wanted to close her eyes again, to pull a blanket over her head and pretend she was young, she was having a nightmare, and if she could just wake up, everything would be set right.

"I don't—" Ellis began to say. Then he halted. As if he did not know what to say. His hands fell, releasing his mother. "She must have brought me back before the cauldron cracked. Before the magic was distorted. I don't know—if breaking the cauldron won't end this, I don't know what will."

The dead woman smoothed her bony hands over his chest, straightening his shirt.

And something in Ryn's mind finally came together. It wasn't just the cauldron that had bound the dead here—it had been her. A woman who had lost her son: first to death, and then to distance. Ellis must have wandered away after he was resurrected—or perhaps the thief even stole him, only to lose the child in the woods. She supposed they would never know the truth of it.

But this was true: Ellis's mother remained here. Even after she'd died, after the magic brought her back, she'd waited. For Ellis.

"Ellis," she said. "She's your *mother*."

"I know!" He spoke through gritted teeth. "We've established that."

"No," said Ryn. "I mean—she's your *mam*."

The word startled him. Confusion flickered across his face. He looked between Ryn and his mother, his brow creased.

"She stayed here," said Ryn, "waiting for you to come back." There were tears running down her face; she only realized when she felt them fall.

Ellis's mother had lingered in the house, while her flesh rotted away, in case it meant seeing her child again. She'd clung on even when death tried to take her.

And there was something so human in that, so recognizable, that a sob hitched in Ryn's chest. She knew what it was to cling on, to grasp those small fragments of memory and try to live in them. Even if it meant not living at all.

Ellis remained still. His eyes roamed over the bone house, as if trying to find something in it. He was crying, too, Ryn saw. Silent shakes of his shoulders, his mouth crooked open as if he wanted to speak but didn't know the words.

Then his gaze jerked back up to the bone house's face.

To the woman's face.

To his mother's face.

His lips were bloodless when he finally spoke.

"Mam?"

The bone house looked up. Moonlight shone across the cheekbones and jaw.

The dead woman leaned closer, until the ridge of her brow was pressed to Ellis's. As if she wanted to feel the warmth of him.

Ellis spoke the word again, his voice shaking apart. "Mam?"

The bone house wrapped him up in her arms, held him close. And then she did something that Ryn had never expected. Something the dead should not have been able to do.

She *spoke*.

"Ellis." Her voice sounded like that of any woman—her words preserved by the same magic that had kept her lingering here. She spoke again, and her voice was overfull. "My Ellis."

"Mam." This time it wasn't a question. Ellis made a small, broken sound and he hugged her back, pressing his face to where her shoulder should have been. Like a child who wished to shut out the world and to remember only the one place where he had always found safety.

Ryn remembered tucking her own face into her father's shoulder, feeling the strength of him, and sitting in her mother's lap, feeling utterly secure. And perhaps—perhaps this was why she'd retreated to the forest after her own parents were gone. To love someone was to lose them. Whether it was to illness or injury or the passage of time.

It was a risk, to love someone. To do so with the full knowledge that they'd leave someday.

Then to let go of them, when they did.

Ellis cried out suddenly, and Ryn blinked through her tears. His mother was swaying, her arms loosening. It was as if the magic that had kept her alive was draining away. "No, no," said Ellis, and he was choking on the words. His face collapsed in on itself, twisting with unsuppressed pain.

His mother sank to the floor; Ellis sought to keep her upright, his arms locked around her, but it was to no avail. His mother was fading, the magic slipping away. Her fingers traced his cheek, and then clattered to the floor.

Everything went quiet.

Ryn stepped forward. On shaking legs, she knelt beside Ellis and put her arms around him. She felt as if the sobs might shake him apart, and she clung on, knowing how it felt. How the grief swelled up like a tide, threatening to sweep a person away.

She held on, knowing that sometimes that was all a person could do.

CHAPTER 31

THIS WAS HOW the bone houses were defeated.

With a whispered name.

The After

CHAPTER 32

WHEN THE STORY of the bone houses was told, it would go something like this:

There was a young woman. She was a fearless creature—a girl who would chase death into the mountains. With only an axe for company, she slipped past pwca and afanc, fought through lines of dead soldiers, and found the old woman responsible for the curse. There was a great battle, and the young woman beheaded the dead woman, ending the chaos.

Or, there was a young woman and a young man. They'd eloped, because the woman's family didn't approve, and took her younger brother and sister with them. They went into the mountains seeking refuge, only to find Castell Sidi. There, they ended the curse by melting down the cauldron.

Or, there was a young criminal. She stole a map of a mine,

hoping it would lead her to great treasure—but instead, it led her into the mountains. She stole the cauldron and, in her own ignorance, accidentally shattered it and ended the curse.

Or, perhaps it went something like this: A goat ended the curse. It got tired of its humans being distracted by hordes of dead soldiers, so it went into the mountains and ate the cauldron.

Years later, Ryn would confront Ceridwen over that particular version of the story. Ceri disavowed all knowledge.

But for all the variations, the stories never mentioned what happened *after* the curse was ended. Even in Ryn's own mind, the details blurred together.

There were a few days of cleanup. Dead bodies were strewn about the fortress and Ryn couldn't just let them be. She found the tools of her trade in one of the outlying buildings, and she began work the next morning. It felt almost natural to find places in the rocky soil where graves might be dug, to clean the bodies as best she could, to wrap them in cloth and lower them into the ground.

To give these dead the peace they deserved, but had never known.

Ryn worked until her fingers blistered, until the weak autumn sun made sweat gather on her neck, until her clothes were stained with dirt.

On the first night, she looked out over a row of burial mounds and felt something like satisfaction.

She found the bone goat on the second day, curled up beneath a tree, as if in sleep. But she was dead—well and truly, this time.

Ryn buried her as well. She left wildflowers on the mound.

It was a strange few days. Living in Castell Sidi, burying long-dead bodies by day, and sleeping in an old barracks by night.

Ellis slept in the cottage.

Ryn went by a few times, but he didn't speak, so she didn't press. She did bring him a bowl of hare cawl, thick with potatoes and leeks. She left the bowl beside the front door. When she returned again, the bowl was empty.

He must have been trying to place the cottage in his memories. She saw him a few times, wandering about the grounds. He'd trace a wall with his fingertips, as if he were trying to map out its structure with hands alone. Then he'd vanished into the cottage again.

On the third day, Ellis returned to the fortress. Ryn was taking a well-earned midday break. She kept a good distance from the Llyn Mawr, choosing to wash her hands in a nearby stream instead. When Ellis approached, Ryn scrambled to her feet.

His eyes were red and shadowed, and he moved with that restless grief that Ryn knew so well. Platitudes and reassurances meant nothing, so she didn't offer them. She waited for him to speak, instead.

When he managed it, his voice sounded rusty and unsure. "I—I want to bury her," he said. His throat jerked in a swallow. "Can you help?"

Ryn gave him the smallest of smiles. "That's one thing I'm well equipped to do."

Ellis found a place behind the cottage. The soil was thick with old rocks, and it took half the afternoon to dig the hole. Ellis wrapped his mother in a clean linen sheet and they lowered her into the earth.

When they were finished, the sun was low in the sky and Ryn's back ached. Ellis didn't speak, but laid a hand on the pile of rocks. "She wanted me," he said softly. "She—she spent years holding on because she wanted to find me again." There was a tremor to his words, as if he hardly dared believe them.

Ryn placed her hand between his shoulders. His back was warm, damp with exertion. "Of course she did."

She felt a shudder run through him. He turned and she pulled him close, felt his breath rustle her hair when he exhaled. He smelled of fresh earth and sunlight.

That night, he slept in the barracks.

They left Castell Sidi with full packs of food, ancient swords, and very little conversation. Ellis had taken a few things from the cottage—an embroidered shirt, a book, and a blanket.

As Ryn walked out of the great hall, she glanced over her shoulder at the living statue of the Otherking, one hand raised as if in welcome—or farewell. In the spring, fresh leaves would awaken the hall, make it into something breathing and green and wonderful. It was beautiful even now, with the starkness of winter and rain in the air.

They would go around the lake this time. As Ryn trudged along the broken-shale shore, she found a half-collapsed skull sitting amid the rocks. With a grimace, she picked it up and tossed it back into the water.

What she was not prepared for was to see an axe fly out of the lake. It flew at Ryn's head and she lunged to one side.

The axe thudded into the ground, blade sinking into the soil.

For one long moment, neither she nor Ellis moved. She looked at the lake, looked at the axe, and then back at the water. "What," she said flatly.

"Don't the otherfolk dislike iron?" Ellis reached down and picked up the axe. He flicked a stray leaf from its blade before he held it out to her.

"Thanks," said Ryn.

The axe handle had toothmarks on it. But she shrugged and hefted it over her shoulder.

The journey home took longer.

For one thing, going around the lake added another two days to their journey, and it was hours of grueling climbing over jagged peaks and slipping on patches of damp lichen. They took care not to touch the water, relying on flasks until they reached the river.

From there, it was slow going through the mountains.

But it was also peaceful. There were no dead things crawling about. Ryn and Ellis slept at night and walked during the day.

Even the mine had little fear left in it. It was dark and damp, and Ryn's heart beat a little fast as they passed through it, but there was no terror. No waiting for a hand in the dark. It was just an abandoned mine.

She closed her eyes, wondering where her father was resting. She would have liked to bury him.

But at least he *was* resting now.

They all were.

The villagers at the old mining encampment were burning their dead. This time, the fires did not have the sweet cook-fire scent as they passed—no, these were pyres. Ryn and Ellis kept to the fringes of the camp, skirting the edges through the forest. They dared not go too close to the camp; Ryn remembered Catrin's fear and desperation. Grief could turn to anger, and Ryn knew how easy it would be for those people to wield that anger like a weapon.

She wondered if they would remain at the encampment or if they would find somewhere else to live. Perhaps some of them would come to Colbren.

As for Colbren—they found it battered but alive.

Ryn walked into the village and saw Dafyd was at work rebuilding a door. When he caught sight of Ryn, he spat out a curse before clapping her on the shoulder. "Knew you'd amount to something, girl," he said, and then gave Ellis a hearty embrace that made the young man gasp for breath.

"How did you know?" she said, baffled.

"Your sister's been braggin' to anyone who'll listen." He smiled broadly. "Said you went into the woods to fix the curse. And the day after, most of the dead cleared out. The armored ones just left, and the stragglers were easier to deal with."

She understood. The dead soldiers had been here to find Ellis—and they must have followed him back into the forest. Ellis's gaze dropped to the ground, and she saw the smallest flicker of guilt cross his face. She took his hand and squeezed.

Morwenna grinned when she saw them and then went back to her forge. It looked as though she were working on new bars for a fence.

Ryn's house was a mess. Their door was broken, and there was a chicken waiting in the kitchen, merrily eating spilled grain.

Ryn stood in her home, breathed the familiar scents, and something loosened in her chest.

"Ceri?" she called. "Your chicken is in the house!"

A shriek came from one of the back rooms. Then a clatter, the thud of bare feet against wood, and Ceri slammed into her. They swayed and fell—and Ceri still did not let go. She was crying and laughing, using her small fists to shake Ryn. "—should have told me," she was saying, "—should have said good-bye, you foolish, you unthinking—" She buried her insults against Ryn's shoulder, and Ryn held on tight.

Gareth was in the backyard, repairing the pantry door. He had a nail tucked between his teeth, and he seemed intent on his work—at least until Ryn said his name.

The nail dropped from his bloodless lips.

Neither moved for a heartbeat.

Then he held out an arm and Ryn stepped into it, hugging him back.

"You did it," he said simply.

"We did," she replied. "I think Ellis gets a fair share of the thanks."

She stepped back, giving him a once-over. Gareth looked older than she did now—the last few weeks were evident in his eyes and mouth. "You managed to keep Eynon from taking the house?" she said, smiling. "And I see the village is one piece. Mostly."

Gareth huffed out a breath, turning away for a moment. When he looked back, his face was an odd mixture of irritation and amusement. "Eynon came here a few days after you left, to say we were being thrown from the house. He said with Uncle dead, we had no legal claim to the graveyard, which meant we would never be able to pay him back. But when he began shouting, Morwenna overheard him. She came over and said that the dead man couldn't be our uncle—not if he was her long-lost father."

"What?"

Gareth shrugged. "Dafyd also said that the body bore a distinct resemblance to a second cousin of his."

"Dafyd doesn't have any cousins."

"The courts won't know that."

"You can't be serious."

He nodded. "After you left, Ceri would tell anyone who listened that her big sister had set out to stop the curse. And when the bone houses left, it seemed like a miracle. People will live, because of you. And even if word of your deeds never makes it out of the village, people here know. As for our debts... well, I expect Eynon can wait a few weeks for payment. There are quite a few bodies that need burying, and Enid made it quite clear that if Eynon tried to evict us anytime soon, she'd let her chickens into his bedroom."

Ryn glanced away, trying to hide sudden dampness around her eyes. She'd never thought as much as she loved the village—she'd never anticipated they would come to her aid like this.

"As for Uncle," said Gareth, "I believe... it is better that he be named among the missing." A small shrug. "After all, that dead man could have been anyone."

A pang went through her. She had never liked her uncle, but he deserved better than to die unmourned and unremarked upon. "I should—"

"You should talk to the villagers soon," said Gareth, breaking in. "There are still dead about. We keep finding them in odd places—a bone house managed to crawl into the space beneath the Red Mare, of all things. And people are tired of burning them—the smell has gotten *atrocious*. I think they'll be wanting the services of a gravedigger soon." He nodded in the direction of the graveyard. "And I thought that would be the first place you visited."

She followed his gaze. Before, she would have gone there at once. Visited her mother's grave mound, checked the others. But the dead would keep now—and the living needed her more.

She dug into her pocket and withdrew two halves of a wooden love spoon. Gareth drew in a sharp breath.

"Later," she said. "I need to tell you something first."

Ellis went to see Eynon the following day.

The fine home was a mess. The windows were broken and the garden uprooted.

Ellis walked into Eynon's study and found the older man sitting at his desk. His eyes were sunken and his hair tangled. He looked as if he had not slept in several days. "You," he said. "What are you doing still here? I thought you'd gone back to the prince."

"Oh, right," said Ellis. "I'm a spy. Forgot about that."

Eynon frowned at him.

Ellis was not afraid of him. Not of the man's disapproval nor of his power. And if word got back to Caer Aberhen of this encounter...well. He wasn't too worried about that, either. His smile was sharp edged and his fingers rapped the oaken desk. "You," Ellis said, "are going to forgive Aderyn's family's debts."

Eynon let out a derisive laugh. "Am I?"

"Oh yes," said Ellis. "You are."

"I don't see—"

"For all that you're a greedy, grasping bastard," said Ellis, "you're not very canny. If you were, you never would have threatened me." He leaned in a little closer. "You accused me of being the prince's spy. And then you threatened me. I must say, if your aim was to appease the prince, that's the wrong way to go about it." He straightened and walked a circle around the office. He surveyed the scattered papers, the broken wine bottle, and the fallen books.

Eynon became the color of a sickly mushroom.

"I—I never," he sputtered.

Ellis's smile widened. "Of course you did. And that's precisely what I'll tell the prince in my letters to him. He's rather fond of me, you see."

Eynon's breathing sped up; he looked as though he might faint—or throw something at Ellis's head.

"What," he said, "do you want?"

Ellis turned to face Eynon. "What I want is this: You're going to forgive Ryn's debts. Oh, and the mine. You should reopen it."

A moment of disconcerted silence, and then Eynon said, "Th-th-the mine. Can't be done—the people we've lost there—"

"The dead will no longer be a problem," said Ellis. "We made sure of that. That *was* the problem, after all? The one you never mentioned to the prince. You said it was the collapsed tunnel, but really it was the dead that came after. You couldn't tell him that, though, without sounding a bit mad. Well, the dead are gone. And the remaining tunnels are stable. I went in there myself."

The smallest flicker of greed appeared in Eynon's face before he made an effort to stifle it.

"This isn't for you," said Ellis. "Don't think this was ever for you. The mine reopening will make Colbren a center of trade again. There will be jobs and coin—and the villagers will see most of it." His voice lowered. "No more taking from the villagers what should stay with them."

“And if I do not do as you say?” asked Eynon.

“Then,” said Ellis, still smiling, “I am going to return to Caer Aberhen with a rather fascinating story about a lordling who endangered his village by not reporting a curse, by removing the iron that protected it, and who has been lining his pockets with coin that belongs in the royal coffers.” He nodded at Eynon. “Are we in agreement?”

Eynon’s gaze jerked from side to side, as if he were searching for a way out.

There wasn’t one, of course.

Eynon’s jaw worked, and Ellis heard the creak of muscle and bone. “Fine,” the older man ground out.

“Don’t act like this is a hardship,” said Ellis. “The mine will keep you a wealthy man. And as for the rest of the village... they’ll be more comfortable as well.”

He turned to leave, but Eynon called after him.

“You never did tell me what your surname is,” said Eynon.

Ellis glanced over his shoulder.

The answer came to his lips easily—and for once, painlessly.

“I don’t know,” said Ellis. “And it does not matter.”

Ellis stayed with Ryn’s family for a week.

He helped in the house; he swept floors, assisted Ceri with the cooking, and offered to help Gareth with the washing up. Ryn caught him in quiet moments, when he thought no one was looking. He would touch the fringe of his hair, pushing it back behind his ear, the way the bone house had touched him. There was a distance to him that had not been there before—but also a surety.

They ate meals together. They walked the rounds of the graveyard together, and he listened as she pointed out the mounds where her grandfather and grandmother had been buried. He listened, his fingers twined with hers, as they walked the edges of the forest.

"How's your shoulder?" she asked. "I know our cots aren't that comfortable."

He gave her a small smile. "It hurts. As always. But pain is something I've come to live with." He drew in a long breath. "I used some of my coin to purchase willow bark, but you'll have your payment."

"Payment?" she said, confused.

"For guiding me into the mountains." He nodded toward the forest. "We did agree that I'd pay you, after all."

She bumped his good shoulder with her own. "Oh, stop."

"You did say something about looting my body should I die on the quest."

"And yet, we both came out alive." She gave him a small smile. "I think we're settled on the matter of payment." Her smile dropped away. "What brought this on?"

"I've been thinking. Of what comes after."

She looked at him. "After death?"

"No, after the next few days," he replied with a brief smile. "I mean, we accomplished the impossible. I'm not sure what comes after."

Ryn considered it. "I think...if all goes well, it means Ceridwen grows up. I get to keep digging graves. We keep our house. Gareth works on the ledgers. As for yourself..." She slid him a look. "That's up to you."

"I have to return to Caer Aberhen," said Ellis with a small sigh. "The account of what happened here—I'll need to tell them. The prince will want to know that the mine could be reopened, and I'll tell him of the curse. Not all the details. I think my having come back from the dead would be a little too much."

"Ah. So you'll go home." She stopped walking, and her fingers tugged on his. He halted beside her, his gaze searching her face. She tried to hide her disappointment, but he seemed to understand.

"Caer Aberhen will always be dear to me," he said. "But I don't think it's home. No more than Castell Sidi is—not anymore." He gave her hand the smallest squeeze. "It still bothers me."

"What?"

"The map that brought me to Colbren," he said. "The paths were badly sketched, and the measurements were off. Other people could get lost if they use that map. And they can't always depend on a dashing rescue from a lovely gravedigger."

"True," she agreed, and her heart beat a little faster.

"I should redraw those maps," he said. "That way Colbren might actually have some trade again. Without the bone houses—and with a proper way to find the village."

She inhaled. Just a sharp little breath. "How long...does it take to make a map like that?"

He shrugged. "It could be a while. Weeks, even months. I'll have to find a place of my own to stay here. And maybe someone to guide me about the forests. A person who knows this land better than anyone."

She wanted to laugh. Rising up onto the balls of her feet, she took hold of his shirt and drew him close.

When she kissed him, the corners of her mouth were crooked in a smile.

This—this was what came after. Living.

She would carry the dead with her, but now she wouldn't be burdened by them. They were a weight that would lessen with every step; not because the memories would fade, but because she'd be stronger for bearing them.

And perhaps this was the truth about the dead.

You went on.

They'd want you to.

ACKNOWLEDGMENTS

Hello, dear reader. We meet again.

We have reached the end of the book. So—first of all—thank you for reading it. I truly appreciate your support. Books take quite a few people to create, and readers are a vital part of the process.

Secondly, I have to give a shout-out to Lloyd Alexander. When I was pretty young, I was given the second book in his Chronicles of Prydain series, thus starting a lifelong habit of (a) reading series out of order and (b) a love for fantasy. When I was older, I considered writing to Mr. Alexander to tell him what his work meant to me, but he had already passed away. This novel is my nod to him.

Thank you, Mr. Alexander. I hope you would have liked this book.

This book would never have existed if not for my wonderful publishing team at Little, Brown Books for Young Readers. To my lovely editor, Pam Gruber, who heard my pitch of "gravedigger versus medieval zombies" and understood my vision for this book even before I did. To Hannah Milton, for all her tireless work and energy. And a big thank-you to Marcie Lawrence, Marisa Finkelstein, Chandra Wohleber, Clare Perret, Erika Breglia, Stefanie Hoffman,

Natali Cavanagh, Valerie Wong, Katharine McAnarney, Victoria Stapleton, Alvina Ling, Jackie Engel, Megan Tingley, and the wonderful Sales team. If I ever had to pick people to survive a zombie uprising with, it'd be all of you.

To the Adams Literary family, thanks for being in my corner.

Another big shout-out must be given to the traveling companions that traipsed through Wales with me: my mother and Brittney. Thank you for accompanying me through abandoned copper mines and old castles.

To all the booksellers who gave their early support to this book: Kalie Young, Sami Thomason, Alena Deerwater, Anna Bright, Zoe Arthur, Jane Oros, and so many others. Thank you so much.

To the Tillabook crew—Alexa, Rosiee, Kat, Mary Elizabeth, Lainey, and G'Norm the Gnome. We had some great writing times.

To s.e. smith, for being the person who would discuss both plot and rotting bodies with me.

To the lovely people at OwlCrate. I didn't get to thank you in the acknowledgments of my last book, so I'm doing it here.

To all of the bloggers, BookTubers, Instagrammers, and Booklrs—you are an awesome part of the book community and I appreciate you so much.

To my family. Mom, Dad, and Diana—sending you all hugs.

And lastly, to Josh of the Conwy Tourist Information Centre—without whom I could not have written this book because I'd still be trying to figure out the Welsh public transit system.

Diolch yn fawr.